BURIED SECRETS

Buried Secrets Series #1

Rafe Escobar and Alek Belanov

BRINA BRADY

M/M/ Gay Romance

BRINA BRADY

BURIED SECRETS

AUTHOR'S NOTE: This book contains spanking and graphic gay sex.

DEDICATION

Thank you to all my awesome Beta Readers.

Cj Lewis

Debby Demedicis Elliott

Tori Wall

Anita Ford

Austin Daniels

Jean Paquin

Doreen Frantz

BURIED SECRETS

BURIED SECRETS

BRINA BRADY

CHAPTER ONE

Alek Belanov

Alek Belanov finished dying his blond hair dark brown. He didn't look bad with darker hair, but it wasn't who he was. As a matter of fact, he could get used to it as long as he didn't look into the mirror. With all the threats he had on his life, no one would recognize him from a distance. Leaving his possessions behind with his two armed security guards, Alek exited the motel room and waited in the parking lot for Uncle Sacha.

Within five minutes, a black limousine pulled up in front of him. The driver was Uncle Sacha's other nephew, Pavel, who was twenty-four-years old, two years older than Alek. When Pavel opened the side door without saying a word, Alek stepped into the limo, hurting from his cousin's slight. After all, they had been very close at one time, and they hadn't seen each other in two years.

Uncle Sacha wasn't smoking a cigar, which normally dangled between his lips. Silver-gray, perfectly groomed hair covered his head and the edges of his round face. He had a strange scar looking like a washed-out fishbone that ran from under his eye to his chin. Gray stubble complemented his cheekbones beautifully and covered

9

most of his scar. Uncle Sacha stood tall among others despite his bulky frame. Most men feared him and with good cause.

"Good evening, Uncle Sacha," Alek said.

Alek bent over and kissed Uncle Sacha on both cheeks to show his love and respect in the Russian way. His uncle returned a kiss to each cheek.

"Sit." Uncle Sacha pointed to the seat across from him.

Immediately, Alek obeyed his uncle's order while he sized up the older man to gauge his temperament at the moment, but his expression was blank, devoid of all emotions.

"Alek, you'll go to this party as I've discussed with you on the phone. Tell Valerik Korsak your name at the door when he asks. He's a tall, gray-haired Ukrainian man. Do whatever he wants you to do within reason. In the end, this will be the best way for you to stay safe and live your life in the manner closest to your sexual preference." Uncle Sacha's stone-cold blue eyes penetrated through Alek, the same way they had done when Alek was a child.

"I don't understand. What kind of party is this, Sir?" Alek's stomach contracted into a tight ball.

"Let them enjoy you, so one of the men will take you home. This party is your last chance for protection. You were safer in prison." Uncle Sacha's strong Russian accent fought against speaking English, especially when he was exhausted from overwork and stress.

Cold perspiration broke out across Alek's forehead when he attached meaning to Uncle Sacha's words. The unknown completely shrouded his environment once again. Uncle Sacha demanded respect at all times and made Alek's life miserable when he didn't show it. The absolute panic of displeasing his uncle persisted whether he was in or out of his uncle's presence. Even after two years in prison and away from him, the fear remained.

"Did you sell me to a man for my protection, Sir?" Alek chewed on his bottom lip, lost in thoughts of the dire consequences for his protection.

"Don't speak about selling. You will attend this party for the sole purpose of finding a male protector. This arrangement is nothing more than a business exchange. Your protection will cost more than money." Uncle Sacha's eyes displayed deep sadness and loss.

"What do I have to do for my protection?" Alek asked, terrified he'd be going from one prison to another. Freedom would never be in his future, and he had to learn to live with it, one way, or another.

"I did a full investigation of this rare protection society of men to meet your special and sensitive needs. If one of the men finds you pleasing, he'll become your protector." Uncle Sacha lit his cigar.

"Tell me what I must do for my protection, Uncle Sacha," Alek repeated, swallowing hard in the hope of stopping any unwanted tears from escaping.

"Nothing you haven't done before in prison. So make it happen. Do I make myself clear?" The way his eye twitched was enough to tell Alek to stop pressing for answers.

"Yes, Sir." Alek didn't understand why his uncle had sold him to a stranger. Certainly, he had enough money to pay for his security without any sexual favors from Alek. His life was in serious danger from two feuding Russian crime families. Hopefully, the new situation would be better than he had with Trigger when he had been in prison.

"Remember, you're no longer under the Belanovs family protection. You lost that when you got involved with the wrong man. This will be the last time we can safely meet." Uncle Sacha closed his eyes as if he were in pain.

"Why are you banishing me?" Alek shoved his hair out of his eyes with fierce anger and was unconvinced he wouldn't bring whatever danger followed him to wherever he was going.

Pavel stopped the limo in front of a mustard-colored adobe home with bright turquoise trim set behind trees. He stepped out and opened the door.

"Alek, I have to do this, so I don't put you or our family in any further danger. Stay safe." Uncle Sacha's voice cracked, full of regret and guilt.

"Thank you for raising me. Remember, I'll always love you, Uncle Sacha, and I'll never forget you." Alek's voice was soft, almost fragile, as if it and his heart would break any minute. Perhaps his heart was already broken.

Alek stepped out of the limo, and Pavel walked him to the bright turquoise front door. A chilly bleak silence surrounded Alek. His face flushed with humiliation and a deep sense of shame from Uncle Sacha throwing him away like the weekly garbage. He didn't have any other choices at the moment, but realistically how far would he get without a hole in the back of his head? He must carry on as he had done in prison. One day, he'd be free again.

Alek sucked in a shaky breath, feeling his throat constrict. Panic rose like bile in his body. He stood at the door, staring blankly up at the terror before him. His palms were clammy.

13

Pavel rang the doorbell since Alek was incapable, lost in his morbid thoughts. They waited in silence for a few minutes when a tall, gray-haired man, wearing a black mask covering his face, answered the door. Pavel waited beside Alek, preventing him from running. His cousin worked for his uncle Sacha in many capacities without disobeying his orders. Ever.

"Who are you?" the masked man asked.

"Alek Belanov, Sir," he managed to say, the words rolling out of his mouth like tumbleweed.

"I'm Valerik Korsak. Address me as Mr. Korsak for now." The tall man signaled him to follow.

Pavel's last parting words to his cousin were, "He should have taken you out with the rest of them, Alek. Once a traitor, always a traitor."

Alek glared at Pavel in response, not knowing what to say, so he kept it short. "Fuck you."

The *he* word stuck in his head. Who was Pavel talking about? What traitors? His cousin wanted him dead. What had Alek done to him? Not a damn thing. Pavel got what he always wanted. He had replaced Alek, and now he was Uncle Sacha's favorite nephew. His uncle didn't have a family. Alek had lost his uncle's favor and love. His head throbbed, and his stomach ached from the stress of losing his place in the Belanov family.

"Come along, Alek," Mr. Korsak said.

One last time, the two cousins held a death stare like two bulls ready to plow through one another, neither moving.

"Alek, come inside," Mr. Korsak shouted, aiming a gun at Pavel. "And you leave my property or I'll use this."

Pavel turned around and walked to the limo without looking back. The man slammed the door and said, "Why do you hate him?"

"He's my cousin. I don't really hate him, but he's caused trouble between my uncle and me."

"Follow me."

Reluctantly, Alek straggled behind the man to a side room. Dark furniture with lots of bright orange and reds decorated the room. A large framed painting of an inferno blaze hung on the wall across from a dark desk. It reminded him of Bosch's work depicting hell. Naked people were boiling in a huge cauldron while others hung upside down with flames everywhere. Alek hoped these paintings weren't a bad omen predicting his immediate future, even though he had landed in hell when he was born.

Mr. Korsak smelled of tobacco and whiskey. Nothing made sense about this masked man. He wasn't even Russian, so why did Uncle Sacha trust a Ukrainian man with Alek's life? His uncle had hated Ukrainians until now. The thought crossed his mind that there was a slight chance that he had hired Mr. Korsak to take him out. Many times, Alek had overheard the gruesome stories detailing his uncle's killings, but he'd shoved the bloody specifics out of his mind. Something about Mr. Korsak's demeanor frightened Alek and yet there was something familiar about him. Above all, he wouldn't displease Uncle Sacha if he wanted to stay safe, preventing the others from finding him.

"Remove all your clothes and wear this red collar around your neck," Mr. Korsak said with a definite Ukrainian accent. The collar resembled a mini-belt with a buckle to fasten it. Were these people going to treat him like a dog? What had Uncle Sacha gotten him into?

Alek hesitated about undressing. The man hid part of his identity behind the mask, meaning only one thing to Alek: it was a sign indicating depravity would soon follow. Alek had been used to taking orders, remembering punishments from times at home and in prison when he hadn't obeyed. Mr. Korsak motioned for him to begin undressing. Alek unbuttoned his white shirt and laid it

16

across on the back of a chair. He kicked off his shoes and socks, unzipped his jeans, and stepped out of them along with his briefs. He set the rest of his clothes on the chair and put his socks inside of his shoes and under the chair. Alek buckled the red collar around his neck, ashamed of being naked in front of this Ukrainian stranger.

Alek felt ridiculous beside this man dressed in his suit and mask. At this wretched point in his life, Alek accepted how weak and alone he was without any ground to stand on.

When he'd been imprisoned, he'd have been dining with Trigger in the chow hall by this time, and after that, he'd fuck Alek until his ass was raw in front of his friends. He still had nightmares about Trigger fucking him and forcing him to give blowjobs to him and his friends. He'd been out of prison for only a week. He had never expected to be sent away from the Belanov family. Not by his beloved uncle Sacha.

Mr. Korsak inched a step closer to Alek and pulled him into his arms while two very cold thin fingers pinched and kneaded his ass. Uncle Sacha had said, 'Let them enjoy you, so one of the men will take you home.' Alek wiped a few tears away, wishing the man wouldn't touch him. The rejection from the man, who had raised and loved him, had hurt him more than he cared to admit.

The man stopped pinching his butt, took Alek's hand, and led him to the party area in a large room with a bar and at least twenty small tables with two chairs at each one. Another four framed fire paintings decorated the walls of the open room. Animals and flames eating men and women with all sorts of horrific scenes depicted the suffering in hell. The fire-themed paintings he once loved now disturbed him.

Uncle Sacha hadn't mentioned the men would be wearing black facemasks or that there would be other naked young men available for what he didn't quite know. But then, he never fully disclosed everything to him. Obviously, the naked ones needed protection, and the ones in suits were the protectors.

Not only was Alek aware of the exposure of his ass but also of the weight of his dangling cock and balls. He glanced at the length of his dick and watched it flopping between his legs as he walked. Alek was grateful he wasn't hard, but it was difficult not to get excited. Naked men traipsed around the room while he admired their bare asses and swaying cocks and balls.

"You're wearing a red collar for a reason. Your protector will be wearing a red tie to match the color of your collar," Mr. Korsak said. "It's the same for the other naked boys and their protectors, but as you can see, not one boy shares the same collar color."

Alek scanned the room looking at the men wearing black suits and black shirts without ties. The naked guys wore different colored collars as Mr. Korsak had said.

"Sir, no one in a suit is wearing a tie."

"The men will talk and play with you to see if they want to become your protector. At the end of the evening, the men will choose one of the ties from the tie table to match the color of the collar of the boy they want to protect. Each protector will wrap his tie around the chosen boy's neck to show he will be their protector."

"Should I stand here and wait?" Alek didn't much like this game, but a drink might ease his anxiety. *Suppose no one picked up a red tie?*

Other naked young men were roaming around and talking to men in suits. They were his competition. The naked guys were all ages, sizes, and shapes, but the suited men stood tall and broad-shouldered.

"Order a drink first and sit at the bar." Mr. Korsak pinched his ass again.

"Yes, Sir." Alek was sure he had heard Mr. Korsak's voice before in his past, but he couldn't quite place when or where.

A young naked bartender, wearing a bright green collar and a matching tie around his neck, stood behind a large fully stocked bar. A protector had already claimed him. The cute bartender had tousled dark brown hair, which was thick and lustrous with a slight curl. His gorgeous dark eyes were a mesmerizing brown with long, thick eyelashes.

Alek double-checked the room again and saw that each man wore the same black suit and matching mask. Some had different shaped noses. A few of the masked men spoke Spanish. Others spoke English with a heavy Russian accent like his uncle Sacha. Still, something didn't feel right about these men. Why were they hiding their faces?

"Alek, your job is to entertain the men until you're selected." Mr. Korsak tone was flat and cold.

"Yes, Sir."

"Excuse me; this is Alek Belanov. Don't forget to play with him," Mr. Korsak shouted at the men in the room.

The men roared, laughing and whistling at him. Bad memories returned of many of the prisoners laughing at him because everyone had known he didn't belong there with violent criminals. Too many cigar smokers in one room polluted the air. For a moment the tobacco smell reminded him of Uncle Sacha. He counted nineteen naked men and twenty men dressed in black suits.

Alek sat at the bar on a stool, uncomfortable with his public nakedness.

"What would you like?" the bartender asked.

"Vodka on ice."

"These are yours," the bartender said as he pushed a pack of Marlboro Red and a lighter in front of him.

"How did you know I smoke this brand or that even I smoke?"

"They know everything about you. It's a good thing."

"Thanks."

Alek opened the package of Marlboros, pulled out one cigarette, and lit it. Without knowing what else to do, he focused his eyes on the mirror behind the bar to view behind him, smoking his cigarette and waiting for someone to come.

"Don't look so scared, *amigo*. These men are well vetted. While each may have different kinks, you'll be safe." He paused to put an ashtray on the bar top. "You must be running from enemies or the law like the rest of us naked *chicos*. All the protectors are gay men, but you can't

21

tell by looking at them. They behave like ninja assassins and will kill to protect you after you're bonded to them."

"How do you get bonded?"

"Your protector will spell it out to you because it's different with each one. If you don't accept the bonding, then no protection."

"How did you get your tie so fast?" Alek asked.

"I went to another party and was picked. Look behind you across to the wall. My protector is the blond man talking to the man who's been watching you from the minute you sat down."

Alek turned around and saw two men talking. At least someone might be interested in him.

"What's your name, by the way?" Alek asked.

"Emilio."

"I guess you figured out I'm Alek." Every time Alek checked on the dark-haired man, another protector walked up to him. He seemed never to leave his position.

"I didn't figure it out. The owner, Mr. Escobar, informed me when he showed me a picture of you. Your hair is darker, though. He provided the cigarettes and lighter for you. I hope you get chosen tonight, and maybe we can be friends."

"I don't have any friends, but I'd like one. What happens if I don't get picked?" Alek cringed when a man came behind him, reached around, and yanked on his cock.

"They'll house you at the camp until the next party, and if you do get picked but don't bond, then you will be sent to the camp for another chance." Emilio ignored the man touching Alek.

Alek saw the dark-haired man talking with all the new boys. So much for looking at Alek all night.

"I don't know if I should want to be picked tonight or not." Alek felt the brawny man squeeze his nipples. He was too afraid to turn around to look him in the eye.

BRINA BRADY

CHAPTER TWO

Alek Belanov

Emilio didn't bat an eye at the man molesting Alek in public. "Look around. You're gorgeous. Hopefully, they won't fight over you."

Emilio left Alek to make his drink while the man's rough hands continued touching him all over. His hands played with his cock as if he were a doctor checking him for flaws.

"Suck me off, boy," the black man said.

Alek froze and was unable to move. The man smelled like whiskey and cigars.

"On your knees. Now." The man's deep masculine voice commanded so gruffly that Alek shuddered.

He slowly stepped off his stool and dropped to his knees between the man's legs. Reaching up and unzipping his slacks, Alek pulled out his huge brown cock.

"Put it in your mouth, boy," he commanded.

Shivers went through Alek at the word *boy*, taking him back to his prison days. The man's fierce brown eyes followed Alek's every move. As Alek's head inched closer to the veiny brown cock in front of him, the man put his hand on the back of his head and guided him to it. He

25

crammed the man's hard cock into his mouth, his tongue caressing the bottom of it as he attempted to inhale it. Alek couldn't get much of it in before he gagged. It was just too big.

"Take all of it, boy."

Alek took the large cock into his throat once again, sucking and licking as much as he could. It tasted bitter at first, but it was clean. He wanted the guy to shoot quickly to ward off his humiliation, but another side of him wanted the man to wrap a red tie around his neck.

"There you go, boy, nice and easy. Suck it all."

Alek continued to suck him, using his hand to make up for the inches he couldn't swallow. After several minutes, the man bucked his hips and face fucked him until Alek gagged as he pushed his head down further. His uncle Sacha had told him to entertain the men so one would take him home and this was his last hope to attain protection. He knew it was his only option to stay safe, so there was no room for complaints. It was merely an exchange of services, plain and simple, with no emotion.

Alek realized he had no control to regulate his movements with the man's hand holding his head, and then the man pushed his cock down Alek's throat again. He coughed, spraying precum around the base of the man's cock and balls.

"Nice touch, boy. I like that."

Alek returned to sucking when the man moved his cock out of his throat. Taking the man's balls in his hands, Alek massaged them at the same time. A few of the protectors surrounded them and watched him taking the man's cock into his mouth. Sucking this stranger in public was no different from being in prison, except the audience's apparel had changed from orange jumpsuits to black business suits and masks. Alek peeked in between the standing men and saw that a few other naked boys were doing the same thing he was. *No big deal*, he supposed.

When Alek couldn't take it anymore and needed to take a deep breath, he pulled his mouth away from the man's cock, inhaling the smoky air.

"Get it back into your sweet mouth. Keep me wet with your throat juices, boy."

Alek's cock pulsated hard at the sound of his words. He couldn't come in front of everyone because Mr. Korsak hadn't told him he could take that liberty. Reluctantly, he returned to sucking the dark man's cock and shortly after, he spilled his seed down Alek's throat.

"A plus blowjob."

27

He pulled his cock out of Alek's mouth and said, "Clean it, boy."

Alek licked the man's wet dick clean. Without any other exchanges, the stranger zipped up his slacks, turned, and walked away toward another young man with light brown hair and pretty green eyes. For some reason, the man talked to this guy first and they both seemed to enjoy their private conversation.

Apparently, Alek didn't deserve a conversation. The black man had ordered him to suck his cock without getting to know him first. Crushed from his first rejection, Alek returned to his stool and felt like he'd failed in some way. He had thought he'd suck his way into going home with him. Emilio made him a fresh drink because the ice had melted in the other one.

"I guess he found someone better." Alek caught a glimpse of the stranger getting another blowjob from the young man he had a conversation with.

"Stop worrying." Emilio said. "You don't want him anyway because he's a Dom and into BDSM. Someone will pick you tonight. Check out the man staring at you. He's standing by the wall. I know who he is because he ordered a drink while you were blowing that burly man. I heard his voice."

"Who is he?" Alek chugged down his drink and wondered why Emilio was talking about this one man who was staring at him.

"He's Rafe Escobar and is in charge of this Gay Protection Society. This is the first time I've seen him at one of these mixers. Trust me, he's hot!"

When Alek turned around, he saw the dark-haired man was still watching him as he stood against the wall with a drink in his hand while he was talking to yet another man in a black suit. *Emilio said he had been watching me, so maybe he had.*

"Naked boys line up here," Mr. Korsak said.

"Hey get me another drink before I have to stand in line, please."

Emilio raced across the bar, made him a drink, and set it in front of Alek.

"Hurry now."

Alek drank the vodka in one swig. "Thanks."

"Good luck, Alek."

Alek jumped off the stool and made his way to the end of the line. They stood side by side as though they were on an auction block. *How could Uncle Sacha make me go through this?*

"Bend over and stretch your cheeks open, so the men can check your pretty holes," Mr. Korsak ordered.

Everyone bent over, and Alek did the same, feeling violated, similar to what he'd been through in prison. These men, circling around the row of bent-over, young men crushed Alek's dream of falling in love at the party. He wanted his happily ever after, and he knew he was for damn sure not going to find it here.

The protectors wore a new set of gloves as they moved from one to another boy. Each man took turns poking their fingers inside their holes without the naked boys knowing whose fingers were inside them. Some of the protectors played with their cocks and balls.

When all the protectors had checked each boy out, Mr. Korsak said, "Sit at the table decorated with the color of your collar."

As Alek scanned the room for the table with the red tablecloth, Rafe Escobar stopped him. He wore a red tie around his neck. Mr. Escobar grabbed Alek's cock in a death grip and rubbed it until he was sporting a major erection. Alek lowered his eyes, displaying how embarrassed and degraded he felt.

"Bring me a Jack Daniels on the rocks," Mr. Escobar ordered.

Fully erect, though not by choice, Alek rushed to the bar.

"How are you doing?" Emilio asked.

"I'm getting through it. I need a Jack Daniels on the rocks for Mr. Escobar."

"What about you? You should have a drink too."

"Vodka on the rocks, please."

Emilio returned with the two drinks and set them down.

"Thanks. I think my night just improved. Mr. Escobar just talked to me, and he's wearing a red tie."

"That means he's extremely interested in you if he's wearing the color tie that matches the color of you collar. I figured he'd take the best one here."

Mr. Escobar wasn't where he'd left him, so Alek scanned the room. He focused on the men's hair color to figure out who was who because all the protectors dressed alike made it difficult. Most of the men had various shades of brown hair and a few had gray. Was this the reason Uncle Sacha had ordered him to die his hair dark brown? Was he trying to pass Alek as a Mexican, so he could fit in with the rest of them? If that were true, why would Russians be here too? Then again, he didn't want Alek easily spotted by his enemies. Hopefully, no one from the Pavlenko family was hiding out here.

"Hey, Alek, he's at your table with the red tablecloth." Emilio pointed to where Mr. Escobar was sitting.

"Thanks, you're a lifesaver." Alek carried the two drinks to his table and sat across from Mr. Escobar.

"So, I hear your name is Alek. Tell me about yourself," Mr. Escobar said.

For the first time, Alek saw Mr. Escobar's sparkling brown eyes. He had wide shoulders, defined muscles, and strong legs. He reminded Alek of a marine in a suit looking like a bouncer from a rough biker bar. Up close, he stood much taller than he appeared from a distance. The man went to the trouble to find out his name. Alek listened for an accent but didn't detect one.

"I don't know where to begin, Sir." Alek inhaled his intoxicating scent, a mixture of lime and some sort of tobacco, but not cigarettes or cigar. Maybe he smoked a pipe.

"Tell me about your parents."

"They were murdered along with my two older brothers when I was four years old." Alek picked up his glass and downed his drink in one gulp.

"I'm sorry to hear that. Where were you when that happened?" He took a drink from his glass.

"I hid inside the toy chest in my bedroom closet. My father told me to hide there if I ever heard gunfire." Alek paused to take a breath. "They shot everyone in the head in a matter of minutes. Blood was splattered everywhere."

"How did you get out of there?"

"Uncle Sacha found me and carried me to his home. We had to walk past my dead family in the living room. I'll never forget those gruesome images. My uncle ended up raising me."

"Did you ever find out who did this to your family?"

"My uncle Sacha said my father was working with a Mexican cartel. Something went wrong, and they put a hit on him and his family. That's the story I've been told since I was a small boy."

"But they didn't go after you?"

"Well, as of now, they haven't put a hit on me that I know of."

"My question is why didn't they take you down at a later date?"

"I was under Uncle Sacha's protection, so no one touched me. He's the head of our family."

"Tell me why you need protection now. Be completely honest with me. I need to know about all your enemies to protect you."

"It started when I was a teen. I fell in love with a man who was twenty-two. His family was feuding with my family. My uncle forbid me to see him, but I didn't listen. We were together until his father found us. That bastard called my uncle and made him pick me up at their home. His Russian mobster family is still after me."

"What's the name of the man you were in love with?"

"Does it matter? He's dead." Alek's pain and loss over his lover washed over him in waves, engulfing and overwhelming him into immobility. He dared not indulge himself in his eternal grief.

"It matters. What's his name?"

"Burain Pavlenko."

"When was Burain murdered?"

"A little over two years ago."

"Why isn't the Belanov family protecting you anymore?"

"They believe I betrayed the Belanov family when I was with Burain."

"Why now and not two years ago?"

"I was in prison for two years for selling cocaine. Someone from the Pavlenko family planted it on me after Burain had been murdered. They blamed me and my family for his death."

"And you had nothing to do with it?"

"Look at me. Do I look like a person who would kill someone? I loved him." Alek wished he could get dressed and Mr. Escobar would remove his damn mask.

"I want you to do to me what you did to the other man before I make my decision." He motioned to the dark man across the room.

"You want me to give you a blowjob?"

"Yes, that's what I said."

"Can you remove your mask?" Alek asked.

"No. Get on it, *mi angelito*." Mr. Escobar pushed his chair away from the table. He unbuttoned and unzipped his slacks and hauled out his huge cock with precum shining at the slit. He pulled out his balls too, for good measure.

Alek walked around the table to where he was sitting. His legs were spread apart while Mr. Escobar was pulling on the cockhead. Alek knelt there staring at the huge cock pressing downward along his upper thigh. He just stared at it, not doing much of anything. It was the most beautiful cock he'd ever seen, and he had seen many in prison, too many. He wanted to claim it as his. Alek's cock was literally standing up. No way could he hide his desire for this man.

He took hold of the hard cock, licked the head, and made slurping noises. Alek ran his tongue over the slit and the precum wetness on the head.

Mr. Escobar moaned. "Lovely tongue."

Alek used his hands to fondle and gently pinch this hot man's balls. He tasted delicious, intoxicating like his scent. Alek's tongue swirled around the large mushroom head, and he dug his tongue inside the slit. He nailed it with his tongue, in and out with deep, slow strokes.

"Ah, yeah, that's it... Oh, fuck, yeah – use your spit, too."

Alek spit on his cock and sucked the shaft up and down. He licked Mr. Escobar's balls leaving a wet trail. Bobbing his head, he deep throated that cock so far it made his eyes water. Unable to breathe each time his cock hit the back of his throat, he fell into a regular rhythm allowing him to catch his breath. Mr. Escobar's cock throbbed inside his mouth as he yanked at Alek's hair.

"Ah... yes... keep doing that." He panted.

Mr. Escobar's steel erection pulsated as it plowed deeply into Alek's mouth. His entire body was soaking wet and his knees quivered and trembled. Alek felt how tight his balls were. He was very close to emptying them. He wanted to please this man because he knew this was the man he wanted to go home with. The other protectors and the naked guys stood around watching. Out of nowhere, Mr. Escobar pushed Alek's head away from his cock and zipped up his slacks.

"Stop. We're going to finish this later." Mr. Escobar removed the red tie around his neck and went to put it around Alek's. "I promise to protect you, Alek. Do you accept my protection?"

"Yes, Sir." Alek wondered if they were bonded.

"Call me, Rafe. You and I are going to be tight, so we're going to be on a first-name basis."

Alek nearly cried when Rafe put the red tie around his neck. This sexy stranger wanted to protect him. Emilio was right; this man was smoking hot.

"Thank you, Sir." Alek stroked the red tie with his fingers, grateful this particular man had chosen him.

"You don't have to 'Sir' me. We're not in the military."

"Can I get dressed?"

"Follow me. I have clothes for you."

"What about the clothes I came in?" Alek asked, wondering if this stranger already knew his sizes, but then maybe they wouldn't fit.

"Someone saw you wearing those clothes. We're going off the grid tomorrow."

"Off the grid?"

"I love that big erection you have when I'm talking to you," Rafe said.

"Thank you." Alek looked down at his stiff cock, still sticking straight up, unable to hide his feelings. Rafe took his hand and led him to a room down the hall.

"Get dressed."

"Can I keep the red tie?"

"Sure you can."

Alek saw the navy blue jeans, shirt, and hoodie. He quickly dressed and laced up his combat boots. All the clothing and the boots fit perfectly. Rafe removed his suit and dressed in the same kind of clothing he wore. So they were going off the grid dressed like twins.

"Are you going to take off your mask?" Alek was dying to see what his face looked like.

Rafe inched closer to Alek. "You can take it off."

Alek slowly removed it from Rafe's face and gasped. "Wow, you really *are* hot. Emilio was right."

"Emilio said that?" Rafe laughed.

"Yes."

"He's my little cousin. You two will see each other again when they meet up with us."

"Emilio never mentioned you were his cousin."

Rafe pulled Alek closer to him and pressed his lips on his.

"Here's your wallet." Rafe handed it to Alek.

CHAPTER THREE

Rafe Escobar

Rafe jumped into his car after he made sure Alek had fastened his seatbelt. Staring at the blond streak highlighting his dark brown hair made Alek seem all the more adorable. *Someone did a fucked-up job of dying his hair.* Rafe imagined fucking this beautiful man. Alek's eyes lit up the room when he smiled, and the way he rested his pouty lips, slightly open when he finished speaking, tugged at his heart.

Another captivating characteristic about Alek was that Rafe could not remember ever seeing anyone with such sad eyes.

At times, Alek's voice was heavy with shame, the same way his guilt weighed down upon his shoulders. Rafe planned to change all that by helping Alek find his inner soul and the power within him. He'd start with trying to ease the seriousness of his dire situation with many fun activities. The poor guy needed to laugh and have some fun after what he'd been through for the last two years.

"Can you tell me where we are going?" Alek asked.

"For now, we're heading toward my home, but tomorrow we're leaving to live off the grid for thirty days."

"Where do you live?" Alek leaned his head against the door window.

"Ojai, tucked away in the trees and hidden from people. We have an hour to drive. Ask me any questions you want. Don't be afraid of me."

"I'm kind of nervous about this protector bonding. Could you explain it to me?"

"It means I have to trust that you are truthful to me at all times. So far you've been honest. Believe it or not, I know more about you than you do. To bond means I'm fucking you and no one else. That hasn't been established yet, but I'm not worried about that part. Are you?"

"No, I guess not. Did you know you were going to pick me before the party?"

"I read all the new boys' applications and decided you needed me the most. I'd say you're in more danger than the others. You don't have one gang after you or the law. Your threats involve two feuding Russian mafia families. I'm including the Belanovs. I don't trust them."

"Did my uncle Sacha hire you?"

"He did. I spoke to him on the phone, not in person."

"Why don't you trust him?" Alek asked.

"I don't trust anyone and neither should you. My job is to keep you safe, and yours is to keep my dick happy. That's our deal."

"Are you saying I shouldn't trust you?" Alek looked confused for a moment.

"You must trust me for our arrangement to work, and I need to trust you. So there can be no lies between us. If you fuck up, I'll punish you."

"Punish me?" One brow curled up, and his mouth opened into a perfect 'O', giving Alek's attractive face the look of a question mark.

"I'll whip your ass with my belt. Don't do anything wrong, and your ass will never be introduced to it. My dick, however, will fuck your ass anytime I want. Do you have a problem with that arrangement?"

"No, I eventually became used to getting fucked a couple of times a day in prison." Alek closed his eyes as if he were trying to rid the terror of his prison memories.

"I bet you were, but I won't humiliate you or hurt you when I fuck you. If I do, tell me."

"How do I know what you consider fucking up?"

"It's real simple. Do as I say the first time, every time and never risk your safety."

"My uncle Sacha made me take STD tests." Alek changed the subject abruptly as if he didn't want to continue discussing rules and consequences.

"I have all your paperwork. Your uncle was quite thorough sending your files."

"So you knew everything about me before you asked me questions?" Alek smirked.

"That was a minitest to see if you were honest. If you'd lied to me, I wouldn't have given you my red tie. I'd have sent you to the camp, and you'd have had to wait for the next party." Rafe continued, "We don't get many Russians here. They usually take care of their own."

"Are you Mexican?" Alek asked.

"No. Not everyone who can speak Spanish is Mexican. My family is from Colombia. I'm bilingual and was born and raised in San Diego."

"Colombians are in charge of the drug cartels," Alek said.

"That's my family you're talking about. Like you, I was kicked out of the Escobar family, but I have my brother Mateo and my cousin Emilio with me," Rafe said.

"I like Emilio."

"He's a love. He's in the program because my family put a hit on him when they found out he was gay. Emilio

44

and I were always close when we were growing up. He's much younger than I am."

"How old are you?" Alek asked.

"I'm thirty-four years old, and he's eighteen," Rafe said.

"Why did you get kicked out then?" Alek asked.

"They kicked me out before they found out I was gay. I didn't announce it or come out to them or give them any reason to think I was gay. I hid it by dating girls."

"So why then?"

"Long story. The short version is I refused to take part in the family's drug cartel business. They didn't want me dead like… just away from them."

"What about your brother?"

"Mateo didn't want to get involved with the cartel either. He's working with me, but he's not gay. He's protecting a young woman. You'll meet her. Her name is Anouska Asimov. She's Russian and around your age or younger. She'll probably tell you her story one day."

"When we go off the grid, are we going to be alone?"

"Never alone. We travel in a group of ten. So basically there'll be five couples. Besides us, our group will include Mateo and Anouska, Kaden and Emilio, Valerik and Liam, and James and Dante. You'll meet all of them when we meet up tomorrow."

"Is this Valerik, Mr. Korsak?"

"Yes, that's him. You can call him Valerik. James is the one you gave a blowjob to."

"Oh, fuck," Alek said. "And you let him?"

"You weren't mine, yet. I wanted you to take full part in the party. It's traditional for our new members. He won't go near you anymore."

"Didn't Dante get pissed?" Alek asked.

"Dante is new like you. I guess James liked Dante's blowjob better than yours." Rafe paused and watched Alek's smile fade. "Ha-ha-ha." He burst out laughing.

"He told me I gave him an A plus blowjob. I guess he lied, but I'd rather have you than him." Alek's smile returned, but he didn't laugh.

"James already knew I was going to protect you. I could have stopped it, but I didn't want you to know everything was set up before the party. I wanted to see how you naturally responded to me without knowing my imminent plans. By the way, I loved your first reaction to me."

"I get it."

"When we're off the grid, no electronics. None. No communication at all. Do you have a phone?"

"Not anymore."

"Good. I like you already." Rafe winked.

"What about clothes? I only have what I'm wearing."

"Don't worry. That's my job, and it's been taken care of. Everything is packed for tomorrow."

"Thanks," Alek said with a smile.

"Your uncle paid me a shit load of money. He wants you safe, but mostly he wants you happy, something we have in common."

His uncle Sacha had known everything about Alek, right down to the cigarette brand he had smoked and what alcohol he drank. Rafe had taken care of his cigarettes, Stoli Vodka, and Amstel beer. His uncle Sacha had said to make Alek happy, so the old man could die in peace when it was his time. *Was he sincere or was he guilty about something? It was clear the old man never wanted to see Alek again.*

"I love Uncle Sacha, even though he banished me. He wouldn't even allow me in his home when I was released from prison. He stuffed me in a motel for a week. I know it wasn't easy for him, but he's responsible for all the Belanovs, not just me. My crimes against my family haven't been forgiven and apparently never will be." Alek slumped into his seat.

"Sometimes, those we love the most aren't who we think they are. Remember that." Rafe wished he could blurt out the truth, but Alek had enough to deal with right now.

As soon as Rafe parked his car, they walked to the porch. "What do you think?"

"It's beautiful here."

Alek followed behind him as if he were terrified someone would take him out any minute. The poor guy didn't feel safe, but he would soon. They went to the kitchen and sat down.

"So let me tell you about our next thirty days. Hey, do you want a beer?"

"Sure, but I'd like a cigarette too."

"You can't smoke inside, but you can on the back porch. Let me get our beers first." Rafe pulled two beers out of the refrigerator and handed one to Alek.

"Thanks."

Rafe slid the door open, stepped outside with Alek behind him. They gazed at the beautiful sparkling lit pool. Chaise lounges dotted the pool's concrete skirt. He scanned the mini forest, looking past the Jacuzzi. The ten-foot-high fence kept strangers out. No one could see anything in the yard or on the porch since there were no nearby houses and plenty of mature trees. Regardless, the fence stood high enough to provide them with complete privacy.

They sat on the chairs around the pool. Alek lit a cigarette and Rafe lit his pipe.

"Where are we going tomorrow?" Alek asked, sipping his beer.

"Fawnskin. We have five cabins there. The others in our group will be there too. As I said, we work in teams of five couples."

"Fawnskin. Where is that? Is that in California? I've never heard of it."

"That's the point. It's near Big Bear."

"I've never been there either. My uncle took me to Russia a lot. We have family there. He also took me all through Europe."

"Do you know how to use a gun?" Rafe enjoyed looking at Alek under the night shining on his face. He seemed more relaxed than he was at the party. Though he had managed himself very well.

"Yes, my uncle taught me how to shoot with all kinds of weapons. I don't really like them all that much." Alek drank his beer, looking at the view.

"You're going to need one when we come back. Right now, you're a high-risk target, so that's why we need the thirty days off the grid," Rafe said.

"Where do we go when we're not off the grid?" Alek inhaled the smoke from his cigarette and exhaled.

"We'll move around a lot. We have places all over the US. So we rotate, but not in any specific order. We can't leave any traces or establish a pattern."

"Will I be able to work?"

"What do you do?" Rafe laughed to himself. Alek would never have to work, but it was admirable that he wanted to.

"I was attending USC Berkeley, but I've never worked."

"What did you study?"

"I was majoring in Veterinary Science. My uncle hoped I'd go into his business at some point, but I wanted to be a veterinarian. I never got past the basic classes before I was sent to prison."

"Well, the only way you can attend school is online right now. We'll see how it goes. The Belanovs live in San Geronimo, California. So it's possible we could locate where you can attend school. Maybe another state or Southern California when things get stabilized."

"So, what about working?" Alek asked again.

"I don't know, but we can get jobs in other states depending on many things."

"I want to do something with my life besides running from Russians."

"Well, you'll be doing something. Running might be in your future for a while, but you won't be alone."

"How could falling in love cause so much shit?" Alek asked.

"I don't know. I've never fallen in love, so I'm the wrong person to ask." He swigged his beer.

Rafe's cock was stirring. He wanted Alek to get on his knees and make him go to town on his cock and balls again. He needed to get off. He'd been waiting all night for this to happen. When he peered at Alek, Rafe saw he was looking at him intently.

"Would you like me to finish sucking you off?" Alek asked as if he were reading his mind. It was casual as though he was asking Rafe to pass the bread.

"Fuck yes. I was just thinking about that, you little mind reader." Rafe gestured for him to get on his knees.

"You had that look on your face." Alek stood and walked around to Rafe, kneeling between his legs. He

51

unzipped Rafe's jeans, shoved them down, and grabbed his stiffening cock.

As soon as Rafe's hands were free from the bottle of beer he'd been holding and his cock freed from his pants, he took control. His erection was thick and long enough that it stretched Alek's mouth open as he slipped into it. He managed to take it. When he slid deeper, Alek swallowed, accepting all of him.

"Take it. Take it all," Rafe shouted, tugging Alek's hair.

Sliding out slowly Rafe then pulled Alek back until he was once again deep inside his throat, then pushed his cock in and out, harder and faster. Alek's throat was going to be as sore as his asshole was about to become. He continued hammering into Alek's throat taking that momentary pause before coming, feeling it swell as it prepared to erupt. He needed this.

A loud screech of tires on the driveway blasted, then a car door slammed. They heard footsteps, followed by someone trying to open their front door.

"Shit, who the hell is that?" Rafe pushed Alek's head away, put his cock back into his pants and zipped up his jeans. Taking his gun from his pocket into his hand, he turned and ordered Alek, who was still kneeling on the floor, a directive. "Stay here and for God's sake stay down."

He inched toward the sliding door and stopped. "Oh fuck, it's just Mateo and Anouska. I forgot they were spending the night, so we can get an early start."

Rafe unlocked and opened the sliding door.

"There you two are," Mateo said. "I thought you'd be in bed fucking."

"Very funny. This is my beautiful Alek Belanov."

"Oh, now we have three Russians in our group," Mateo said.

"Technically, Mr. Korsak is a Ukrainian. They aren't part of Russia anymore," Alek said.

"That's true," Mateo said. "You know you can't be any safer than with my brother Rafe. He's the best."

"Where's Anouska?" Rafe asked.

"She's in the kitchen fixing us a snack," Mateo said.

"Of course. Sounds just like her," Rafe said.

Anouska soon returned carrying a tray of salted cucumbers and tomatoes, setting the two dishes on a round umbrella table.

"Come and sit." Her Russian accent was stronger tonight. When Rafe had thought about it, she had a similar way of emphasizing words as Sacha Belanov. *It made sense. They were both Russian. It would be great if Alek could have a friendship with her, and he already liked Emilio, but who wouldn't? He was so endearing and lovable.*

They all sat at the table under a blue umbrella.

"Anouska, this is Alek Belanov," Rafe said. "I'm protecting him now."

"Hello, Alek, that's such a lovely name. I'm happy we have another Russian in the group. Do you speak Russian?"

Alek nodded. "I'm not perfect at it, but I spent vacation time in Russia with family."

"What part?" Anouska asked.

"Saint Petersburg."

"That's where I was sent to live for a couple of years."

"That's interesting," Alek said. "I haven't had salted cucumbers and tomatoes in a while. I love them. These are great."

Mateo got up to get two bottles of beer for him and Anouska.

"What time are we leaving?" Mateo asked.

"About five. We'll stop on the way for breakfast," Rafe said.

"I set up the coffee for us in the morning," Anouska said.

"Thanks," Rafe said. "I think we need to turn in early. Are you ready, Alek?"

Alek finished his beer and stomped out his cigarette. "Sure."

"See you guys at five," Rafe said.

CHAPTER FOUR

Alek Belanov

Alek enjoyed meeting Anouska. There was something about her that was familiar and by listening to her, he felt peaceful. It could be the accent similar to Uncle Sacha's. But her eyes. Her kind eyes reminded him of someone, but he couldn't place who as of yet. The way she moved around him, the more he enjoyed her energy, and it wasn't anything sexual.

"Since you attempted to give me a stellar blowjob twice, I think I'll pass on the blowjob tonight and go straight to fucking," Rafe said.

"Sounds good to me."

"I was tested at your uncle Sacha's request, and he sent me your recent tests, so I know you're all clear. Is it okay for me to fuck you without a condom?"

"Sure. Can I take a shower first?" Alek was touched by Rafe's question. Of course, his uncle Sacha would make sure Rafe was cleared of any diseases. Now, he understood why his uncle had taken him to the Russian doctor for all those damn tests. He'd already known he was going to send him away, just like Rafe had already known he was going to choose him, but he had made him go to that crazy party anyway.

"Alek, what's wrong with you? How do you know I was tested because I said so? Don't you realize that you must be more careful when it comes to your protection?"

"I didn't know I had the right to demand to see your tests," Alek said.

"If it involves your safety, physical, emotional, or medical, you need to see proof and demand it."

"Can I see your tests, please?" Alek asked, uncomfortable with demanding anything from another person. He'd have to work on this part for Rafe.

"That's a good start." Rafe pulled out a paper from his top drawer and handed it to Alek. "Read it."

Alek read the results and returned the paper to Rafe. "Thanks, Rafe."

"Want to shower with me or alone?" Rafe asked.

"Do I have a choice?" Alek asked, surprised he was asked and not told what to do.

"It's your choice."

"With you."

"Strip off your clothes," Rafe ordered like a drill sergeant.

Alek rushed to obey; still shocked he had been given a choice. When they'd finished undressing, Rafe pulled Alek into the bathroom and turned on the water, still holding Alek in a tight grip. When the water had warmed, he pulled him inside. Standing side by side, Rafe was a good five inches taller.

"You're beautiful," Rafe whispered to Alek, "but why did you dye your hair?" he asked while he poured shampoo onto Alek's hair.

"My uncle Sacha told me to do it." Alek was soaping his body with shower gel.

"The color is bleeding out," Rafe said.

"Shit. I forgot. It's that temporary hair color that washes out when you shampoo it. It's already washing out." Alek pointed to the dark color of the water coming from his hair. "You're about to see the real me."

"You don't need dark hair anymore. Leave it the color you were born with."

"I'm sorry for getting the shower dirty." Alek lowered his eyes, ashamed of the mess he had made.

"Don't worry about it."

"I don't understand why Uncle Sacha wanted me to dye it in the first place." After Alek finished flushing the dark water down the drain, he soaped up Rafe's back for him.

"I didn't ask him to make you dye your hair if that's where you're going. I imagine he thought you might be recognized when you left the motel for the party. It's good in a way, because your cousin Pavel saw your darker hair."

Alek was blindsided that he knew his cousin. "How do you know about Pavel?" *Had Mr. Korsak told him about the incident with Pavel at the door?*

"Like I said, I know more about you than you do." Rafe rubbed his hand along his trimmed beard. "I like the way you scrub my back."

"Thanks. I don't know if that's a good thing that you know so much about me or not." Alek loved Rafe's beard, it was so sexy.

"It's all good. The more I know the better I can protect you. Keeping you safe is my primary objective."

"I guess you need to know everything, but sometimes it's a little creepy."

"Can I shave you?" Rafe asked.

"Where?"

"Everywhere, but not the gorgeous hair on your head."

"O... kay?" Alek liked it when Rafe suggested something he'd never done. It made it seem kinky from his limited experience, which mostly consisted of bend over and take it vanilla.

Rafe turned off the shower, shook the can of shaving foam, and applied it to Alek's chest, armpits, and down to cover the rest of his body. He applied more to his ass and the back of his legs.

"I want you to feel everything I do to you," Rafe said.

"I don't have much hair on my chest, and for sure there's none on my ass."

"Doesn't matter. I want your skin completely smooth and hypersensitive. I want you to feel my touch on your body."

Rafe's voice carried authority. Coming from the six-foot four-inch stature only magnified it. Everything he said felt like an order, like a whip against wet skin stinging just a bit, but at its most tender, it relaxed him like the aura from singing angels.

"I hope no one else will ever be allowed to touch me," Alek whispered, lowering his eyes and unsure he had the right to say anything.

Rafe didn't respond, leaving Alek's mind to spin with worry. He was pleased they were in the shower and Rafe was concentrating on shaving him. Two tears silently rolled down his cheeks and he wiped them away with the back of his hand.

Finding out Mr. Korsak would be part of their group concerned him, but he was teamed up with Liam. Uncle Sacha must have known him from some place in his life. Another concern was James and that blowjob Rafe had watched him give. Certainly, Rafe didn't expect him to give him any more blowjobs?

"Hey, are you okay?" Rafe asked.

Alek nodded unable to speak without getting emotional.

"Are you sure?"

"I'm okay."

Rafe shaved Alek everywhere. He took his time, removing every hair from his body; there hadn't been much to begin with. When he reached his balls and pubic hair, Alek tensed up but remained quiet and still. He wanted to do this right and not fuck up any part of Rafe's plan up, grateful that he'd taken an interest in him. Rafe moved behind him to finish his back and run the razor over his already hairless ass. After he'd finished, he rinsed every part of Alek's body with warm water.

Bending down, Rafe rubbed his ass in a loving, caring way, kissing each cheek.

"Part of my bonding is to mark you. I'll use my hand on your ass, so we have a visible sign between us. Are you okay with that?"

"I want to be bonded with you. Yes, I'll do whatever it takes."

Without warning, slaps hit the cheeks of his ass, right above where his thighs began. Rafe smacked repeatedly on the same area over and over. Alek felt the burn much more because Rafe had shaved him, leaving it extra sensitive to any stimulation. Rafe didn't let that stop him. He continued slapping Alek as if he would never stop. Alek bit his lip to prevent himself from screaming, and then the spanking abruptly stopped.

"Perfect!" Rafe said.

"What's perfect?"

"My handprint on your ass." Rafe stepped out of the shower and toweled himself.

"I like the idea of being bonded to you." Alek rubbed his ass.

"Get out, so I can show you," Rafe ordered.

As soon as Alek stepped out, Rafe toweled him dry and held up a mirror to show him the handprint.

"Wow!"

"Do you like it?" Rafe asked.

"Yes. I love it. So, is that it? Are we completely bonded?"

"Bonding isn't something to rush. You're safe here with me. I'm not going to return you or send you to the camp."

"I'm sorry for bringing it up so much."

"You can bring up anything what's on your mind. If things between us stay good for one week, we'll be bonded."

"Does that mean you'll be fucking other guys during the week?"

"We're going off the grid with our group. We stay with our assigned partner. No switching."

"I don't know how it all works."

"Are you afraid I'll pass you around to the other protectors?" Rafe asked.

"I thought you might do that."

"Were you passed around in prison?"

Alek nodded. "I can't talk about that in too much detail. I'm sorry."

"Don't worry about such things. You're out of prison. No one is going to fuck with you like that because I'm protecting you. I promise no one will fuck you."

"Thank you for explaining it to me."

Rafe nodded in response. "Get into bed," Rafe ordered.

Looking at the bed Alek naturally was drawn to the side he was used to sleeping on, but this was different. He needed to sleep on the side Rafe wanted him on. "Which side?" he asked.

"The side away from the window and while you're at it get on your stomach." Rafe lowered the blinds and closed them.

Alek flipped over the comforter. Lying on his stomach with his head on the pillow, he inhaled the fresh scent of the sheets mingled with a hint of Rafe's cologne. Alek remembered when he had been told to lie on his stomach or bend over a bathroom sink in prison. There had been a line of men waiting to fuck him. This was different with just Rafe. Alek could do this for him. He had to own up to his part in this deal. Alek was safe and this man wouldn't hurt him like the ones from the last two years.

Rafe pulled a tube of lube from under his pillow. He spread some on his palm, and around Alek's opening, inserting one, then two fingers, almost frantically. Alek winced from the surprise at the rough entry. He arched into Rafe's prying fingers, needing more.

Rafe blew on Alek's ear, sending chills down his body. "You okay?"

Alek nodded.

Sneaking a kiss, Rafe continued slowly pumping his fingers, hitting just the right spot to open Alek. With his other hand he reached around and gently played around the exterior of Alek's nipples. The mixture of pain and pleasure had Alek sinking fast. Rafe licked the outline of Alek's tattoo on his lower back.

"What does that Russian writing tattoo mean?" Rafe asked.

"It's an abbreviation for mother in Russian. I got it when I was sixteen to honor my mother."

"I'm going to tattoo your ass. And you know what it'll say?"

"Not my entire ass?" Alek asked.

"No, something small, but big enough to warn any fucker who even thinks about touching *mi angelito's* sweet ass to think again. It'll say, 'This ass is the sole property of Rafe Escobar.'"

"When are you going to do that?" Alek asked.

"I'm kidding, you." He rumpled his hair. "I'm not your master nor are you my slave. I'm your protector taking some dick liberties with you. Your safety is my primary concern."

"Too bad. It sounded hot."

"We'll see then. Give us time."

Rafe pulled out his fingers slowly, aimed his dick at Alek's opening, and moved in slowly. Inch by precious inch his hard cock disappeared inside Alek until his pubes were crushed against Alek's skin. Then, while still moving fast and deep, he pulled Alek's ass up off the sheets, wrapped his hand around his cock, and stroked it, moving in the same rhythm as his hips.

"I love your firm ass, and your cock is so nice and big. I love playing with it."

"Hmmm."

Alek moaned through uneven breathing and made unintelligible loud gurgling sounds. Rafe continued to bang his prostate, driving him crazy, until he shot his hot load deep inside.

"Come, *mi angelito*," Rafe managed to say through the aftershocks of his orgasm.

Alek's ass tightened and pulsed around him, until, without saying a word, he shot into Rafe's hand. Some of his cum splashed down onto the sheets, creating a wet spot they both would want to avoid sleeping on.

"Tomorrow, we're going to talk about things," Rafe said.

"What things? Did I do something wrong?"

Alek worried he wasn't a good fuck for Rafe, which meant they'd never be bonded, since part of the bond meant they would be monogamous. Alek knew he tended to think that anytime someone handsome fucked him it meant he loved him or at least was on his way in that direction. He could kick himself in the ass for being so damn foolish. Even after spending two years in prison, he'd learned nothing about alpha men. Was it so difficult to ask not to be passed around? He hated the idea of Rafe fucking another man. *What's wrong with me?*

"Nothing's wrong," Rafe said. "I just want to update you on some information. I'm taking you into my confidence. That means what I tell you is never to be repeated."

"I'll never betray you. You don't have to tell me anything until you can trust me if that would make you feel better about it." Alek wondered what kind of information Rafe was going to share with him. Possibly something to do with his uncle Sacha or something even worse he knew nothing about.

"I'll decide what I share, not you."

Rafe kissed him, smothering the questions he must have known were coming. Alek loved the feel of his lips.

"Sleep. We have to get up early," Rafe ordered.

68

"Hey, were you ever in the military?" Alek asked. The man sure knew how to shout out orders.

"Four years in the Marines," Rafe said with pride.

Alek yawned as he tried to get comfortable. "Thought so. Good night."

"See you in the morning," Rafe said.

Feeling unsure of his future with Rafe, Alek turned his back to him and closed his eyes with the hope he'd get through sleeping without disturbing nightmares.

***

In the morning, Alek crawled under the comforter quietly as not to disturb Rafe's sleep. The clock beside the bed read four forty-five. Leaning over Rafe's sleeping body, Alek moved his lips onto Rafe's massive cockhead. Soft moans told Alek that Rafe had woken up and was enjoying his warm, velvety mouth. It appeared that Rafe wasn't upset that he'd taken the liberty. He flicked his tongue in the slit, moving it in and out. With his hand, he gently jacked Rafe's cock while trying to stuff as much of it into his mouth as possible. Pulling back, he bathed the cockhead with his tongue, making it wet and warm.

"What a way to wake up," Rafe whispered.

Rafe reached down, taking Alek's head in his enormous hands and pushing it deeper until his cock hit the back of Alek's throat. As he released Alek's head, Alek pulled off Rafe's cock, and his lips traveled back down to the thick cockhead, tasting the clear juices. The already tight skin of Rafe's cock stretched and tightened further as Alek's lips slid across the head. He planted kisses on the crown and the side of his hardness. Rafe encouraged him by pushing his hips forward, letting him have his entire length. Alek could easily get used to Rafe's taste. Like everything else about this man, he craved it, never getting enough. Was this sexual attraction or was it amplified because he felt so safe with him?

Alek accepted the cock deeper into his mouth until Rafe's pulsing cockhead touched the back of his throat again. Alek's cock throbbed from the feeling of Rafe's thick cock sliding down his throat. Alek's lips closed tightly around the base of Rafe's shaft until his nose was buried in his pubic hair. As he deep throated him, he gently caressed Rafe's balls in both hands. Rafe threw the comforter back and sat up against the headboard, pulling Alek with him with his cock still buried in Alek's throat.

"I took home a dark-haired man and woke up with a blond in my bed," Rafe said, as he watched Alek serviced him.

Alek trembled when Rafe dropped kisses on his head and as his balls tightened, he knew he neared exploding. He could feel Rafe restraining him in place and holding his head firmly with his cock still buried in his throat. Rafe lifted Alek's head, then pounded back against his throat until he spilled his seed deep inside Alek's mouth.

"Fuck, that's perfect. Swallow it. Take all of it, *mi Angelito*." Rafe groaned and tugged Alek's hair.

Alek relished swallowing Rafe's semen while he held him in place. He swallowed as quickly as possible. At first, he struggled with the copious amount of his cum. Alek accepted his release, sucking harder now to empty him. After swallowing the cum, Alek found that some had escaped onto his chin. With a swipe of his finger he slid it into his mouth. It tasted salty, and he hunted for a hint of anything left on the tip of Rafe's cock, taking it one last time into his mouth. With great care, Rafe pulled free his slippery dick.

"I can get used to having you in my bed," Rafe said.

"I wanted to make sure you got your blowjob, since yesterday didn't work out."

"Oh, it worked out."

Alek's cock demanded attention, but he couldn't ask for it. He seemed to understand that it was not his place to hint at asking to be sucked off.

"I love your pretty mouth." Rafe kissed the top of his head. "I'm going to take really good care of you."

Then Rafe surprised Alek by leaning over him. Rafe swallowed Alek's cock in one go. He sucked, making loud noises, enhancing the experience. Rafe massaged his balls, licking every inch of Alek's cock. He pulled away and pulled one of Alek's balls into his mouth, gently sucking and licking.

Alek's grunts morphed to moans. He swayed his hips forward as Rafe's swollen lips sealed around his balls. Rafe drew the other side of Alek's sack into his full, wet mouth, being careful not to bite. He released Alek's balls and returned to his cock, licking and sucking the shaft. It didn't take him long to spill his sweet cum into Rafe's mouth. He swallowed it and licked his cock clean.

"I'll do better when we have more time," Rafe said.

"It was awesome." Alek laid back, closing his eyes.

Rafe let his eyes linger for a fraction longer. Sure enough Alek opened his eyes and gazed back, unguarded and calm.

CHAPTER FIVE

Rafe Escobar

After they had showered and dressed, Rafe said he had to take care of a few odds and ends with Mateo, so Alek went to the kitchen. The air was thick with the scent of coffee. He did a double take when he saw Anouska sitting alone at the table sipping her coffee. When she noticed him, she jumped up gesturing for Alek to sit at the table.

Anouska had straight blonde hair. This morning it touched the middle of her back, not too thick or thin, much different than the night before when her hair sat on top of her head in a bun. This morning she looked like a completely different woman. She wore cut-off jeans shorts, and a blue ruffled tank top that accentuated her eyes. She looked much younger than most women did in their early twenties.

"Do you take sugar or milk?" she asked.

"No. Just black, please."

She poured the hot coffee into a red mug and placed it in front of him. Alek inhaled her flowery scent, which smelled as if she'd bathed with roses. When she sat across from him, she smiled. She had full lips accented with warm pink lipstick contrasting with the pale creamy tone of her skin. Alek treasured being in her presence without comprehending why, since he just wasn't into girls. Her very presence brought comfort to him. It had to be the Russian connection between them, but he knew something deeper drew him to her, and it had nothing to do with sex.

"Where's Rafe?" she asked.

"He said he had some loose ends to take care of."

"How are you doing?" She sipped her coffee with the daintiness of a ballerina.

"I guess okay. I don't know how I'm doing or feeling. I wasn't expecting to be on the run. None of this was my choice." Alek said more than he probably should have.

"Did your uncle force you to come here?"

"Yes." Alek knew that he sounded like a weak loser.

"When I first came here, I lost some of my sadness, and things changed for the better. Mateo and I bonded right away as if we were made for each other. Love at first sight. Rafe and Mateo will find things to entertain us. I doubt there will ever be a boring moment while we're off the grid. You'd think there would be, but we all get along. It's really fun," Anouska said.

"If you say so. Rafe has been good to me so far," Alek said.

"Rafe hasn't had anyone to protect because he usually organizes everything. He assists protectors in our group and other groups as well. Mateo was as surprised as I was that Rafe took you on, but I'm delighted, and Rafe looks that way too." She smiled and batted her long dark eyelashes.

"I didn't know that about him. I always thought my life would take a different turn. I never expected to end up here. I messed up, so it's my fault I'm here."

"What grave sin did you commit, if you don't mind me asking?"

"I fell in love with a man. Our families don't get along, and that's saying it mildly. Some members of my family want me dead. So my uncle sent me here to keep me safe from them. That's what I think anyway, but I don't really know."

"What happened to the man you loved?"

"Dead. Someone took him out. His family blamed me for his death and put a hit on me. That's the other reason I'm here. I just got out of prison for a crime I didn't commit."

"Did you think someone set you up?"

"My uncle said my lover's family set me up to get rid of me."

"I'm sorry for you. I'm sure it wasn't easy to deal with."

"It's been two years. Some days, I'm over him and other days not so much."

Rafe and Mateo entered the kitchen together. Mateo had the same colored hair and eyes as his brother but was about two inches shorter than Rafe. Mateo wasn't a male model, but he should have been. He had lush, dark hair that he apparently groomed carefully. One big difference was that Mateo didn't have a beard. He was slenderly built and wore his clothes well. His perfect lips were ripe for the kissing.

"You guys ready?' Rafe asked.

"Sure, I put four cups of coffee in the tall traveler mugs for the road." Anouska pointed to the kitchen counter.

"Do I have time to have a cigarette?" Alek asked.

"Sure, I'll go outside with you," Rafe said. "We'll be right back."

"Oh no, another desperate smoker," Mateo said with a smile.

"That's fine. I'm going to tidy up the kitchen," Anouska said.

Mateo moved up, standing right behind her and kissed her neck. "I'll help you, my sweet princess."

Alek opened the sliding door to the porch with Rafe at his heels. Putting a cigarette between his lips, he inhaled deeply.

"Do you like Anouska?" Rafe asked.

"Yes. I feel good around her. I can't really explain it."

"Are you bisexual?" Rafe teased.

"No. Not even a little bit. I just like her, that's all. There's nothing sexual going on if that's what you're thinking."

"I was kidding you. Anouska feels like a younger sister to me. I love having her with us."

"Do you own the party house?" Alek asked.

"No. We rented it for the day. The parties are once a month in different locations. Why do you ask?" Rafe pulled Alek's cigarette from his mouth, took a drag, then returned it.

"I wanted to know about the artist of those paintings on the wall," Alek said.

"The artist was an unknown Portuguese master during the early 16th century. The one in the bedroom is titled, *Hell*. They're reproductions. The originals are at the National Museum of Ancient Art in Portugal. I asked the owner the same question when I rented the house for the weekend. I found those art pieces fascinating."

Rafe picked up the ashtray, carried it to the kitchen, and threw the cigarette down the garbage disposal running the water while he washed the ashtray.

They each picked up their coffees, locked up the house, and hiked on the path to the car. Mateo and Anouska were already sitting in their car. Alek waved as he jumped into the car with Rafe. He placed his hand on Alek's thigh.

"What's going to happen when we get there?" Alek asked, sipping his hot coffee carefully.

"There're five cabins that are all close together. In the middle there's a fire pit to make a bonfire at night and roast marshmallows. We'll probably just sit around the fire pit and visit for a while, so you can get to know everyone. Then maybe we can go on a hike or even go boating."

"Do we have to go grocery shopping?"

"All done. Kaden did all the shopping for the cabins. The protectors put in their orders."

"Is Emilio with Kaden?"

"Yes, they left last night."

"How long has Valerik been with Liam?"

"He's new too. Why?"

"No reason."

"Hey, no secrets between us."

"He pinched my bare ass when he got a chance."

"Well, that makes sense. Valerik was interested in you, but I told him you belonged to me. I talked to him during the party, and he was happy with Liam."

"That's good. I sure don't want that old man touching me again."

"I'm much older than you are. Do you consider me an old man too?"

"At thirty-four, no. I don't know how old Valerik is, but he has gray hair and he's a little mean."

"His hair isn't all gray. He has some gray hair," Rafe said.

"I didn't like his accent."

Rafe adjusted the rearview mirror again and noticed the same black SUV was following with two men in the front. They had been driving for thirty minutes. The vehicle drove closer.

"Alek, get down," Rafe ordered.

Alek dropped to the floor and covered his head with his hands. "What's wrong?"

"It might be nothing, but this SUV is following us."

"So, an SUV is following us?"

"Yes."

"What color is it?" Alek asked.

"Black."

"What does the guy driving look like?"

"He's young, like you, same color hair as you, and that's all I can see," Rafe said.

"That could be Pavel and his brother."

Rafe threw his phone to Alek. "Phone code is 1976. Go to favorites and call Mateo."

"What should I say?"

"Tell him we're being followed by a black SUV and that we're taking a detour. We'll meet them later."

Fumbling with shaking hands, Alek tapped the phone and finally tapped Mateo's number.

"What's up?" Mateo asked.

"This is Alek. Rafe wants you to know a black SUV is following us. He's going to take a detour, and we'll meet you guys a little later." Alek's voice trembled.

"Does he need help?"

"He wants to know if you need help," Alek said.

"Tell him no," Rafe said.

"He doesn't need your help."

"Stay safe." Mateo ended the call.

"Don't worry, Alek. I'm going to get them off our tail. Your stupid cousin has nothing on me." Rafe took his phone back and put it in his shirt pocket.

Taking the next exit off the freeway, Rafe increased his speed and made a left turn to return to the freeway. The SUV followed by taking the next exit, leaving him farther behind than he had been. At the end of the ramp, the SUV stopped at the red light. Rafe took this time to enter the freeway and crossed over to the farthest left lane. He drove twenty miles faster than the speed limit.

Checking his rearview mirror constantly, Rafe could see that the SUV had lost them. As soon as an exit sign was close by, he crossed over to the right lane and exited off the next ramp, turning right onto the service road. He stopped at a car rental place and parked in the back of it.

"Stay down. I'm going to switch cars. Don't poke your head up for anything." Rafe handed Alek a Glock 17.

"What am I supposed to do with this?" Alek asked.

"Use it if you're threatened. I'll be back shortly."

There was no line inside, so he didn't have to wait for someone to help him. He rented a silver SUV for a month. While the salesman filled in all the paperwork, he sent a message to one of the protectors in the area to pick up his car. When the salesman handed him the keys, he hurried

81

back to get Alek, who was where he'd left him down below the dashboard by the front seat. He knocked on the door and peered inside so he wouldn't startle him, then motioned for him to come outside, Alek stepped out of the car with the gun in his hand. Rafe took the gun and put it in the pocket of his hoodie.

"Grab the suitcases," Rafe ordered.

Alek and Rafe moved the luggage to the new SUV's trunk, ran around, and jumped inside.

"Good job," Rafe said.

"What about *your* car? You're just leaving it here?" Alek asked.

"No. I sent a text to one of the local contacts in the area to pick it up for me." Rafe noticed the change in Alek's expression, sad and upset.

"Do they have the keys?"

"No, but they know where to get them."

Alek leaned his head against the window.

"Hey you, talk to me. What's up?"

"Pavel. That bastard wants me dead. He's…" Alek couldn't finish.

"Alek, he was following us. If he wanted to take you out, he could have started shooting at us on the freeway. I don't trust him, and you shouldn't either. It doesn't matter that you two are blood cousins or that you shared your childhood with him."

"Would you say that about Mateo or Emilio?" Alek asked.

"No. Mateo and Emilio love me as much as I love them. It's different because your cousin made threats to you. Mateo and Emilio never did anything like that."

"You know what I can't stop thinking about?"

"What? Tell me. I need to know."

"I know so you can protect me better, right?" Alek smiled.

"Right. Tell me, please. I can see you're upset."

"When Valerik opened the door for me at the party, Pavel had walked with me to the door. He said that *he* should have taken me out with the rest of them. Once a traitor always a traitor."

"Wow! He conveniently labeled you as a traitor because he wants your uncle Sacha's favor. That's pure bullshit. Were you two close when you were young?" Rafe really wished he could tell Alek who the *he* was.

"We were until he realized I was gay. He was like an older brother to me. We did everything together. He traveled with us and spent a lot of time at my uncle Sacha's house."

"You never noticed that he wanted what you had?" Rafe asked.

"No. I thought he loved me like a brother. I'm always wrong on love matters. Always the fool."

"You're not a fool. I don't think Pavel can do anything to you. Your uncle didn't pay for your protection so Pavel could take you down. You're safe with me."

"I feel like everyone's abandoned me. I don't belong anywhere."

"You have our group and me. Remember, your ass is mine. Nobody is going to fuck with you."

"Thanks," Alek whispered and leaned his head against the window again.

"We have another hour; then we'll be there," Rafe said.

Alek licking his lips reminded Rafe of his blowjob. Rafe's dick twitched in his jeans. He grabbed his covered cock and squeezed it. Turning to Alek, he could see the outline of the cock in his jeans. Then he looked back toward the road.

"Damn, Alek! I feel like pulling over."

"Do you need to take a piss?" Alek asked.

"No. I need to fuck you again."

"It's your call." Alek smiled.

"The things you do to me."

CHAPTER SIX

Alek Belanov

While hiking up the dirt road, overgrown with weeds, Alek saw the five cabins that could have been carbon copies of each other. Each one looked like it was straight out of a fairy tale or a child's picture book. They each carried two suitcases while trekking up the path to the cabins. Emilio and a buff blond man with tattoos met them halfway.

"Alek, you made it," Emilio said, taking one of the suitcases.

"I'm glad to see we're in the same group, but you already knew we would be. Didn't you?" Alek said with a smirk.

"Of course, I knew, but I wasn't allowed to tell you. Sorry," Emilio said.

"Not a problem. And you were right about Rafe," Alek said.

The blond tattooed man with Emilio stepped up and extended his hand. "I'm Kaden Donagan, Emilio's protector. We're both glad you've made it up here without any major incidents."

Alek eyed him up and down, then shook his hand, applying excessive pressure to hopefully give the impression that he was tough; not to be mistaken for any weakness. Kaden applied equal pressure and released his hand with a killer smile. The six-foot man had snake tattoos on both arms. His tight black short-sleeve shirt accented his muscled arms.

Kaden scanned Alek's body with bloodshot blue eyes like he was working off a hangover from the night before. At first glance, he looked like Alek's vision of a bouncer in a rough biker bar. These protectors must lift weights daily because Alek had never seen so many men with muscular upper bodies, wide shoulders, and strong handgrips. Kaden had longer hair than the other men and seemed likable right away. No wonder Emilio had spoken highly of him at the party.

"Everyone else went on a hike, so we're the only ones here right now," Emilio said.

They dropped the suitcases at the front door. "We'll let you guys settle in first. We'll be outside in front of our cabin," Kaden said.

"Thanks for the help and going shopping," Rafe said. "We'll be out in a little while."

He unlocked the door and stepped inside with Alek behind him. The interior was bright and airy. The wooden walls and floors were typical of a country cabin. The door opened into the living room with a stone fireplace on the outside wall. The room was furnished with a brown leather couch and two matching recliners, but there was no TV. Stacks of books and magazines decorated the coffee table, but all the walls were empty.

Dropping the suitcases, Rafe said, "Let's check out the kitchen for something to drink."

Alek followed him into a small kitchen with a tiny stove, two small wooden chairs, and a matching circular table.

Rafe opened the refrigerator and pulled out two beers. "We need one, after that crazy drive." He handed Alek a beer and asked, "So, what do you think?"

As Alek looked at the beer bottle, then in the fridge, he laughed. "Did my uncle Sacha tell you I drink Amstel beer?"

"Yes, he did. He sent me a list of what you like and don't like. He marked certain items with an asterisk, meaning this is the only brand."

"He didn't need to do that. I hope you don't think he has spoiled me because he hasn't."

89

"No. That man has never spoiled you, but he has a complicated relationship with you. I'm trying to figure him out and your relationship."

"Don't. Nobody has been able to figure him out yet. He was acting like he was giving away his dog to a better home along with a list of his favorite dog food."

"I guess that makes you my pet now. Let's check out the bedroom," Rafe said.

They carried the suitcases into a tiny bedroom. The oak furniture had the same woodsy smell like the rest of the cabin.

"I forgot how damn small the beds were here," Rafe said.

"Do you want me to sleep on the couch?"

"Fuck no. It means you'll be sleeping much closer to me."

"That's good. For a minute there, I thought you didn't want me to sleep with you," Alek said.

"You'll sleep with me every night, no matter what. Put your clothes away." Rafe's voice shifted to commander's mode on the second sentence.

They finished unpacking and returned to the living room to finish their beer.

"We need to discuss a couple of things," Rafe said.

"I'm listening." Alek worried about what dirt Rafe had found out about his family.

Rafe sat on one of the recliners, and Alek sat on the other one.

"As I said, there will be no electronic devices of any kind. That means, there will be no communication with anyone outside of our group and then only in person," he said.

"Rafe, I don't have any personal possessions with me. Don't you remember you walked me to a room while I was naked and gave me these clothes? I don't have any electronics."

"That's true. You'll be glad to know that I do have some electronics and more clothes for you at my home. There'll just be no devices on this trip."

"Did my uncle send you my laptop?"

"Yes, he did and a few other things as well. I'll show them to you when we get back home," Rafe said.

"That was thoughtful of him," Alek said without smiling.

"Don't go anywhere without me. If I have to check the perimeter, you're not to leave this cabin."

Alek didn't appreciate the tight rein Rafe had over him. He wanted to walk around, check things out, and talk to whomever he wanted. Spending so much time with one person disturbed him. *What if we run out of conversation?*

"Okay. So, are you saying I can't walk around on my own?"

"Not until we check the perimeter. We do that on the hour and take turns."

"Am I your… prisoner?" Alek tried to stop the shock and sadness showing on his face.

"In a way you are, but I'll try to make it fun for you."

"Sure," Alek said unconvincingly. *I'll never be free unless… unless what? I have no idea what needs to change for me to live my life. I want to be with Rafe, but not like this.*

"Remember when I told you that I knew more things about you than you knew?"

"I remember." Alek wished he'd just spit it all out instead of hinting to him or revealing one thing at a time. He definitely knew something about his family.

"Don't be so sure that the Pavlenko family was responsible for setting you up. That's not how Russian mobsters work. If they'd put a hit on you, you'd be dead like Burain."

"What are you saying?" Alek asked.

"I'm saying I'm not so sure they're after you or if they ever were."

"Then who is?" Alek asked

"Who would gain by you going to prison? That's the question," Rafe said.

"I guess Pavel. If I'm out of the picture, he gets Uncle Sacha and takes over when he's gone."

"You're out of the picture now, so he doesn't need you dead. That's all I'm saying. I'm still working on the other members of the Belanov family. Someone else wants you out of the way permanently."

Alek wondered why Rafe thought Pavel was behind it. Maybe it was someone in the Belanov family who had set him up to go down for selling cocaine. Then why did his uncle tell him the Pavlenko family had set him up? Wouldn't his uncle know if someone in the family would do this to him? Pavel didn't even want to talk to him. Alek didn't like what he had said about how someone should have killed him too. That could only refer to his parents' and brothers' murders. Why did Pavel and his brother follow them? Someone was lying to him, and he didn't know who.

"I need a cigarette after all this shit talk," Alek said.

"Let's grab another beer and go sit in the front outside with Emilio and Kaden. You can smoke outside."

Kaden and Emilio were talking when Alek and Rafe showed up.

"Is everything okay?' Emilio asked.

"Let's sit over there so we can talk." Alek pointed to the rockers on the front porch, far away enough from their protectors to have a private conversation.

Alek and Emilio walked over and sat on the rockers.

"So, what's up?" Emilio asked.

"I don't know if I can live like this," Alek said.

"I've been with Kaden for a month. Dante and Liam showed up the same day you did. We're all new except Anouska and Mateo, but they were already a couple before they joined the protectors. We'll get through it because we have to, and the alternative isn't acceptable," Emilio said.

"What were Rafe and the other protectors in our group doing before picking us?"

"Rafe is in charge of all the groups, so he rotated from one group to another. The others had other guys, but they left. From what I understand, some guys come for a shorter time than others do. Kaden said his last guy got a new identity and moved to another state."

"Why don't we get a new identity then?" Alek asked.

"I don't want a new identity because I don't want to live without my family. Rafe and Mateo want me with them, so I have no choice. I don't know how to be on the run all alone. They don't think it's safe for me to live by myself. Now, in your case, Russian mobsters are after you, and they dish out really gruesome deaths, so I wouldn't take any chances if I were you."

"I want to return to school and become a veterinarian. I want a nice quiet life with a man who loves me. I guess that's too much to ask." Alek wished Emilio hadn't reminded him of the way Russian crime families kill people. That was something he'd seen firsthand when he was only four years old. He knew only too well how brutal and merciless they were.

"I want to finish my high school diploma. I was about to finish my senior year when this happened," Emilio said.

"You will. You're still young."

"Don't you like Rafe?" Emilio asked.

"I do, but I'm just a job with dick liberties to him." Alek rolled his eyes.

"Give it time. Please? I don't want to read about the police finding your body parts spread all over the state," Emilio said.

"Emilio, don't be so dramatic." Alek couldn't bear to think about the details of an angry Russian mobster, and it was best to deny it existed.

About that time James and Dante walked over to the porch.

"Hi," Alek said, checking out Dante's green eyes.

James left Dante with them on the porch, and he joined the other guys.

"I saw you give James a blowjob," Dante said.

"So what?" Alek said. "I guess he liked your blowjob better because he didn't pick me." He wasn't about to listen to Dante brag about how he'd won James.

"No, it wasn't about that," Dante said

"I went home with Rafe."

"Can I bum a cigarette from you?"

Alek handed a cigarette and his lighter to Dante. In prison, cigarettes made Alek several friends, and since his uncle put money on his books, he could afford to buy them. Then the damn prison went to a no-smoking facility.

"James is a Dom, and he managed to find out I was a sub before we even met, so it's perfect for us," Dante said.

"I don't know anything about all that Dom and sub stuff," Alek said.

"You ought to," Dante said.

"Why?" Alek asked.

"James gave me a BDSM book to read, and it's really good stuff. I'll let you borrow the book after I finish it," Dante said.

"Sure. Thanks." Alek needed all the friends he could get at this point, and there was no need to be rude to him. He remembered Uncle Sacha telling him to maximize his friendships and minimize his enemies.

As they sat there smoking, Valerik showed up with red-haired Liam.

"Hey, boys, this is Liam," Valerik said with his Ukrainian accent. "He's new like you two."

Alek couldn't forget Valerik Korsak pinching his ass at the party. He wondered how his uncle met him. They greeted Liam with a thumb-up.

"Everything okay, Alek?" Valerik asked.

"Yeah." Alek paused and bit his lip. When Valerik moved to leave, Alek said, "No, actually could I talk to you alone please?"

Liam shot Alek a death stare.

"Sure." Valerik gestured for him to follow.

They walked to the back of the cabin and stepped down into the yard. The twigs crunched under their boots as they made their way to the brook. A pair of bluebirds screeched high up in the canopy of the trees.

"What's up?" Valerik asked.

"How do you know my uncle Sacha?" Alek asked.

"Who said I knew him?" Valerik displayed a blank expression.

"He did." Alek folded his arms.

"Oh."

"I want to know how you know him."

"Sacha and I go back to the old country. Actually, we went to school together, but I was much younger and in a lower grade. That's where we first met. He protected me, so no one touched me. In Russia, you might as well be dead if you're gay."

"He said you were Ukrainian."

"Yes, my family moved to Saint Petersburg when I was two years old, so I'm as good as Russian."

"Why did my uncle care about you?" Alek asked.

"Sacha wants to be the savior of the world. He saved me from the older boys who wanted to abuse me. I worked for him in the States for a while. He told me about this protection society and thought it would be a good fit. Sacha was right as always."

"Did you know I was his nephew?"

"Sacha told me that you were his son, not his nephew. He called me about you and wanted to know if I thought you'd be a good fit here. I told him you would. You're perfect for our society," Valerik said.

"Did he tell you why I had to go into hiding?" Alek asked.

"I can't discuss that with you." Valerik turned around to walk back to the cabin.

"That's not fair," Alek shouted as he quickened his pace and caught up with Valerik.

"Tough. This conversation is over," Valerik said as he split at the path and sat with the protectors. Alek returned to the porch.

"What did you want with Valerik?" Liam asked, obviously not yet comfortable with the idea of Alek wanting to talk with Valerik in private.

"I just asked him some questions about my uncle. He used to work for him."

Looking at the picnic table, Emilio squinted. "Hey, Anouska and another lady I've never seen are setting the table."

"Who is that?" Alek asked.

They wandered over to the picnic table where the women were preparing for dinner.

Anouska said, "I bet you're wondering who this is."

"Yes, who is she?" Emilio whispered.

"Boys, let me introduce Sara. Mateo found her walking the perimeter. After talking to her for a while, he asked her if she wanted a job for a month," Anouska said.

"Did she clear her security check already?" Alek asked.

"Mateo made sure she didn't have any weapons. He did a quick background check on her, and it turned out she's illegal. She's not connected to any Mexican gang or cartel, so I think we can trust her." Anouska said, shooting a smile to Sara. "I'm happy we have another woman I can talk to."

"I'm here to work, nothing else," Sara said in surprisingly good English.

She looked to be upset. Something was wrong, and Alek was determined to find out what. No one looked this disturbed on the first day of employment. She looked like she had secrets.

Alek didn't trust anyone, especially strangers.

"Where is she going to sleep?" Emilio asked.

"She'll sleep in the empty cabin," Anouska said.

Alek suddenly heard raised angry voices and looked over where the protectors were sitting. Rafe and Mateo were arguing, so Alek walked over to see why. Emilio followed right behind him. Alek was sensitive to people fighting or arguing. Uncle Sacha had argued with his brothers often, frightening him. As far back as he could remember, he'd always tried to be a peacemaker. He hated it when people fought.

"We need to leave tonight," Rafe shouted. "We can't be taking in strays no matter what."

"I'm sorry," Mateo said. "I checked her out, and she's an illegal looking for a job."

"No. She could be a mole for the Escobar family looking to take down Emilio. I'm going to set something up, and we're all moving on. Take Kaden with you. I'll keep Emilio and Anouska with us until you return. Get rid of her now. Drive her somewhere and get back here because we're leaving."

"What's wrong?" Alek asked.

"Pack up our things. This place has been compromised. You two go inside while I get Anouska," Rafe ordered.

Alek and Emilio walked back to the cabin and went inside.

"That doesn't sound good, does it?" Emilio asked.

"No. I bet Anouska will be upset about Sara," Alek said.

"What about all this food? Kaden and I shopped for three hours for all this food," Emilio said.

"I don't know. I guess we could pack some things." Alek didn't know what he should do.

"I think we better wait for Rafe. He's not to be crossed when he's in one of his moods," Emilio said.

"Well, I'm going to pack our clothes since he said we have to move. I won't touch the other things."

Alek went to the bedroom, packed their clothes, and set the four suitcases near the front door. Emilio was reading a motorcycle magazine on the couch while he drank a beer. It seemed he was used to living in chaos.

"He's still not back?" Alek asked.

"Nope."

CHAPTER SEVEN

Rafe Escobar

Rafe followed his brother to the picnic table. He took one look at the young woman and knew he'd seen her before in San Diego where he'd grown up. His family had something to do with her being here. There was little doubt that she was looking for Emilio and Mateo. She'd already seen Emilio here, but he didn't know what to do with her. She was so damn young that shooting her was out of the question, but he had to do something to keep her from revealing Emilio's whereabouts.

That stupid fuck! What had Mateo been thinking when he did his perimeter check? This is the reason for the damn checks on the hour. He brings the enemy right to us.

"Look Sara, I don't know who you're working for, but you're not welcome here," he said.

"You don't understand," she said. "I'm here to work for you, and that's all," Sara said as tears rolled down her cheeks.

"No. Stop the bullshit. You're not just working for me."

As Rafe pulled a handgun out of his pocket and pointed it at her, she screamed in terror.

"I come to work, nothing else," she repeated.

"And just what do you think you're going to do here?" Rafe asked.

"Stop it! What do you think you're doing? Don't hurt Sara," Anouska shouted.

"Making sure we're out of here before they find her," Rafe shouted.

"Find her how?" Mateo asked.

"You don't understand. I only come to work, please," Sara begged again through her tears.

"Anouska, go to my cabin and wait with Emilio and Alek," Rafe ordered.

Anouska mumbled incoherent Russian words through her hands, choking as she sobbed.

"Go to my cabin, now," Rafe ordered in a loud, angry voice.

Mateo put his arm around Anouska and whispered something to her. Then she hugged Sara and whispered to her before she hiked to the cabin, leaving Sara to Rafe.

He'd managed to make both women cry, which wasn't his original intention.

How could Mateo be this stupid?

"This is getting very messy," Rafe said. "Get me some rope."

"Are you sure that's a good idea?" Mateo asked.

"Don't fucking question my orders. The alternative is worse, and you know that. Look at her. She can't be more than sixteen years old. They're using her to do their damn dirty work and for their advantage," Rafe said.

"Who'd be using her? She's a damn illegal immigrant," Mateo raised his voice.

"The Es… co… bars," Rafe said, allowing it to sink in slowly.

"Oh shit! I never thought of that." Mateo covered his face with his hands out of frustration.

"No. You never think first. That's the problem, so don't start now. Get the rope and meet me inside your cabin."

"I'm sorry. It won't happen again," Mateo said as he walked toward the shed.

Rafe stood behind Sara with his gun still pointing at her. Speaking to Sara in Spanish so she'd understand, he ordered, "Walk to Mateo's cabin."

She trembled as she walked; tears were flowing while she prayed in Spanish.

Rafe opened the door, shoved her inside, and pointed to a piece of furniture in the corner. "Sit on that damn chair."

"Don't kill me, please. I only wanted to work," Sara repeated like a broken record.

"What's going to happen here is that you're going to stay in that chair tied up until I call someone to free you."

"How long?" She wiped her tears away with the back of her hand.

"Three hours. You can tell my father or whoever sent you here to spy on me, to fuck his own ass. Do you hear me?" Rafe shouted in Spanish.

"I promise I will."

"What was the fucker's name who hired you?"

"Mr. Escobar. He'll kill me now."

"No, he won't. He'd never kill a woman. Never."

Mateo entered the cabin with the rope in his hand. His dark eyes were dull and empty, yet they told the story of his regret and despair. His shoulders were slumped as he dragged his feet across the room. Sweat dripped down his face from his forehead, and he wiped it away with the back of his hand. Rafe hated to admit that Mateo wasn't cut out for this type of work, but he was going to have to toughen up.

"Tie her to the recliner," Rafe shouted to his brother. By this time, he was enraged at Mateo's stupidity for hiring a stranger while they were off the grid.

On what level was he thinking that this was a good idea?

Sara yelled for help in Spanish, and Rafe wanted to slap her to shut her up. He put the gun to her head as her eyes filled with fear. He wanted to use her to send a message to the Escobar family not to fuck with him. They weren't ever getting Emilio. His heart beat fast with hate and anger.

"Shut up," Rafe said. "Tie her hands in front of her first."

Mateo wrapped the rope around her wrists four times, knotted it, and cut the rope with his knife.

"Wrap rope under her breasts and around the chair. Do that six times. You have enough rope."

"I hate this shit," Mateo said as he ran the rope around the girl, strapping her to the chair. She was too frightened to move. With her eyes closed, she began praying in Spanish again.

"Next time, don't pick up strays," Rafe said.

Once Mateo finished tying her to the recliner, he took a deep breath and sighed.

"Pack up your things and load your car," Rafe said. "I'm going to make a call. Come to my cabin when you're done." Then he turned and stomped out of the cabin, slamming the door on his way out.

James, Kaden, and Valerik were standing on Mateo's front porch. He wondered how long they'd been out there and why were they there in the first place. "What the fuck are you guys doing here?" he asked.

"We're just here to tell you we're almost packed and ready to go," James said.

"I'm going to make a call to make reservations for us. James, go to my cabin and make sure they packed up my car. Valerik, help Mateo load up his car," Rafe ordered.

"Sure," Valerik said as he turned to enter the cabin.

"Don't forget to pack up the nonperishable food," Rafe ordered.

"What about me?" Kaden asked.

"Come with me to the brook," Rafe said, "I need to make a call."

As they headed toward the brook, Rafe pulled up the number of his local contact, Nacho. Once there, Kaden leaned against the tree and waited as Rafe made the call.

"Hey, what's up?" Nacho asked as he answered Rafe's call.

"I need five traveling vans. We'll be by in an hour or two."

"No problem."

"Thanks." Rafe ended the call.

"Mateo really fucked up this time, didn't he?" Kaden asked.

"Yes, he did," Rafe said, pressing his fingers at his temples, hoping to delay the throbbing headache he really didn't need just then.

Kaden handed him two painkillers from his pocket, offering a drink from a bottle of water he'd been holding. He always seemed to know what Rafe needed.

"Thanks," Rafe said as he tossed the pills into his mouth, swallowing them with the water.

He was angry with Mateo for picking up that girl. All this crap was an unnecessary expense of time and money. He was going to have to clip his brother's wings, so he wouldn't be making any more irresponsible decisions. Suddenly, his brother had become a problem. He'd expected there would be some kinks with a new crop of boys, but he didn't imagine his brother would fuck up so badly.

He lit his pipe and sat on a rock overlooking the streaming water. He'd wanted to spend time here with Alek. He needed the peace and serenity of Fawnskin, and now, he was going to be gypped out of it. He'd take him to another place where he can recharge and enjoy his time.

"You know I love it here, and now we can't ever return," Rafe said.

"I know you do. It's not safe anymore for our group. At least the others can use it, right?"

Rafe nodded. "That's not the point. I wanted to spend time here with Alek."

"There are other places we can go," Kaden said.

"I know. I know. I'm just pissed at my father. He won't let up until all three of us are dead."

"Stop talking like that. Nothing like that will ever happen. I won't let it and neither will you. Together, we're strong and can fight this."

"I wish my brother were as strong as you. We have to toughen him up."

When Rafe and Kaden returned to the cabin, everyone stopped talking. Anouska was sitting with Alek.

"Did you guys pack the nonperishable stuff?" Rafe asked.

"Yes. Everything is packed and in the car," Alek said.

"Round up everyone and meet me at the fire pit. I'll explain our next move. I'm going to lock up."

Rafe rushed out the front door, checked and made sure all the cabins were locked. He stopped by Mateo's cabin and walked inside. Sara was crying, still bound to the recliner when he walked passed her looking for Mateo.

"Where's Mateo?" he asked her in Spanish.

"He packed up everything and left. Please let me go," she begged in Spanish

"You'll be fine. Three hours. Who do you want me to call?"

"*Mi esposo*. The number is in my red purse. It's on the couch."

Rafe dumped the contents of her purse onto the couch since the coffee table was covered with magazines and books. He went through the empty purse, found a zippered pocket, opened it, and found her phone. Then he slipped it into his pocket to check it later.

So much for Mateo checking her for electronics. That dumbass.

"Where's your fucking number?"

"On the pink card," she said.

He immediately found it and put it away. "Don't fuck with me ever again, *pequeña perra*."

"I won't. I promise… never."

"You know, if you report this to the police, they'll just send you back to Mexico."

"No police."

Rafe left the cabin unlocked and took his time walking back to the fire pit. They were all there waiting for him.

He stood in front of them and announced, "Everybody up! We're going to San Bernardino to pick up traveling vans."

As the group rose to their feet he continued, "You'll access the directions under 'Rental 1920.' The reservations are under the name of Fuller Christian Church. Everything's paid. Just drop your car in the back parking lot. From there we're going to meet near San Bernardino National Park. Access your phones for directions under Community 1920. We'll sleep in the vans, but we'll be eating out until Kaden can shop again. Any questions?"

"What about Sara?" Anouska asked.

"Don't worry about her. She'll be fine," Rafe said.

"Did you know she's pregnant?" Anouska shouted.

"She's what? Could this get any worse?" he yelled to no one in particular. It was the last straw for him.

Anouska was hysterical. "If she loses her baby, it'll be on you."

Rafe disliked her accusatory tone and the way she began pointing angrily at him as she spoke. "Shut up, Anouska. Don't talk to me like that ever again." Rafe paused. "I can make you disappear faster than you can blink an eye. No one talks to me like that. I won't tolerate it. Mateo, keep her quiet."

"I'm sorry. I'm just worried about her baby," Anouska said.

Mateo leaned over and whispered something to her.

"The rest of you, don't pick up any strangers and drive safely. See you soon."

As they headed to the cars, Rafe was thinking about Sara's pregnancy. It made this entire quagmire worse than it was.

I can't keep her there tied up for three hours. I'll have to call someone to stay with her until… until I figure out what to do with her.

Sixteen years old and pregnant. What the hell had she been thinking?

"Didn't you just rent this SUV?" Alek asked.

"Don't tell me what I already know. Right now, I'm still pissed at Mateo for being such an asshole. Was he thinking with his dick?" Rafe adjusted his shirt, pulled out his black sunglasses, and slid them over his eyes.

"I hope not. He has Anouska." Alek pulled his sunglasses from the top of his head and put them on.

"Mateo is her protector, not her husband. He's doing a damn piss-ass job of protecting her."

"Do you always get this angry when things go wrong?" Alek asked.

"Nothing usually goes wrong. I trained Mateo, but I don't know what he was doing. I told him never to pick up strangers when we're off the grid. It's so damn simple. What would be the point of going off the grid if we take in strays? Not one damn thing in his training points to anything like this."

"What did you do to Sara?" Alek asked.

"What did Anouska tell you I did?"

"She said you held a gun to her back."

"She's in Mateo's cabin. He tied her to the chair. I'll call someone to watch over her. After three hours, she can go wherever she wants. By that time, we'll be long gone. She'll be fine."

"Why do you even think she's a threat? She's just a teenager."

"I'm positive my father sent her to find Emilio. I've seen her around in San Diego. She might be my father's maid's daughter. I know he wants Emilio dead, but that'll

114

never happen under my watch. He does shit like this to us all the time."

"I don't think Sara would take Emilio out, do you?"

"No, but she could pass it on to whoever sent her here. In one week, I'm going to get them both deported because I'm fucking pissed."

"That's really kind of mean," Alek said.

"It's better than blowing her head off."

"You're scaring me. You sound like my uncle. He talks like that often."

"Then let's not talk about such things. Hell, I thought we'd be fucking again by now. Tonight, we're going to fuck all night. Only instead of that small bed, we're going to be in a van."

"I don't care where we fuck as long as you fuck me," Alek said.

"I like the sound of that."

"What's going to happen to all the food?" Alek asked.

"I just didn't like wasting the money on all that food. When I call my contact, he'll turn the food over to the churches or food banks."

"Are we going to stay longer here?" Alek asked.

"We have to be able to pick up and leave at a moment's notice. The new boys and my brother need the damn practice to suddenly pick up and leave."

"Are you going to forgive Mateo for fucking up?"

"Of course. He's my brother and I know he always sees the good in people. He's new at this and it's not natural to him. The others have been with me for five years. So they're the crème of our society. We take the ones with the biggest threats like you."

"So, you think they want to take me out?" Alek asked.

"Why do you think your uncle placed you here?"

"I thought maybe he wanted to get rid of me hanging out at his house. I don't think he thought it through. He took me in when my parents were slaughtered and spent a lot of time with me. I don't know. He never made me feel unloved, and he was always there for me."

"What happened when you told him you were gay?" Rafe asked.

"I never actually told him. He found out. I don't know how. He had security guards watching me. Maybe one of them told him."

"Maybe Pavel did," Rafe said.

"Pavel could have. I've never discussed it with him. He has made comments about why I didn't date girls."

"I want to find out more about Pavel," Rafe said. "Something doesn't seem right to me."

"What difference will that make? I'm already banished for good."

"Are you hungry?" Rafe asked, changing the subject.

"Starving."

"Let's stop at that restaurant up ahead."

As soon as Rafe parked, they made their way inside, sat at a booth away from the window, and waited for the server. The menus were already on the table.

"I don't even know what you like," Alek said.

"I eat everything. I'm not fussy. I know what you like and don't, thanks to Uncle Sacha."

"I want the cheeseburger platter and a beer," Alek said.

"I love a man who knows what he wants. I'll have the same. I'm too damn stressed to think about food."

"I wish you weren't. You're a lot more fun when you're not angry."

"I'm responsible for lives here, and I thought my brother was ready. Maybe he's not meant to be a protector. I know he's upset about his fuckup, and he won't repeat that one again, but what if he fucks up something else?"

"He needs your support, not your anger," Alek said.

117

"Yes, you're right. I need to be more patient with him."

The server took their order and took their menus. Shortly after, she brought their beers.

"So I can't wait until tonight when we're all settled in again," Rafe said, picking up his beer.

"I want to take part in my protection, but I don't want to kill anyone. That's where I draw the line."

"Don't worry. I appreciate you listening to me, but I don't need you to do anything like that. All I want from you is for you to follow my orders. I don't give them to fly on alpha power. I do it for your protection and the others. There'll be times when I'll be short with you. Don't take it personally. I have to internalize shit that way."

"If I could live with my uncle, I can live with anyone."

"Was it tough living with your uncle?"

"Sometimes. He was always there for me, but there were times when he got very dark and moody. We had tons of Russian men in and out of our house. They didn't include me. Uncle Sacha always sent me to my room. He protected me from his lifestyle. When he got angry with me, he'd stop speaking to me for a couple of days. He'd never discuss his anger. He just went silent on me," Alek said.

"That's better than how my father treated Mateo and me. He was violent and shouted at us often. We knew when he was angry and why."

"Uncle Sacha never touched or hit me," Alek said.

"We had a horrible childhood. I'm glad we're away from him."

"I'm sorry you two had lived like that when you were kids."

The server returned with their order, and they ate in silence. When they finished, Rafe paid the bill. They walked to the SUV without speaking. Alek smoked a cigarette and gave one to Rafe since he looked like he needed one.

As soon as they both stumped out their cigarettes, they jumped into the car and drove in a comfortable silence, relieving the stress of the day. Rafe stopped at the rental place and parked in the back parking lot. Mateo was already standing there with a lit cigarette. Alek pulled the luggage from the trunk.

What the hell is he doing? He doesn't smoke.

Mateo had left Anouska in the car and was walking toward the rental office when Rafe jumped out of the SUV.

"Mateo," he shouted.

"What's up?" Mateo yelled back.

119

"Come here. I want to talk to you."

Mateo walked to Rafe and continued smoking his cigarette as if everything was perfect, like he hadn't just single-handedly blown all their cover on the first day.

"I was very upset with your decision to hire Sara without my permission. Don't make any decisions without asking me. Reread the rules on 'off the grid'. Did you know she was pregnant?"

"Not until Anouska said something," Mateo said.

Rafe pulled out a blue card and handed it to Mateo. "Call this number. It's one of my local contacts. Tell him to pick up Sara at the cabin right now. Be sure to mention that she's pregnant. Tell him to drop her off at the hospital with an envelope with five hundred dollars and leave."

"I'll call now. I'm sorry," Mateo said.

"I know you're sorry. Think before you do shit." Rafe left him in the parking lot and went inside to get the keys to the new van.

Sometimes, Rafe wondered if he was doing the same thing his father had done to his brother. Mateo was better suited to a life as an English teacher, with his love of books and more gentle nature. He struggled to do what is right in a world where threats, anger, and violence overruled kindness every step of the way.

With deadly threats from his father, Mateo had to learn how to protect himself as well as keep Anouska safe. Rafe's decision to bring Mateo into the protector's group made it difficult for his brother to reach his true goal of becoming an English teacher. He was nowhere near his goal, thanks to Rafe.

CHAPTER EIGHT

Alek Belanov

Alek was delighted when they exchanged the SUV for the traveling van. They had to drive to the next location before they could relax, but sitting in a high-back swivel chair was comfortable and unexpected. Alek had never been in a traveling van or gone camping for that matter. He didn't think he'd enjoy traveling all over without knowing where he'd rest his head at night. Sitting beside his handsome protector Rafe was exciting in an alarming way. He'd kept Alek safe, but he'd also spoken harsh angry words about Mateo. Like Uncle Sacha, he'd gotten over it quickly.

"Anouska was terribly upset at the cabin. She thought you were going to kill Sara," Alek said.

"Are you asking me if I would have put her down like a sick animal?" Rafe's voice rose.

"I don't know you well enough to know what you'd do or if you'd tell me. I lived with my uncle since I was four, and he had his share of violent behavior toward people he felt threatened him and his family. He didn't always tell me the whole truth, but I listened to what he told my uncles and sometimes those stories were very different. I think he

123

thought I was weak. I guess I wondered if you'd leave out certain details, thinking I was too weak to hear the truth.

"I see." Rafe paused and gripped the wheel tightly. "I told you what I did with Sara. As a matter of fact, I told Mateo to call a contact to take her to the hospital for a checkup. You don't ever need to compare me to your uncle. He was raising you and wanted to protect you from his lifestyle. I promised I'd tell you the truth because there's no room for lies if we're going to work as a team. Remember, you were a boy when your uncle didn't tell you the complete truth. If you believe nothing else, you need to know that I don't think you're weak in any way."

"My uncle is still lying to me." Alek swiveled in his chair, enjoying the space and comfort.

"I see you're enjoying twirling in your seat." Rafe changed the subject. He always did when he didn't want to discuss a topic, regardless of Alek's desire to continue with the same subject matter.

"I've never been in a van with a bed, mini kitchen, and bathroom."

"Didn't you ever go camping?"

"No. Uncle Sacha said camping was for people on the run, and he would never run from anyone."

"When I was a boy, we used to camp in our sleeping bags on the beach in Mexico. It was great waking up on the beach." Rafe adjusted his rearview mirror.

"I never did anything fun like that," Alek said.

"You went to Europe and Russia. I haven't done that."

"Those trips were more educational than fun. It's not that I'm ungrateful, but there are so many things I wanted to do but was never allowed to do them."

"What kind of things weren't you allowed to do?"

"I couldn't join any school activities, sports, nor have any friends visit me at my home. He wouldn't even allow me to get my driver's license. I had to wait until I was twenty."

"Well, we're going to have fun, even though our focus is your protection."

"Right. I find it hard to believe my uncle couldn't control the Belanov family. It doesn't make sense. He never made me feel unworthy because I was gay. The real problem started when I fell in love with a guy from one of our enemy's families. I blame myself for Burain's death."

"Don't. You didn't do anything but love the man. Break free from that guilt you're carrying. You can't punish yourself for things you had no control over. We don't get to choose who we fall in love with."

"Are we here?"

"Yes and it looks like everyone else is here already," Rafe said.

Alek spotted the others sitting on chairs in one big circle. They jumped out of the van, walked to the others, and sat in two empty folding lounge chairs.

"About time you two showed up," Kaden said. "I picked up some things for dinner and these chairs so we can sit outside and talk."

"Thanks, Kaden. I appreciate that." Rafe paused and turned his attention to his brother. "Mateo, do you have anything to report to the group?"

"Sara is safe," he said with some distance in his voice.

"Thank you for taking care of that delicate and unfortunate situation. I want to go on the record and repeat that we don't pick up or hire strangers when we're off the grid. From here on in, no one will hire anyone or bring them to their base unless you ask me first. I don't want any more fuckups when lives are on the line. With the security breach at the Fawnskin campsite, this group will no longer be able to stay there. The other groups can. The Escobar family is aware of the campsite, so it's unsafe for all the Escobars in the Gay Protection Society, and there are three of us," Rafe said.

126

Mateo held Anouska's hand while she stroked his back. Alek hoped to have a relationship like theirs before long.

"Dinner will be ready in three hours." Kaden paused," James and I are going to barbecue chicken and boil corn on the cob. Anouska and Emilio are going to make the mashed potatoes. Valerik is going to make us a killer fruit drink. Liam, Dante, and Alek are on clean-up duty. We're eating on paper plates to keep the work down."

"What about me?" Rafe asked.

"You need a break from the stress of the day," Kaden said.

"Thank you. In that case, Alek and I are going to take a walk. We'll be back before dinner."

Rafe and Alek hiked along the dirt path through the rocks and grassy area. Rafe took his hand and led him to the stream.

"What do you think of this place?" Rafe sat down against a tree, and Alek sat beside him.

"It's beautiful and calming," Alek said.

"Yes. Just what I need after today."

"I'm impressed how quickly you changed the plans and how everyone in the group flowed right along with the changes."

"That's how it is when you're hiding out."

"It makes me very sad that your father would put a hit on Emilio."

"Emilio has always been bullied when he was little because he couldn't fight. He's smart though. Like you, he hasn't been able to finish school. At some point, he needs to finish it up.

"He's a good bartender," Alek said.

"I taught him how to bartend. The Escobar children all learned how to be bartenders at a young age. My parents made us serve them and their friends."

"I didn't have jobs at home. My uncle forced me to read a lot. He sent me to additional classes after school. He wanted me to be educated so I never had to do what he does for a living."

"You'd get along with Mateo because he wants to be an English teacher, and he loves to read."

"I'll have to talk to him about books sometime." Alek pulled out his cigarettes and lit one. "Do you want one?"

"No." Rafe pulled out Sara's phone and read the messages sent by his father.

"Is there anything important on Sara's phone?"

"Same old shit from my father. 'Call when you see Emilio, Mateo, or Rafe.' She returned his messages with

'All three are here.' She also gave him the address of each of the cabins."

"I guess it's a good thing we left as fast as we did. Did you tell Mateo about those texts?"

"No, but I will. Don't say anything to Emilio. I don't want him to worry."

"I won't."

Rafe was quiet for a minute, then looked at Alek and gently kissed him, pulled away and said, "This place is too open, and the others might take a hike too. Otherwise I'd fuck you right here."

"We could go in the van and close the curtains," Alek said, jumping up to his feet.

"Let's go," Rafe said as he stood.

Their van was parked far away from the others, so no one noticed their return. Alek closed the curtains while Rafe locked the doors.

"Get naked, pretty man," Rafe ordered as he was removing his shirt.

Alek had stripped all his clothes before Rafe had even taken off his jeans.

"Where do you want me?" Alek asked.

"On your hands and knees. Um, I guess the bed. It's too tight to be creative in here." Rafe put some lube on his erection and waited for Alek to get in place.

"I've been waiting all day for this," Rafe said.

"Your cock is doing the talking. No words are needed."

Alek dropped to his hands and knees, doing as he'd been told, and lifted his ass with an arch of his back. Rafe's warm, large hands parted his cheeks, exposing him. The cool air brushed upon Alek's exposed flesh, sending chills throughout his body.

"Oh. such a pretty pink hole," Rafe said.

"That's a funny thing to say." Alek had never heard anyone say that about his hole.

"Drop your chest onto the bed and then use your hands to spread your cheeks apart as wide as you can and make sure your sweet hole is open to me," Rafe ordered.

He put more lube on his fingers and dipped his finger inside that tight hole. Alek's body ached with anticipation, wanting more than just one finger. As Rafe's finger rubbed across his prostate gland, Alek relaxed and Rafe added a second finger, pounding in and out and tapping the secret spot repeatedly, making Alek beg for more.

"Rafe. Please. Fuck me," he panted, knowing Rafe would love to hear him beg for his cock. He'd had enough finger fucking. He wanted Rafe's cock.

Ignoring Alek, Rafe added a third finger and played more. Alek arched his ass up to meet his next fingering thrust. Rafe was toying with him until he decided to fill him.

"Please, just fuck me," Alek begged again.

Rafe removed his fingers and aimed his cock. In one quick movement, he was balls deep. Picking up his pace, he pounded, causing Alek's body to jerk up and down against the pillow. The thunderous banging in the bed caused the van to move, but Alek didn't care at this point.

Rafe wrapped his hand around Alek's pulsating hard-on. Stroking it at the same tempo, he pumped in and out. Alek trembled, tightening his anal muscles around the steel dick still pounding deep inside him. The warm semen in his balls threatened to flow, and he knew he couldn't fight much longer as his body quivered, trying to hold back the climax that was ready to spill out of him.

"Not yet, *mi angelito*. Not yet!" Rafe shouted.

"I... can't stop," Alek whimpered.

His balls throbbed, begging to release, but unable to because of the painful grip of Rafe's large hand on the base

131

of Alek's cock cutting off the flow, allowing only a small dribble to escape.

"I didn't say you could come, yet," Rafe said.

"Please, it hurts. Please." Alek's head bumped the wall each time Rafe pounded his cock inside him.

As Rafe rode him harder, Alek spilled his cum through Rafe's tight grip and all over his hand and on the pillow.

"Oh fuck. Fuck. I can't stop it. Oh fuck." Rafe's balls tightened.

Alek pushed his ass toward the cock beating inside him. As Rafe's warm cum exploded into Alek, both moaned as they came together in full harmony.

"I needed that," Rafe said.

"Me, too."

"I could get used to owning your ass and fucking you anytime I want."

Alek just smiled, not wanting to ruin his afterglow with talking. They rinsed themselves separately in the mini-shower and dressed in jeans and T-shirts.

CHAPTER NINE

Rafe Escobar

Rafe and Alek left the van and soon found the others sitting in a circle by the cabin. They separated when Emilio called for Alek to come over to him. Rafe headed toward Valerik, who was sitting with Liam, whose hair was so red that Valerik made him wear a cap when they were away from their living quarters.

"I need to talk to you alone," Rafe said.

"Sure, my van is empty," Valerik said and turned to Liam. "You stay put. I'll be right back."

"I'm starving, so I won't be going anywhere," Liam said.

They walked to the van and sat in the front seats.

"What's going on?" Valerik asked as he hit a button to roll down both windows.

"Did you get any more information about the project?" Rafe asked, dangling his right arm out the open window.

"You know you're putting me in a compromising position. I owe everything to Sacha, and you're asking me to tell you something that might hurt Sacha and Alek."

"Did you find out anything or not? Was it true?" Rafe watched, but Valerik was stone-faced, telling him nothing.

"It's true," he confessed. "Just as you suspected. You must never tell Alek for many reasons."

"It would break his heart if he knew, but I need to think this through. It might have other consequences, and I'll have to weigh the two telling or not. Did he give you a reason?"

"No, I'm still working on the why. It's difficult, a delicate matter for the family. I don't want to put any of my sources in danger. This whole drama makes me sick to my stomach. Sacha is a protector in his own right. I've told you how he's protected me during my school years in Russia, so it's difficult for me to accept this about him," Valerik said.

Rafe turned to Valerik with a firm request. "Turn your investigation to Pavel. I want to know everything about that bastard. I think he's got to be part of this bullshit."

Valerik thought a moment. "He's always poked fun at Alek. I've seen it myself. He'd belittle him just to make him feel bad."

"I was afraid of that."

"You know Sacha is grooming Pavel to take over one day. He originally wanted Alek to take command, but as the years went by, he knew that would never happen. Sacha often told me that he wished Alek weren't gay. He blamed his softness on his sexuality. He thought Alek would never be able to do what it takes to command something like that. He asked me for advice on how to deal with Alek's sexuality since he knew about me in Russia, but he never made Alek feel bad about being gay. He seemed to understand that he was born that way."

"Why didn't you tell Sacha that Pavel was bullying Alek?" Rafe asked.

"I did, but he was blind to it. He told me they were close and just joking around. He's still blind to Pavel, even today. "

"I have another question. If you were around then, why doesn't Alek recognize you now?"

"I don't know, but it was five years ago. I never spoke to him. I talked about him to Sacha, but he was overprotective. He never exposed him to any of his criminal activities. I think he wanted Alek to think he was perfect. He loves Alek like a son. I don't understand why he sent him away."

"That still doesn't explain why he didn't recognize you," Rafe repeated.

"I was at Sacha's house all the time, but I had much longer hair then, and I went by another name."

"Why two names?" Rafe asked

"That's what Sacha wanted. He said he didn't want anyone to know we'd known each other in Russia. It had to do with me being gay because people in Russia already knew that. Valerik Korsak is my real name."

"Alek's pretty quick. I think it's very odd that he didn't recognize you at all, even with a different name. He may be more aware than he's letting on."

"Actually, he didn't act like he had ever seen me before. I used Borya Gorbunov back then."

"Not to change the subject, but why did you come on to him at the party?" Rafe asked.

"I just gave his ass a pinch a couple of times. That's not coming on to him. I have no interest in him anymore. It's just that I fell in love with him back when I worked with his uncle, so my feelings for him wouldn't have worked then or now. Remember, that was back then, and it was another time. Now I have my beautiful, ginger-haired Liam, who gives great head." Valerik smiled.

"Wait, he would have been in his teens back then, and you fell in love with him? You were what... 45?" It made no sense that Alek didn't remember Valerik working for Sacha. Something didn't fit in this puzzle, and he aimed to find out what it was. Who falls in love with a teenager? *Did he mean love, or is he a fucking pervert.*

"Alek was a hot-looking teen back then, and I knew he was already having sex with Burain."

"Enough with Alek. Let's get back to talking about Pavel." Rafe wondered if Valerik still had some interest in Alek.

"Sure."

Rafe opened the door and slid out of Valerik's van, scanning the group area for Alek or Emilio. He figured they were talking away from the group, but he didn't see them. He made his way to Kaden and James, who were preparing the seasoning for the chicken.

"Did you guys see where Alek and Emilio disappeared to?" Rafe asked.

"They're in my van talking," Kaden said.

"How's it going with Emilio?" Rafe asked.

"He's great. I should be jealous of you. When he talks about you, he makes it sound like you're his savior. He worships you."

"He was in a bad spot when he came to me. I don't understand why my father betrayed me or my cousin like he did."

"I love Emilio already, and I can't imagine why anyone would want to hurt him," Kaden said.

"He was raised by my uncle Reuben, my father's younger brother. He was too strict with him, so Emilio never enjoyed anything. He told me he's happy with you, and that makes me happy, but I still worry that they want him dead." Rafe felt the pain of his words when he had spoken of Emilio's demise.

"Old Colombians with their stupid ways. You know, for cousins, he looks a lot like you."

"The Escobars have strong genes, and we all look similar." Rafe hoped to appease Kaden's questions. Mateo didn't even know.

"That's true because your brother looks like you, too," Kaden said. "I'm really upset with Mateo for putting Emilio at risk."

"You don't know the half of it. Take a walk with me. James can keep an eye on the chicken," Rafe said.

Rafe and Kaden hiked, side by side, on the path to the stream. Kaden was his top organizer. He could depend on Kaden to follow orders to the letter. He didn't look like a guy who'd work at the Gay Protection Society. No one would ever guess he was a protector. He reminded Rafe of a hippie. His blond hair was long. He dressed more casually than the others, and it was difficult to get the guy to dress up, even for the parties. Kaden was the most loyal of the protectors and Rafe's second man in charge. They'd met in the Marines. He'd fucked Kaden a number of times back then until Kaden finally admitted he'd rather top. Since that didn't work for Rafe, they had tossed their sexual relationship aside but kept their friendship. They had a special bond that would never be broken.

"Did you find out anything?" Kaden asked.

"I confiscated Sara's phone. She had messages from my father on there. He demanded to know where Emilio, Mateo, and I were. She responded by telling him our address at the Fawnskin cabin site. Mateo told me he'd checked her out, but he hadn't checked her purse thoroughly. I know he just wanted to make Anouska happy by bringing in Sara, but we can't do shit like that when we're off the grid," Rafe said.

"Does Emilio know about this?" Kaden's forehead creased from worry about Emilio.

"He knows, but he doesn't have the details of my father's messages, and I'd rather he didn't. There's no need to worry him."

"I agree. After a month, he's finally able to enjoy himself. I'd like to enroll him in an online adult school so he can finish his high school education. He's bothered that he couldn't finish. He talks about it constantly."

139

"Actually, that's a great idea, but what address will you use?" Rafe asked.

"I can use your address in Ojai. What do you think?" Kaden asked.

"Yes. That would work. Thanks for supporting him with this. You know I appreciate it," Rafe said.

"He has the laptop you bought him, so he really doesn't need anything else."

"It's not with him, now, is it?" Rafe asked.

"No, it's back at my house. I know how to pack for off the grid," Kaden said.

"Sorry. I know that. I'm just double-checking," Rafe said.

"I understand. I like that he's making friends with the boys in our group."

"I do too. He needs a break. He was so depressed when he first came to me."

"He's doing better now." Kaden smiled and returned to the large fire pit where James was grilling the chicken.

Valerik had helped while Kaden was gone. Rafe sat in the group circle and lit his pipe. His brother and Anouska were sitting with them. He knew his brother was upset with what had gone down at Fawnskin, but he'd get over it and move on. He needed Mateo around him, so he didn't worry about him at a distance. Their father had blamed Rafe for taking Mateo away from him. His father had been optimistic about turning the business over to him until Rafe had made it clear he wouldn't. Rafe would make sure he kept both Mateo and Emilio safe and away from his father.

Rafe returned to the van alone. He sat behind the wheel and punched his father's number into Sara's phone. Immediately his father picked it up as he thought he would.

"Sara, did you find out how long they're staying?" his father asked.

"It's not Sara. It's Rafe."

"Rafe! Listen to me," he said obviously disturbed. "Send Mateo back, and I'll end the hit on your precious Emilio. I want my son back."

"Why don't you get it? Mateo isn't coming back, and you're not going to touch Emilio. He's fucking eighteen years old. Why doesn't Emilio mean anything to you?"

"He's not my son. I told you the day he was born he was a bastard to the Escobar family. And now he's gay. Emilio was fucking for money."

"And you kill for money. What's the difference?" Rafe asked.

"You know nothing about my business."

"If you don't stop this bullshit, I'm going to kill you myself. Leave Mateo, Emilio, and me alone. We want no part of you and your drug cartel."

His father ended the call. Rafe stared at the phone as if he could see his father's face.

CHAPTER TEN

Alek Belanov

Alek and Emilio were sitting in the front seat of Kaden's van with the windows rolled down.

"Did you find out anything else about the breach with Sara?" Emilio asked.

"Nope. Rafe doesn't discuss business with me. It's all about fucking with him right now," Alek said.

"Is everything going okay with Rafe?"

"I guess so. He hasn't yelled at me yet." Alek wondered how long it would last before he made Rafe's shit list the way Mateo had. He had to tread lightly around him if he wanted to avoid his wrath.

"So, do you think Sara is okay?" Emilio asked.

"That's what Mateo said. I don't think Rafe will hurt her, do you?" Alek asked, seeing doubt on Emilio's face and realizing in his own heart that he wasn't completely sure.

"You don't know that much about Rafe. He eliminates people if they get in the way of protecting someone he cares about."

"Eliminating… like murdering them?" Alek asked.

"That's exactly what I mean. All the protectors have killed, but I don't know about Mateo. He's new at this, but I imagine if someone threatened Anouska, he'd either kill them or ask Rafe to do it for him."

"What were Rafe and Mateo like when they were growing up?"

Of course, Rafe was a killer; did he think his uncle would send him to a priest to protect him? The man had to be ruthless, so he had to be a killer, but he wouldn't kill a woman, or he didn't think he would.

"Since they were my cousins, I knew them pretty well. Uncle Sal, who was their father, was a mean bastard. My father was his younger brother, and he hated him. I was afraid of him too. On Sundays when we went there for dinner, he scared the shit out of me."

"Was he mean to Rafe and Mateo?" Alek asked.

"Oh, yes. He did unspeakable things to them. I heard my father talking to my mother about it."

The vision of anyone doing unspeakable things to Rafe angered Alek. "What did he do?"

"He'd beat them with anything he could get his hands on and locked them in a basement for days. Sometimes, he wouldn't even let them eat. They were just little guys. He'd even destroy their toys. Rafe and Mateo never talked about

144

it though. In those days, no one dreamed of squealing on Uncle Sal. Everyone was afraid of him. Uncle Sal is the one who wants me dead because I'm gay." Emilio lowered his eyes. "He even threatened to cut my balls off."

"What about your father? Why didn't he protect you?" Alek asked.

"He told me to find Rafe and he'd get me in protection. He said he couldn't stop his older brother from killing me. So I called Rafe after I got tired of the streets and ran into trouble."

"How did you connect with Kaden?"

"I went to a party like the one where you met Rafe. Kaden picked me, but I think he did it for Rafe. I'm not sure he really wants to be with me," Emilio said.

"When I see you two together he looks like he's into you. He doesn't look like a killer. He seems a lot more laid-back. You know, more casual and carefree," Alek said.

"Looks can be deceiving when it comes to him. He's just as violent as the rest of them, but on a day-to-day basis he's much more laid-back than Rafe and Mateo," Emilio said.

"Is the sex good?"

"Oh, God, yes! The sex is great. I just don't know how he feels about me. I wonder if his heart is into me. I know it's only a month, but I'm in love with the guy."

"What was that? Is that a bell?" Alek asked.

"Yep, that's the dinner bell. Time to eat. Kaden loves ringing that bell," Emilio said.

Emilio locked the van, and they walked to the picnic area, filling their plates and taking their places around the circle. James went around to everyone, handing them each a large paper cup filled with a fruit drink.

"Now that we're all here, I want to talk about tomorrow," Rafe said. "We all need a little downtime. We need to do something fun. I spoke with a few of our other groups in this area. We're going to have a pool party. We're all meeting at one of the houses. The directions are under Party 1920. We've been there before. It's a huge house. Please don't mention the breach to anyone at the party. I'd like to keep that within the group."

"Hey, is that the place where they don't have individual cabins?" James asked.

"Yes, it has five bedrooms, so all ten guys in that group stay there unless there's a threat," Rafe said.

"Can you imagine if we all had to live in one house?" Valerik asked.

"If we had to, then we would. So far, we haven't needed to do that. All the other locations are up for a relaxing day together," Rafe said.

"That sounds fun as long as we don't have to swim naked," Alek said.

"Not unless you want to entertain us." Rafe winked.

"No, thank you."

"Get up," Rafe ordered. "We're going back to the van."

"I'm on it." Alek stood.

Rafe and Alek made their rounds to say good night to everyone. Once they'd gotten inside, Rafe locked the doors and closed the curtains.

"What are we going to do? There's no TV in here."

"Do you watch a lot of TV?"

"No. I haven't watched much for the last couple of years. I've only been out of jail for a week."

"Oh, that's right. What did you do while you were in there anyway?" Rafe asked.

"Nothing I want to talk about. I just don't want to relive that time. My only good memory was when Uncle Sacha visited me. He came about once a week and occasionally wrote letters to cheer me up. It didn't make any sense that he was so considerate while I was in prison

147

and then sent me away as soon as I got out." Alek hadn't been prepared for his uncle to cast him aside. His abrupt rejection still hurt.

"You know that was for your protection. If he didn't care…well, you know. Not to change the subject, but what do you think of Valerik?"

"He reminds me of someone, but I don't know who. Sometimes I feel like I know him, and other times I don't."

"He worked for your uncle."

"I know that. He told me he'd worked for him, but I don't remember him." Alek scrunched his nose.

"Are you sure you don't remember him working for your uncle?"

"There's something about his voice, but he sounds like all the other Russians who come to America."

"But earlier you said he was Ukrainian. So his accent has to be a little different, right?"

"He told me his family moved from Ukraine to Saint Petersburg when he was young. Maybe his Ukrainian accent is weak and more Russian."

"When did you speak alone with him?"

"At Fawnskin when the boys were all sitting on the porch and the protectors were sitting together."

"Oh, I guess I didn't notice that."

"Are you still angry at Mateo?"

"I'm afraid so. Let's get some sleep."

***

When Alek opened his eyes, it was still dark. Half asleep, he got out of bed and entered the tiny bathroom. As he emptied his bladder, he checked his face in the mirror. He had a slight headache, and after flushing the toilet and washing his hands, he searched the cabinet for some painkillers but found none. Right, he thought. I'm in a van in San Bernardino —not at Rafe's home. As he looked through the window, he saw everyone was up and already drinking coffee. He took a quick shower and dressed. Rafe was still sleeping, but Alek wanted a coffee. Either he had to wake up Rafe, or he'd have to wait. He didn't like either scenario, so he went to the front area and sat in the passenger's seat.

"Alek?" Rafe said.

"I'm here. I'm sitting up front," he said as he rolled down the window to get some fresh air.

"If you want to get some coffee, go outside and get some. I can hear them all talking out there."

"Do you want me to wait for you?" Alek asked, always wanting to please.

"No. I'm gonna shower and make a few phone calls. You go ahead."

"Okay." Alek wondered why Rafe hadn't been interested in sex the night before, and even though he woke with morning wood poking at the sheet, he still seemed to be thinking about other things.

Alek was still haunted by the murder of Burain. He missed him, more each day. *How can I move on when I feel like this?*

Feeling rejected by Rafe and thinking about Burain made him realize that nothing would ever be the same.

As he was about to hop out of the van, Rafe said, "Alek, come here first."

Alek went to the bed, and Rafe pulled him on top of him. "Did I ever tell you that I love having you around?"

"I don't think so." Alek wondered where this was going.

"You give me energy and make me feel like doing shit around here. I can't wait until we go out tonight. I love being around you."

"I didn't know that. I thought you were doing your job and sex with me was just part of your payoff."

"I don't protect just anyone. Many factors came into play before I made my decision about taking you on. The

150

person I choose must first need my protection and turn me on. With you, it's something I can't put into words. It's more than that. I knew I wanted to protect you when I read your files and saw your picture. I saw something in your eyes that spoke to me."

"Did my uncle send you a recent picture?" Alek asked.

"Actually, he sent me a number of them. The one that got my attention was the old one when you were only four years old. Sacha had just taken you into his home. It was the same day your parents were murdered. He told me this was a picture of you on the first day he became a father. The most recent one was when you were in the limo on your way to prison."

"I wonder why he sent you pictures." Hearing Rafe talk about the day he'd had lost his parents added to the burden of losing Burain. He didn't like talking about that day. He pushed it out of his mind as much as he could.

"Those pictures made me believe I could make a difference with my protection. I couldn't wait until he brought you to the party."

"Thanks for telling me this. I'm glad you're the one who chose me." Alek needed a cigarette to smoke away those horrid memories. "Are you sure it's okay for me to go outside?"

"As long as you stay with the group. I'll be out soon."
Rafe kissed Alek as he let him rise to exit the van.

As he stepped out of the van, Alek wondered who Rafe
would be calling. He pulled the cigarettes out of his pocket
and lit one. He went to the table and poured himself a large
cup of coffee and sat beside Anouska.

"How are you this morning?" she asked.

"I'll be better after I drink my coffee. Where's
Mateo?" Alek asked as he sipped his coffee.

"He's talking to James about yesterday. He didn't
sleep all night because Rafe made him feel like shit over
Sara."

"I'm sorry to hear that. Did you sleep okay?" Alek put
his cigarette out.

"No. Mateo and I were up most of the night, talking
about Rafe."

"You know that Sara's okay, so you don't need to
worry about her," Alek said.

"I know she is, but I was really hoping she could travel
with us."

"You can talk to me."

"Thank you. I'm afraid Rafe is going to try to get
Mateo to dump me," Anouska said.

"Didn't someone pay for you to come here?" Alek asked.

"My story is different than that of you and the other boys. I met Mateo at a bar. He offered to protect me before he was here with his brother."

"Do you want to tell me why you needed protection?"

"I ran away from the people who were holding me. My family sent me away to a couple when I was an infant. Those people wanted things from me I didn't want to give. When I didn't do what they wanted, they sent me to Russia, but I didn't want to stay there with strangers. I managed to get away from them and met a man who bought me a one-way ticket to the US."

"Did he just buy you a ticket, no strings attached?" Alek asked.

"No. I had to stay with him for six months first. Then he bought the ticket for me."

"Where did you go when you finally got here?"

"I stayed in a group home for runaways. One night, I sneaked out and went to a nearby bar. I was going to sell myself to the highest bidder. Mateo paid me two hundred dollars for the night, but one night ended up turning into two weeks. Rafe called him, told him he was in danger, and convinced Mateo to join the protectors. He told Rafe he'd

153

come but only if he could protect me. That's how we both joined this group," Anouska said.

"So, he's protecting you for free? Who's protecting Mateo?"

"Not free. Mateo owns my body. Sex for protection, I guess. Rafe is protecting him."

"So, is it real, what you two have, or just a business deal?" Alek asked.

"On my part it's real, and Mateo claims it's real between us. I'm afraid if he had to choose between Rafe and me, he'd pick his brother. That's why I couldn't sleep all night. I know Rafe blames me for Mateo messing up with Sara."

"Rafe told me he loves you like a sister, so I don't think he'd ever ask Mateo to dump you or ask Mateo to make a choice and besides, I want you here with us."

"Thank you for telling me that. I worried all night that Rafe would kick me out. I like having you here too. I feel… connected to you. I guess it's because we're both Russian and come from similar backgrounds."

When Rafe found Alek with Anouska, he tapped him on the shoulder. "Come with me."

"Good morning, Rafe," she said.

"Morning."

"See you later Anouska," Alek said.

Alek got up and left with Rafe.

"Where are we going?" Alek asked.

"We're going to the brook to drink our coffee. Get yourself a refill."

After refilling his cup, they continued to the brook.

Sitting on a wide flat rock, Rafe blurted out, "I talked to my father this morning."

"Why?"

"Because I'm sick of his shit with Emilio and now Mateo. It's all crap, and it needs to end."

"What did you say to him?" Alek asked.

"I wasn't very calm and cool. I threatened to kill him if he didn't stop threatening us."

"How did he take that?"

"He didn't. He hung up on me."

"Oh, God. You didn't start a war with your father, did you?"

"I don't know. He wants Mateo in exchange for Emilio's life."

"Why does he want Mateo?" Alek asked.

"He wants him to run his drug cartel, so he needs to train him. He thinks I brainwashed Mateo."

"What are you going to do?"

"I'm not going to give him my brother, that's for damn sure. Between Kaden and me, Emilio is safe."

CHAPTER ELEVEN

Rafe Escobar

During the ride, Alek sat beside him, not saying much. Something was on his mind and causing his silence. The seriousness of the threats they faced had his attention. Rafe hoped it wouldn't affect his time at the pool party.

"What are you thinking about?" Rafe asked.

"I'm worried about Emilio," Alek said.

"He's with Kaden. He'll be fine."

"Why do you think some people want to kill us because we're gay?" Alek asked.

"I don't know, but in my family, they believe gay people should be taken out because we're living against their religious beliefs."

"Same with the Belanov family, but not Uncle Sacha. He told me that there was no point in trying to force myself to be someone I wasn't. He believed I was born this way, and that's why he taught me how to use weapons to protect myself. He always wanted the best for me... until now."

"I'm not sure what was in his mind, but he told me that the Belanov family and the Pavlenko family were both after you, but for different reasons." Rafe doubted the Pavlenko family was after Alek. They never failed when they targeted a hit. Their targets didn't get to run away.

"Did he say which member of the Belanov family was out to get me?"

"No. I asked, but he said they all wanted you gone because of your relationship with Burain."

"All of them? It doesn't make sense. I never planned to take over my uncle's position in the family. So forget what my uncle thinks. Why do you think they want me gone?"

"In my mind, it's always about money. Someone wants your uncle's money."

"Pavel does. He told me once that since Pavel, his brother, and I were his only nephews, we should divide his money when the time came. I didn't like him talking about Uncle Sacha dying."

"What I'm wondering is why he allowed Pavel to drive you to the party?" Rafe asked.

"I don't give a fuck anymore. When Uncle Sacha did that, he wasn't protecting me, and he promised me he would."

"That's not true. He hired me to protect you. If he didn't want you protected at all, he'd have left you there and let someone blow you away."

"Do you really believe that?" Alek asked.

158

"Of course. He doesn't want any harm to come to you. He paid me loads of money for your protection. He obviously wants you protected, but I wonder why he couldn't control the rest of your family from making threats. That part bothers me."

Rafe parked the van on the street, and they walked to the back of the house where the pool party was. Men filled the yard; some were swimming while others were just talking.

"Hey, Rafe," Eduardo, the leader of the group, said.

"Is everything okay here with everyone together like this?" Rafe asked.

"Yes, but we'd better off with separate buildings. Ten people living in one big house will cause tension."

"I can imagine. The cabins at Fawnskin are available for thirty days. If you want to go there for the month, let me know. I'll also check out the possibility of alternative housing for you guys that's within your budget," Rafe said.

"That would be better than all of us in one house," Eduardo said. "Put us down for Fawnskin."

Rafe pulled his phone out and wrote a note that Eduardo's group would be staying at Fawnskin for one month. Realizing in all the conversation he'd forgotten to introduce Alek, he gestured. "This is Alek. He's under my protection."

"Well, it's about time you did something other than running things," Eduardo teased.

Emilio appeared out of nowhere. "Rafe, can I steal Alek from you?"

Rafe turned to Alek, putting him on the spot. "Do you want to hang out with Emilio?"

"Sure."

"Don't leave the backyard under any circumstances," Rafe said.

"Okay," they chimed back as Alek left with Emilio.

Rafe hoped that the two would bond and become good friends since they were both lonely. They needed someone to bounce their upsets off. Alek was slowly beginning to share what he was feeling. His uncle had really hurt him by sending him away. Who could blame him? The man was the only one who had raised and loved him. Rafe wanted to know the real reason he had taken Alek into his home.

Other uncles, who had wives, could have raised Alek. Uncle Sacha never married, and that seemed suspicious. *Was he gay too?* He had no idea nor did Alek ever mention why his uncle had never married or had children. That was what most straight people did in his family. He scanned the yard for Mateo and Anouska, but he couldn't see them anywhere.

Eduardo left him to help one of his group members with the food. Rafe found Kaden drinking a beer and talking to one of the protectors from the other group.

"Kaden, have you seen Mateo and Anouska?" he asked.

No. I've been looking everywhere for them. I didn't want to alarm you, but I sent him a message, and he didn't respond. I figured they must have stopped somewhere."

"They were supposed to be here an hour ago. It doesn't take an hour to pick up something for the party. Why the fuck didn't he respond to his messages or answer his phone?" Rafe took his phone from his pocket and called his brother. The phone rang until it went to voicemail.

Rafe left a stern message. "Where the fuck are you? You'd better be on your way. Call me back ASAP." He worried his father may have gotten to them.

"What are we going to do?" Kaden asked.

"We have to find them," Rafe said.

"Do you want me to go with you?"

"We can leave Emilio and Alek with James and Valerik."

"Emilio likes Valerik. Alek can stay with James," Kaden said.

"Alek isn't going to like this. But that's tough. He'll go where I tell him. Talk to Emilio and Valerik and meet me at my van."

Kaden nodded and walked over to Valerik, who was in the pool with Liam. Rafe found James drinking a beer beside the ice chest.

"I need to find Mateo and Anouska. They haven't shown up here, and Mateo isn't answering his phone. Can you watch Alek?"

"Of course. Where is he?" James asked.

Rafe pointed to where they were. "He's with Emilio right now. They're sitting on lounge chairs at the other end of the pool."

"Sure. If you don't get back by the time we have to leave, I'll take him with us in my van. He can sleep in a sleeping bag."

"Hopefully we'll be back before then. Thanks."

Rafe walked over to Alek and Emilio. Alek looked up at Rafe with the gorgeous blue eyes that made Rafe wonder if he should be leaving at all.

"Kaden and I are going to look for Mateo and Anouska. They never made it here, and Mateo isn't

162

answering his phone. James's in charge of you and will take over for me until I get back. I hope it's a quick look and find."

"I hope you find them," Alek said.

"Do whatever James tells you to, for now he's responsible for you."

"Yes."

"Emilio, you're with Valcrik," Rafe said.

"I know," he said. "Kaden told me."

Rafe leaned over and gave Alek a kiss, then turned and left them.

Once Rafe and Kaden were in the van, they both checked their phones for messages.

"Do you think he wants to leave the Gay Protection Society?" Kaden asked.

"I don't know, but my father wants him. I'm more worried that he might have gotten ahold of Mateo."

"Call your mother," Kaden said.

"My mother?" Rafe gave Kaden a crazy look. "I haven't talked to her in a long damn time."

"Do you have her number?"

"Of course. She's my mother." Rafe rolled his eyes.

"Call and ask her about Mateo. She'd know if your father had him because she'd want to see him."

163

"You have a point." In a few seconds, Rafe called his mother, and she answered.

"It's Rafe."

"It's so good to hear your voice," she said.

"I'm sorry it's been so long but… well… you know. I have to make this quick. Did Dad find Mateo?"

"Of course not. Would you boys please come home?" his mother asked. "Your dad shouldn't be working anymore. He needs you boys."

"Mom, that's never going to happen. Mateo and I don't want anything to do with his business."

"How is Emilio?" she asked.

"He's fine."

"Did you tell him yet?"

"No. I can't tell him until I know he's safe. He might get pissed off and run. I can't have that," Rafe said.

"You should have told him a long time ago. The longer you wait, the harder it'll be for both of you."

"Would you do me a big favor?" Rafe asked.

"What do you want?"

"Tell that bastard you married to remove Emilio and Mateo from his hit list."

"He won't do anything to them. It's a threat. He said he would call off the hit on Emilio if you return Mateo."

"It's never going to happen," Rafe said.

"I thought Mateo was with you. So why are you asking if your father has him? Is he missing?"

"I got to go. Talk to you soon. I love you." Rafe ended the call, hating that he'd had to leave his mother wondering if her other son was missing.

"I guess that call went nowhere fast," Kaden said.

"She would have told me if my father had him. He's definitely not there, so we have one less worry."

"Where are we going to look for them?"

"We'll go back to the campground and see if he just stayed behind."

"What was that business your mom asked about? What did she mean when she asked if you'd told Emilio? You said he might get pissed and leave?"

"It's nothing bad." Rafe started the van to drive to the last campsite.

"I should know whatever you're hiding from me about Emilio. Can't you trust me? He's with me day and night. I'd never hurt him."

"I know you care about Emilio, and I do trust you with my life. This is just something I never discussed with anyone, not even you."

"It must be really bad, but now I'm scared for him. Tell me. I won't tell him."

Knowing he'd never get out of this without telling Kaden so Rafe gave in. "When I was sixteen, I tried to prove I was a man because I knew I'd die if anyone thought I was gay. So I got the neighbor girl pregnant. She had the baby, but she was going to give it up for adoption. My mother intervened, and we got to keep my baby in the family. My father didn't want him in his house because he was born out of wedlock. So Emilio was raised by my Uncle Reuben and Aunt Carla."

"Emilio is your son? No way. Well, he does look like you. So, you never told him?"

"My aunt and uncle said they would adopt and raise Emilio if I promised never to tell him the truth. I agreed to that, and they raised him as their own. He has no idea, but he always was close to me."

"Are you going to tell him?"

"Yes. Now, that my uncle sent him back to me, I feel they broke our agreement. I don't know when I'll tell him. I'm afraid he'll get upset with me."

"He loves you."

"As his older cousin, but not his father who abandoned him because his own grandfather made me. I was too young to rebel against his authority then, but not now. I'm going to take him down if he doesn't leave us alone."

"Don't talk like that. You're not going to take him down. It's not that I don't think you can, but do you want the Colombian cartel after you and the rest of us?"

"What am I supposed to do with that bastard?"

"I don't know. Just hang low. When will you tell Emilio?"

"Soon. Very soon."

Driving through the campsite area, they didn't see Mateo's van. Rafe parked where they had stayed last night. "Shit, they're not here."

"I bet he took Anouska to a club to dance or a pub to listen to music," Kaden said.

"He could have told us. He's just acting like a spoiled brat."

"Let's go to the city area."

"Good idea. Did he leave a message?"

"No. I just checked."

"Why would he just take off like this?" Rafe asked.

"You humiliated him in front of the group."

"There would be no need for any of this if he'd followed the rules. He lives in a damn dream world. He always has," Rafe raised his voice.

167

"Well, he's not with your father, so they must be okay. Let's check the local bars. They don't have that many for us to check."

"I bet Anouska talked him into leaving," Rafe said.

"I don't think it would have taken much for him to leave after yesterday's fiasco."

Rafe's phone rang, and he quickly answered it, hoping it would be Mateo, but it was James. "What's up, James?"

"The boys disappeared."

"Which boys?" Rafe's stomach turned over.

"Alek and Dante. I left them in the van while I was at the fire pit. Damn, I told them not to leave the van for any reason. Valerik and I are looking all over for them. We're taking Emilio and Liam with us, so we don't lose them too."

"Wait a minute. Are you still at the party?" Rafe asked.

"No. We're back at the campsite. I told them to stay in the van while I talked to Valerik at the fire pit," James said.

"Maybe they went for a walk. How long have they been gone?" Rafe asked.

"I was out for an hour. So I don't know when they left."

"I'm on my way." Rafe ended the call.

"What's going on?" Kaden asked.

"Alek and Dante are missing. They took off."

"Unbelievable. This is a great night we're having."

"No more socials. I'm tying Alek to the bed the next time I have to leave. I'm not going to go through this again."

"James is so good. I can't believe this happened."

"James was sitting at the fire pit. The boys were supposed to be in the van. Somehow, they left unnoticed. I'm going to teach Alek a lesson when I get my hands on him. I told him not to go out on his own without permission. Neither of them has phones."

"Want me to drive?"

"No, Kaden! I know how to fucking drive."

"I know you do. I thought it would give you time to relax."

"I don't want to relax. How could we lose four members in one damn day?" He feared he was losing his edge. Losing clients never happened before, and he had to put an end to this.

"The boys will be back, but I don't know about Mateo."

CHAPTER TWELVE

Alek Belanov

Alek and Dante had left the van without being seen. They hiked to the road to the Circle-K store and picked up a bottle of Jack Daniels and cigarettes. They wandered the dirt road and found a quiet spot away from anyone. Alek twisted off the cap of the bottle, took a few swigs, and passed it to Dante.

Dante eagerly accepted the bottle. "I hope James doesn't check on us," he said.

"We'll just say we took a walk," Alek said.

"I don't think James will buy that, but we need to hurry back." Taking a couple of mouthfuls, Dante returned the bottle to Alek.

"Okay. If you want to go now, we'll go. Out of curiosity, just what kind of relationship do you have with James?" Alek asked.

"He'll discipline me if I don't follow his rules. It's more than that, but you need to read the BDSM book to understand all of it."

"Is discipline part of the BDSM thing?" Alek figured he'd have to read the book because Dante would hound him until he did.

171

"Yes. I'm supposed to listen to James, but sometimes I need to break free. He's putting his life on the line for me. All he asks is for my submission and obedience," Dante said.

"I guess that's not asking for much when you put it like that, "Alek said. "I've been taking Rafe for granted because he's being paid to protect me, but Rafe doesn't really need the money. He's doing this because he believes it's the right thing to do."

"How do you know he doesn't need the money?" Dante asked.

"Don't you know who Rafe Escobar is?"

"He's the head of the Gay Protection Society."

"True, but besides that, his father is in charge of one of the largest drug cartels. He has big money."

"I didn't know that," Dante said.

"Haven't you read about the Escobar family?" Alek asked.

"No."

"My family is into bad stuff too, but I try to stay out of it. Why couldn't I've been raised by normal parents?" Alek asked.

"I know what you mean." Dante had a worried look on his face. "Are you ready to leave?"

"Sure. Let's go." Alek twisted the top back onto the bottle.

"Are you going to bring that bottle back?" Dante asked.

"Why not? Most of it's still here."

"Won't you get in trouble?"

"I don't think so unless James gets noisy about it."

"How will you explain where you got it?" Dante asked.

"Yeah, maybe I'd better leave it somewhere when we get closer to the vans, but I'm keeping these cigarettes."

They walked down the road, passing the bottle back and forth between them, when a van screeched up beside them. Alek looked inside the van. *Damn it.*

"We're caught," Dante said. "That's Rafe and Kaden."

"I can see that." Alek flung the bottle away.

Rafe jumped out and slammed the door. "Get your asses in the van," Rafe shouted and walked around to open the side door for them.

They climbed inside without saying a word. This was the last thing they needed. All they'd done was take a walk, and now their protectors were going to treat them as if they'd committed a crime.

"You're both in trouble," Rafe said. "James is damn pissed off at both of you, and so am I. You both know the rules about leaving without permission, and you've been warned there are consequences for disobeying your protector."

"James will be waiting for you, Dante," Kaden said. "I sent him a text to let him know we have you guys."

Rafe parked his van in the same spot he had before the pool party. When they all stepped out of the van, James and Valerik were standing alongside Emilio and Liam.

"Thank you," James said to Rafe.

"All of you sit in the circle. I'm going to refresh some of the rules," Rafe said.

Alek sat down without saying a word to Rafe.

When everyone had taken a seat, Rafe said, "We had several breaches between yesterday and tonight. This can't happen and won't happen again. Your protectors are putting themselves at risk to help you. There are times when they have to check the perimeter or fight off enemies without you. That means you must obey your protector to the letter. We're dealing with life and death situations here. There's no room for mistakes or childish games. From here on in, if your protector must leave, he'll lock you in a room or tie you down, but you will not leave. Does anyone have a question?"

"What about the good young men who follow the rules? Does this apply to them as well?" Kaden asked.

"It applies to all four of them. If there are no more questions, let's call it a night." Rafe's expression and words were firm. Of course, no one would dare question his decision.

Rafe walked over to Alek. "Get up and go to the van."

Alek could tell by his tone that he was seriously angry over the events of the day. *Knowing the risk he's taking, how can I justify needing to get away for a bit? It wasn't as if we'd disappeared for good, and we were on our way back to the campsite.* Rafe unlocked the door and waited for Alek to get inside first.

"I'm sorry, Rafe. We only went to the store and came right back."

"You're not sorry. You're just rationalizing your behavior. You know that's bullshit and you're not really one bit sorry about anything."

"I thought I was going to be free when I got out of prison. I had more freedom there than I do here," Alek said.

"I warned you that you needed to do as I say. Did I tell you to leave this campsite without permission whenever you wanted?"

"No."

"Did James tell you to stay in the van?"

"He did."

"And you decided it was okay not to listen to James?"

"I wanted to go for a walk. That's all this is about, but you're making this about you."

"What did I warn you that I would do if you didn't listen to me the first time?"

"You were going to punish me."

"How was I going to punish you?"

Alek didn't want to answer. *No one ever disciplined him with a belt. Where did Rafe come up with this idea? Was he part of the BDSM group and had forgotten to mention it?*

"Alek, I asked you a question." Rafe put his hand on his belt buckle.

"You said you would use your belt on me." The very words sent chills throughout his body.

"You have a choice. You can accept your punishment or leave here right now."

Alek thought about what Rafe had said. He could walk out of here as a free man and escape his punishment or he could accept the punishment and Rafe would continue to protect him. He didn't much like his choices and right now, he had no idea where he'd go if he left. He had no one on his side except Rafe and the other group members.

"I'll take my punishment." Alek hoped he wouldn't regret his decision. He wanted to stay with Rafe, or at least he thought he did. He should have listened to him, but how could he? He felt trapped in the van and needed some space outside.

"Bend over the seat." Rafe pointed to the back of the passenger's seat.

Alek bent over the seat. The loud sound of Rafe's belt sliding through the loops made him clench his ass cheeks.

"I'm punishing you for disobeying me. If you move your hands to protect yourself from my belt, I'll start all over again. Do you understand?" Rafe's voice was void of emotion, a distancing Alek feared.

Alek nodded, unable to speak. He heard the snapping sound of the belt as Rafe whistled it through the air behind him. When the thick belt landed on his ass cheeks, he bit his lower lip to keep from making any noise. Rafe wasted no time whipping his ass with the belt. Each strike hurt

177

more than the one before. It felt like he was swinging the belt as hard as he could. Alek arched his back, hoping to derail part of the sting.

He's never going to stop. I can't get away from him. I'm stuck here forever. Why did I need to take a walk? I had better protection in prison. Rafe's crazy with power and control.

Alek never had a chance to catch his breath—Rafe's belt pounded him continually for what seemed to be a long time. He cried silently from the humiliation and the pain. The belt set his ass on fire. He had never known this much agony and humiliation from a punishment. There was no doubt in his mind that he would obey Rafe's orders from now on. His fear slowly turned to hate.

"Go to bed," Rafe ordered.

Alek turned around and made his way to the bed without saying another word. He stripped off his clothes and slipped into bed. Rafe sat in the passenger's seat, rolled the window down, and smoked his pipe in silence. *All I wanted was a little freedom to do as I please. I don't know if I can live like this much longer.* He'd try his best because he didn't want one of his enemies to torture and murder him. *What was so wrong with walking to the store?*

Alek faced the back of the van because he didn't plan to cuddle up with Rafe if he came to bed. He really didn't want anything to do with him right now. Rafe didn't understand him at all.

Within half an hour, Rafe stripped off his clothes and slipped under the covers. Alek could smell the sweet tobacco from his pipe. There was something very soothing about the smell. Uncle Sacha smoked cigars and sometimes cigarettes. The more Alek inhaled the tobacco scent, the more it reminded him of his father. He'd smoked a pipe, but Alek hadn't thought about that for a long time. That was why the scent of pipe tobacco always made him feel happy. *Why did I have to lose my father? For that matter, why did someone slaughter my entire family? Who did this to them?* He was determined to find out when he had access to the internet again.

Rafe shifted in bed and wrapped his arms around Alek. "Are you up?"

"No."

"I know you're angry with me. I can't risk losing you to some crazy Russian. Don't you understand why I punished you?"

"No. I took a damn walk with a new friend. Big deal."

179

"If someone had seen you or Dante, the safety of you both would have been compromised as well as the others." Rafe kissed Alek's neck, but Alek moved away from him. "Don't be angry at me. I want to protect you. Just let me do my damn job."

"We could have had a conversation." Alek turned to face Rafe.

"No. We already had that conversation. I warned you then what I'd do if you didn't listen to me. Don't ignore me. I don't want to lose you… I like having you around."

"I didn't get out of prison to be treated like this by you or anyone. I don't want you to make me feel like your slave."

"You're not my slave. I'm in charge of your safety. If you don't allow me to protect you, what's the point?"

"I'm sorry if I worried you. Maybe we could agree that I need some time with other people. If I need to go to a nearby store, I'll ask you, so you don't think a Russian blew my head off."

"If you need space, we'll work on that, but please don't go off on your own again."

"What happened to Mateo and Anouska?"

"I don't know where they are. Mateo isn't answering his phone."

"When can we have phones?"

"After the 30 days or when we relocate to a permanent location."

"So then you're open to giving me some space?" Alek asked.

"I'm open to allowing you a safe space, but I need to know about it first."

"No one has ever beaten me with a belt," Alek said.

"Really? So, Uncle Sacha never disciplined you?"

"He stopped talking to me when he was angry. He never touched me ever."

"I have a lot of things on my mind. I don't want to add you to my list of failures," Rafe said.

Not wanting to continue the discussion Alek said, "Good night."

"Hey you." Leaning over, Rafe kissed Alek. "We don't go to bed angry."

"Good night," Alek said again, still upset with Rafe.

BRINA BRADY

CHAPTER THIRTEEN

Rafe Escobar

When Rafe turned to face Alek, he pretended to be sleeping. "Wake up, Alek."

"I'm up."

"I'm going to have to talk to Emilio this morning. Kaden will be coming over to stay with you. If you want to go outside, he goes with you." Rafe dressed as he talked.

"How long is this going to take?"

"It's a delicate topic. I'll tell you all about it after I speak with him."

Alek climbed out of bed. "I'm going to take a shower."

"Go ahead. When we're alone, you and I need to have another long conversation about my expectations."

Alek walked into the shower and closed the door. He was still angry, and it would take some doing to make him understand Rafe cared for him. He understood that Alek's reactions were justified, but he was having trouble moving on from his discipline. Rafe opened the door for Kaden and Emilio.

"Alek is in the shower," Rafe told Kaden.

"Don't worry. I'll watch him."

"Morning, Rafe," Emilio said as he stepped outside.

"Morning. Let's walk to the brook where we can be alone."

"Did I do something wrong?"

"No. Not you. There's something I need to talk to you about. Something I should have told you sooner."

Emilio's face paled. "You're starting to scare me."

"It's not anything bad. I'm hoping you'll be happy about it."

Reaching the brook, they sat on a wide rock.

"You know I love you, right?" Rafe asked.

"Yes. You're my favorite cousin."

"That's what I want to discuss with you." Rafe paused trying to keep it all together.

"Are you okay?" Emilio asked

"Yes, this is difficult for me. When I was sixteen, I got a girl pregnant. She was going to give my baby to a church adoption agency. So my mother asked if we could have the baby and she agreed. The problem was my father, as always. He didn't want my child. So my uncle Reuben and aunt Carla adopted him." Rafe's stomach hurt from finally letting go of a secret he'd carried for so long

"Are you talking about me?" Emilio's eyes widened.

"I am. I'm your father." Rafe sat stock-still and watched Emilio to see what his reaction would be. He had replayed these words many times. *He finally knows.*

"I don't know how I feel about this." Emilio's eyes teared up.

Rafe took Emilio in his arms. "I've always loved you, Emilio. I hope you know that. I'd never turn my back on you. I've made a point to always keep you in my life."

"Why didn't you tell me sooner?" Emilio asked.

"I made a promise to Uncle Reuben and Aunt Carla. They told me they'd only adopt you if I never told you I was your real father. I agreed because I didn't want you to be adopted by strangers, and I couldn't bear the idea of never seeing you again."

"Why does your father, apparently my grandfather, hate me so much?" Emilio's brown eyes looked directly into Rafe's.

"It's not you he hates. It's me. I was never what he wanted me to be, so he used you to hurt me. He knows how I feel about you."

Rafe hated to see Emilio hurting from his father's rejection and hate. Their constant fighting about Emilio over the years had taken its toll. His father had wanted him to marry Emilio's mother, which he hadn't been able to

185

bring himself to do. His father had judged Emilio a bastard and refused to recognize him as his grandson.

Later, when he had found out Emilio was gay, his father had pressured his brother, Emilio's adoptive father, to throw him out of the house and disown him. He had refused. There had been no way he could do that, so for his own safety, he told him to stay with Rafe.

"Why did you tell me now?" Emilio asked. "I don't understand." His voice trembled when he spoke.

"Because Uncle Reuben couldn't protect you anymore, so I felt he had broken the agreement we made."

"I feel funny now around you. I mean I still love you, but I just feel strange."

"It's okay. I'm going to keep on loving you. You can still call me Rafe unless you want to call me Dad someday." He wondered what it would feel like to have Emilio call him Dad.

"I don't know about calling you Dad. Can I think about it?"

"Take as long as you like. I'll always be here for you no matter what."

"I know you will. You were always there for me. Did you tell anyone else about me being your son?"

"I told Kaden last night because he's responsible for you and needs to know everything about you."

Rafe's phone rang, so he picked it up. "Hello."

"Rafe, you need to move," Milo, an area contact said. "I got word that some gang members from Los Angeles are looking for Dante."

"Thanks. Where are they now?"

"They're camping at San Bernardino National Park. There're about ten of them."

"Shit. That's nearby. Thanks." Rafe ended the call.

"Is something wrong?" Emilio asked.

"We're moving to the next spot this morning."

"Where are we going?"

"I don't know yet. I'm going to map that out now."

"I guess we better eat first," Emilio said.

Rafe nodded. "I'm happy I can tell people that you're my son. I don't have to hide someone I love anymore."

"I love you either way. I just can't believe you're my father." Emilio smiled.

Rafe hugged Emilio again. "Remember no matter what you think, I've always loved you."

"I know you have." Emilio kissed Rafe on the cheek.

"I'm glad Uncle Reuben and Aunt Karla adopted you even though I didn't see eye to eye with them. I would have

187

gone crazy if you were adopted by strangers and not be able to see you."

"I love them and I never thought I wasn't really theirs. They loved me until your stupid father told him to get rid of me."

"They still love you and I'm sure they miss you."

"Thanks for saying that."

"We need to get everyone at the fire pit now. Tell James and Dante and I'll get Kaden and Alek."

"Okay."

Rafe and Emilio rushed back, splitting up to go to different vans. Rafe climbed into the van, but Kaden and Alek weren't inside. He went to the fire pit to find them drinking coffee.

"There you are! So everyone is here," Rafe said.

"Where's Emilio?" Kaden asked.

"He's getting James and Dante." Rafe looked over at them. "He'll be here soon."

"Did your talk go okay?" Kaden asked.

"Yes. It was just emotional."

After Emilio returned, he poured himself a cup of coffee and sat beside Kaden.

Rafe stood to make the announcement. "We need to move... today. James, keep a close eye on Dante. Word has it a Los Angeles gang has scouts looking for him in this area. We'll keep the vans and move out of state for a while. There is just too much going on in California. I'll enter the schedule with directions and locations of our daily stops. I'll keep the final destination a secret for now. Give me an hour, and I'll have our next set of directions. In the meantime, pack up, and we'll leave."

"What about Mateo and Anouska?" James asked.

"They've chosen to leave us for whatever reason. Mateo knows how to contact me if they want back in, but for now, my priority is the safety of everyone in our group. We need to keep Dante safe. He needs to be extra careful."

Rafe took Alek gently by the arm. "Come with me. I need your help."

Alek said nothing but followed him back to the van and sat in the front.

"So much is going on right now," Rafe said.

He knew that Alek was still upset with him over the discipline, but he couldn't risk losing him to his own carelessness. He didn't understand why it had been so difficult to follow simple precautionary measures. *Why did he leave with Dante? If he needed anything, he could have just asked me, but he chose to ignore the orders I gave him. Something could have happened to Dante, and Alek would*

189

have been in the crossfire. I need to rethink some of the policies of leaving the boys alone when we walk the perimeter.

"What's really happening?" Alek asked.

"We're not safe here. That's why it's so important you guys don't go anywhere without us."

"You made that perfectly clear last night." Alek glared at him.

"I need you to look up campgrounds four hours from here, heading east. Repeat this for three days." Rafe handed Alek his extra phone.

"Is that all?"

"Make reservations for five vans under the name Fuller Christian Group. If you need to put down a deposit, use this card." Rafe handed Alek a prepaid credit card he used to keep from being tracked.

"Why Fuller Christian Group?"

"I have some of my accounts registered with that name. People usually don't bother Christian groups. It's one of our protection layers."

"Why five vans?"

"I'm hoping that Mateo and Anouska will come to their senses and meet us there."

"What happened when you talked to Emilio?" Alek asked.

"It's a long story. I don't want to go into it right now. He'll probably tell you about it before I have a chance. I need my mind clear right now. We need to work on the directions. Tell me when you pick a spot, and I'll put the directions into the phone for the group to access."

"Thanks for allowing me to help." Alek smiled at him for the first time since his discipline.

"No problem. I need your support right now."

A couple of minutes went by while they both worked.

"The first spot is Brown's Millpond Campground in Bishop, California. It's four hours away from here."

"Thanks," Rafe said and worked on the directions for the others.

He handed Alek a notebook and pen. "Put the info in here."

"Are you still upset with Mateo?" Alek asked.

"Yes. I'm sick about it. I have a couple of my local contacts looking for them. So far, nothing has turned up."

"What about your father?" Alek looked worried.

"No, he doesn't have them. I talked to my mother, and she hasn't seen him. If my father had him, she'd know."

"I'm sorry they left without saying anything. I'm going to miss Anouska."

"Sometimes I think Anouska might be a mole for one of our enemies. I don't have any evidence, but the entire fiasco about Mateo falling for Sara makes no sense to me."

"I don't think Mateo would allow her to make his decisions," Alek said.

"I just finished sending everyone directions, so we might as well take off." Rafe was done talking about Mateo and Anouska.

"Can I talk to Emilio and Dante?"

"Sure Alek, but don't leave the campsite."

Alek rolled his eyes as he left the van.

Mateo and Anouska leaving the society made Rafe feel sick to his stomach. He'd spoken harshly to him, hoping he'd finally wake up and take responsibility for his part of the security. As always, Mateo was blind to any trouble, leaving Rafe to deal with all his problems. It never ended with Mateo. Pulling his phone out, he called his brother once more hoping he'd answer. This time he did.

"What do you want, Rafe?" Mateo answered.

"Where the fuck are you?" he shouted.

"We had to get away from you and the society. Things were getting too heavy and dark for me. You know I don't believe in any type of violence. I wondered if you'd have killed Sara if I hadn't been around," he said.

"My primary goal is to protect. Sometimes, when our lives are threatened, we resort to what you call violence. I call it a strong defense. Are you coming back?"

"The only way I can come back is if you exclude me from any gun violence," Mateo said.

"What the hell does that mean? You want me to protect you and Anouska?"

"I guess that's what I'm asking. I can't be a protector if it means I might need to resort to killing. I can't do that."

"Come back, and I'll be in charge of your protection and Anouska's if you listen to me. No going off when we all need protection. The society is a group of ten people who bond together to either protect or be protected," Rafe said.

"I can do something to help you that doesn't require guns or tying people up," Mateo said.

"We're leaving for Brown's Millpond Campground in Bishop. It takes a good four hours to get there. Directions are under Location 1930. I made reservations for five vans under Fuller Christian Group. It's paid for."

"See you there, and we can talk more about my role later."

"Okay. See you then. Stay safe."

Rafe didn't like his brother shirking his responsibilities. He certainly lived in a fantasy world. He had promised Anouska he'd protect her, and now what was he saying? At least Rafe would have his brother with him and wouldn't have to worry about them, but his confidence in Mateo was in question. Leaving without telling him left Rafe cold. With all he'd done for his brother, for him to treat him as if he didn't matter didn't sit well.

CHAPTER FOURTEEN

Alek Belanov

When Alek stepped out of the van he found Dante sitting with Liam, but he didn't see Kaden or Emilio. He poured himself a cup of coffee and grabbed a donut. James and Valerik were standing by the fire pit having a private conversation. James saw Alek looking them over and gave him a dirty look. He probably blamed him for the incident with Dante, and he was right. It was his idea to leave without permission. At the time, he'd felt caged like he had in prison. When he'd told Dante, he'd wanted to go with him.

"How's it going?" Alek said as he sat on a chair beside Dante and Liam.

"We're just passing time until everyone is ready to leave," Dante said.

"Did you get into trouble with James last night?" Alek asked.

"Oh, yes! I don't think we'll be doing that again."

"I got in big trouble with Rafe too," Alek said. "Do you think Rafe might be into BDSM?"

Dante smiled. "I don't know if he is or not. James has never mentioned it. I'd think he would have told me if he was."

"Valerik said it's a serious matter," Liam said. "If we leave the group without permission, they can't protect us because they won't know where we are."

"I hope things change when we settle down," Alek said.

"Yeah, this is crap. It's like being in prison," Liam said.

"Not really quite as bad as prison. We have privacy here, and we're safe," Alek said.

"Have you been in prison?" Liam asked.

"Didn't you know? I was in for two years for something I didn't do. It was the worst two years of my life," Alek said.

"I'm sorry that happened to you," Dante said.

"Yeah, I won't use prison lightly in my conversation anymore," Liam said.

"Liam? Why are you here?" Dante asked.

"I was set up to take the fall for my parents. So the police are looking for me. I don't want to talk about it right now, but I'm innocent."

"I believe you," Alek said.

196

"I do too," Dante said.

"Where's Emilio?" Alek asked, not wanting to discuss his prison experiences either.

"He left for the new camp with Kaden. They wanted to get an early start," Dante said.

Rafe showed up and said, "We're leaving now. See you guys in about four hours."

Alek followed him back to the van.

"You and I need to talk," Rafe said.

"That's what we always do."

"I would have fucked you last night, but... you weren't interested."

"And do you think I should have been after what you did to me?"

"The deal is you're to be available to me when I want you."

"That's a great deal my uncle made for you. I'd like to tell him what I think of this bullshit."

"Look, I can see you're in a bad mood, so what can we do to change that?" Rafe asked.

"Not much, but I do have a question that's been bothering me. Did you want me because of the money?"

"I thought I'd explained that to you. First, if you remember, I don't need the money. My father set me up for life so I'll never have to work. I kept the money because it helps the cause. My cause is protecting gay men who need protection. Your uncle's money was partly for you and of course, he told me you have money in your bank accounts. Money isn't an issue for us. I chose you because I wanted to protect you."

Rafe paused and put his hand on Alek's arm and continued.

"When I saw your pictures, something happened. They touched me somehow, like you were calling me. Now with you here, I know I really do want you. I want you all the time. So to answer your question, money had nothing to do with my picking you."

"That still doesn't make me like you any better after last night."

"Well, maybe this'll help. I have some good news."

"What is it? Are you going to let me leave?"

"No. It's not that good, but I want you to understand that I'd be really sad if you did."

"So, what's the good news?"

"I talked to Mateo when you'd left the van. He and Anouska are going to join us at our next location."

"That's great news. Where were they, anyway?"

"I don't know. Mateo had a problem with my expectations. He wants to change a few things around. We're going to discuss it when I see him."

"Rafe, I feel torn. I used to like you, but now, I'm not so sure."

"In the scope of things, it doesn't really matter if you like me. Your ass is mine, and you'll do whatever I tell you. If you even think about leaving, you need to know that I'll hunt you down."

"Why do you even give a fuck?"

"You know, you're too old to be talking like a spoiled brat. If you don't get things your way, you won't play anymore. Grow up, Alek. Move on and make the best of it."

"I'm only here because I fell in love when I was sixteen. Burain rocked my world. I'll never regret being with him."

"Are you over him?"

"I'm over crying about it, but there will always be a place in my heart for him. I know we'll never be together again, and I do want a new love in my life. I'm open to that."

"With me?" Rafe put his hand on Alek's thigh.

"I don't know. I thought we could, but now I'm not so sure."

"I can't take no for an answer. I'm going to find my way into your heart somehow." Rafe squeezed Alek's thigh. "I missed fucking you this morning."

"Well, if that's going to happen, we have to start with trust. Are you going to tell me why it was so important for you to talk to Emilio?"

"I was getting to that. You see, Emilio isn't my cousin."

"He's not? He thinks you are, and you look a lot alike."

"There's a good reason for that because he's really my son. When he was born, I had to give him up to my uncle and aunt. They made me promise to never to tell him. When my uncle sent him to me, I decided our deal was off. So I told him."

"I don't know what to say. So, you were with a girl?"

"I did it to prove I wasn't gay to my father. In the process, I hurt the girl and myself, but I did get Emilio and for that, it was worth it. He's so important to me."

"I can't understand being with a girl. I don't know if I could get my dick to work. You must have been awfully determined or maybe you're bi."

200

"If you knew my father, you'd muster the determination too. I had to prove I wasn't gay but proved to myself that I was. I'm not bi, believe me."

Alek's anger seemed to be waning. "Even though I didn't have the perfect childhood, I never felt I had to be straight. It must have been difficult to live like that."

"I'm still living it… with him. He won't leave Mateo, Emilio, and me alone."

"I don't understand why other people care about who another person loves. It's got nothing to do with them. I never could figure out their problem."

Rafe stopped at a drive-thru for their lunch. He ordered them both cheeseburgers and fries with cokes.

"Thanks."

Rafe parked and called James.

"What's up?" James answered.

"Are you on the road yet?" Rafe asked.

"Yes, we left right after you. Valerik and Liam left at the same time as we did. We're all having lunch in my van, and then we'll be back on the road."

"Just checking. I was worried about Dante."

"He's in the back of the van on the bed. No one can see him. Valerik let Liam stay with us. They're reading, but it sounds like they're doing more talking than reading."

"That's good. Keep me posted if there's any change."

"Sure will." James ended the call.

"Is everything okay?" Alek asked.

"Yes, but it'd be better if you would be a little nicer to me."

"I'm still pissed at you, but I understand why you did it. I'm just not over being upset with you."

"Want some ice cream?" Rafe asked.

"Maybe later."

Rafe drove while Alek looked out the window.

"We need to find a place where we can all be safe. I was thinking of locating on the East Coast. What do you think?" Rafe asked.

"I guess it would be okay. I've been to New York a few times."

"Not New York. We need to live away from major cities, maybe a college town, so you and Emilio can go to school. Once we settle, you'll have more freedom."

"That sounds a lot better than this."

Rafe turned into a side road and drove to a clearing.

"Are we here?" Alek asked.

"Not yet. I need a… break."

"I can take over if you want."

"Not that kind of break." Rafe smiled at Alek.

"What kind of break did you have in mind?"

"Go to the back of the van, take those clothes off, and I'll show you."

Alek couldn't believe him. He actually just parked somewhere to fuck. What did this man do when he wasn't around? He squeezed between the seats and walked to the back of the van, peeled off his clothes, and watched Rafe walking toward him. He was still upset with Rafe, so this wasn't what he wanted to do. It was part of the deal for his protection though, thanks to Uncle Sacha, so this was going to happen.

"Get on your back," Rafe ordered as he unzipped his jeans, dropping them to his shoes in a single movement, revealing his already erect cock.

"Sure thing, Sir," Alek said as he rolled further back on the bed.

Rafe laughed. "I like the sound of that."

"I'm sure you do," Alek said.

Rafe rubbed some lube on his erection. "Should I let you enjoy this, or should I let you have a rough time of it?"

"Mr. Escobar, you'd better make sure I enjoy this." Alek was aroused when he saw Rafe's throbbing erection.

After smearing some lube on Alek's hole, he slipped his finger inside. "Oh, it feels so warm inside."

203

"Next time, you can cool it off with ice cubes, if you like," Alek said.

"You're kind of kinky and I think I like that."

Alek's cock let go a stream of precum as Rafe rolled his legs up and back causing it to land on his stomach. Rafe spread his legs further apart, kissed his hole, and pulled his ass closer to the edge of the bed. Rafe stood before Alek, and used his fingers to pull at his already erect nipples. Alek moaned as Rafe's rough fingers and hard nails played with them.

"Are you ready?" he asked, squeezing Alek's nipples, knowing he was enjoying it.

Alek moaned, but not with pain. He was anxious to proceed.

"Do you want those nipples pierced?"

"No," Alek said.

Rafe took hold of Alek's cock, giving it some jerks. Playing with his nipples made his cock twitch. He stuck a finger back into Alek's hot opening. Then another, scissoring them to stretch and prepared Alek to receive him.

"I see you like me playing with you."

"Are you going to stop teasing me?" Alek asked.

Rafe bent over so he was close to Alek's face and kissed him, pushing his tongue inside. Alek returned the kiss working his tongue against Rafe's.

Rafe turned and pulled something out of a bag. Alek whimpered when the metal clothespins clamped on the swollen nubs. Alek gritted his teeth but stayed silent. The pain increased his excitement.

"I think you deserve a little pinching for being such a bad boy," Rafe said.

"For some reason, it feels good," Alek said.

"Then maybe I should clamp them on your balls," Rafe said.

"No, thank you," Alek's words came out with a slight edge to it.

Alek's hole was ready. The finger-fuck had done a good job. Now Rafe gave the hole attention with his tongue and lips. The naked and completely smooth entrance was inviting. Alek's cock was superhard again from Rafe's tongue-work.

"Please no more. Give it to me, now please," he begged.

"So, do you like me again?" Rafe asked.

"Yes. When you do this, I like you."

Rafe aimed his cock into Alek's hole and grunted like an animal. He was as excited as Alek was. "This time, I'm going to fuck you raw."

"Yes, fuck me, Sir. Be hard on me. Make me come."

Rafe changed between long strokes and short. He was balls deep and stayed inside, letting his balls nestle on Alek's.

"Feels so good," Alek said, realizing that having sex when Rafe wanted to wasn't at all like the guys in prison.

Rafe pulled the clothespins from Alek. He whimpered as he felt the blood rush to his nipples.

"Ahh…Ahh…" Alek moaned.

He was close to the edge but wanted to please Rafe even more.

"Push your ass up." Rafe held Alek's hips tighter, marking his skin with his nails.

Alek pushed up his ass so hard that Rafe almost lost his balance.

"Damn." Rafe squeezed Alek's hips harder to get a good grip and steady himself, then plowed his steel cock in and out, panting and moaning with each thrust.

"Is this hard enough?" he asked.

"Yes. Please. Keep doing it. Don't stop."

"Now I'm going to show you who owns your ass." He brushed his cock along Alek's prostate.

"Ahh… that, do that. It feels so good," Alek moaned.

He moved closer and lifted Alek's legs over his shoulders. He pulled all the way out, aimed his cockhead back at the puckered entrance, and drove forward. Alek groaned as the slick cock entered him again, but it felt too good to complain. His cock had been leaking precum for several minutes, but watching Rafe fucking him was hypnotizing. Rafe's cock hammered his prostate again. Alek moaned softly as Rafe's thrusts became faster and harder. He stroked Alek's cock making sure he enjoyed everything.

"You have such a sexy ass."

"I can still feel the fucking sting when I sit."

Soon Rafe was fucking with long, hard thrusts.

"You like being fucked by my big cock, don't you?"

"Oh, God, yes. Don't ever stop. Fuck the cum out of me." Precum dripped from his cock as Rafe continued his pounding.

As Rafe's thrusts came faster and faster, sweat dripped from his forehead onto Alek. Then Alek cried out, "I'm going to come."

Rafe slowed his thrusts and cupped his hand under the head of Alek's cock to catch his cum as it shot out. He sat back, brought the pool of nectar to his mouth, licked it from his palm and swallowed it. Without wasting any time, he held Alek's thighs with both hands and resumed his fucking. With a final deep thrust, he gasped, flooding Alek with massive amounts of cum. He pulled out of Alek, breathing deeply. They smiled at each other. Rafe slid Alek's legs from his shoulders, bent over, and kissed him. Rafe dropped onto the bed beside him and wrapped his arms around Alek's waist, kissing him on the top of his head, moving to his lips.

"I love being with you," Rafe said. "I've never felt like this before about anyone. It's not good enough to fuck just anyone anymore. For me, it has to be you. I want only you."

"If you want me and my heart, I want you to treat me better by listening to me."

"I always listen to you. Your safety is more important than my sexual need. I'll do anything it takes to keep you safe from your enemies. Please don't take it personally when I do things to make that happen. I know how to do my job, and now even more because I'm protecting you."

"If this is going to work, we need to do more negotiating about things we do."

"Just talk to me. I'll be listening. I want you, and I want you to be happy."

"Time will tell if I still want you," Alek said with a grin on his face.

"Playing hard to get, are you?"

Alek grinned, feeling much better about Rafe than he had before they had sex.

After they rested and cleaned up, Rafe squeezed back into the driver's seat, and Alek sat beside him in the passenger's seat.

CHAPTER FIFTEEN

Rafe Escobar

When Rafe and Alek left the van, they found the others sitting in the circle of folding chairs drinking sodas or beer. Mateo and Anouska were there as well. Rafe stood facing the group while Alek took a seat beside Anouska.

"We're going stay here for the night. Plan to leave by ten in the morning. Tomorrow I'll let you know where we're going. We'll be moving for a while until we reach an area we can call our home. I'm looking for a place where Emilio and Alek... and anyone else can return to school. I may be able to help... financially. Just talk to me about it so I'll know how you plan to use that education for your future careers. We'll be able to work at the final location. Our funds aren't low yet, but we don't want to reach that point Any questions?" Rafe asked.

James said, "I want Dante to go to school. He's finished high school, but he wants to study something."

"Great. When the time comes, I'll talk to Dante, and we'll see what we can do about that. Please watch over him. The scouts are trying to find him right now. We may have to change his name, but we'll wait until we get where we're going."

211

"He'll love the chance to go back to school."

"Thank you," Dante's voice cracked from overwhelming emotion.

James put his arm around Dante, holding him close to him, gazing into his eyes with an approving smile on his face. It was clear he didn't want to lose Dante and they shared something special. It was beautiful to watch.

"I only need to finish one more semester to become an English teacher," Mateo said.

"You have the money so you won't need my assistance. Now it's just a matter of finding the right school for you too."

"Thanks."

"Anyone else?" Rafe asked.

Liam raised his hand.

"Liam," Rafe called on him.

"I want to go to school too. I went for three years, so I only need one more year for my degree."

"Since you can't afford it and attended college already, you qualify."

"Anyone else?" Rafe asked. "Anouska?"

"No." Anouska paused to rub her hand on Mateo's knee. "I don't want to go to school. I'm going to stay home and take care of Mateo."

"Okay." He watched his brother kiss Anouska, so tenderly.

"I picked up dinner for us," Kaden said.

"Thanks. So, what's for dinner?" Rafe asked.

"I bought steak to celebrate the unveiling of the true relationship between you and Emilio."

"What relationship?" James asked.

"Sorry, I didn't realize it was still a secret," Kaden said.

"It's okay. It's not anymore."

"I guess not," Mateo said.

Still standing, Rake made the formal announcement. "Today I told Emilio that he is really my son and not my cousin."

Mateo looked at Rafe. "Wait a minute? Why didn't I know about this?"

"I'm sorry I couldn't tell you, Mateo. Uncle Reuben and Aunt Carla made me promise not to ever tell anyone. Since they've sent him back to me, I decided that agreement was null and void, so I told him. I've always loved him."

"That's fabulous," Mateo said, addressing Emilio, who smiled. "That makes me your uncle then."

"I hadn't thought about that. I guess you are," Emilio said.

"Congratulations!" Valerik shouted.

"Yes, congratulations," James said.

"Thank you," Rafe said. "We're free to rest here until Kaden hands out the jobs for this little celebration."

Kaden said, "Tonight James and I will be grilling the steaks. Anouska will be making the dessert, hopefully something special. The four boys will be on clean-up duty, and Mateo will be in charge of the French fries. Rafe will be free to take charge of traveling and the accommodations at our final destination."

"Okay, then you're free until dinner, which is exactly when?" Rafe asked, obviously looking forward to the special meal.

"We're eating at six. Be here, or we'll eat it all," Kaden said.

As the celebration talk waned, Rafe walked over to Emilio. "Hey, are you okay? You seem... different."

"I guess so. This realization of who I am is all new to me, but not in a bad way. I just wonder what it would have been like if you'd been the one to raise me."

"I've thought about that since you were born. That's why I made sure we had you on Sundays."

214

"You know, I was afraid of those Sundays. Your father… uh, my grandfather seemed to hate me for no reason."

"Your grandmother loved you more than you'll ever know. She's the one that arranged for Uncle Reuben and Aunt Carla to adopt you, so we'd still have you around us."

"I never knew that. They never did tell me I was adopted. I figured I looked like them. I mean, it never dawned on me to question it."

"That's because they got you at one week old."

"Where's my birth mother?" Emilio asked.

"Well, she used to live next door, but they moved away. She was a pretty girl and very smart too. I guess she's married by now. I never did look her up."

"What's her name?"

"Caitlin Callaghan. She's Irish. So maybe that's why you have red highlights in your hair."

"Did she have red hair?"

"She did and a face full of freckles. She was cute, but I'm just not attracted to women."

"Do you have a picture of her?"

"I do." Rafe pulled out his wallet and removed the photo. He paused for a moment to look at her picture. He would feel forever guilty for using her to prove something

215

to his father. He had been so stupid and weak when he was a teenager. He pushed away the leftover fear of his father. It had been wrong, and he had no idea how to make it right for her. It was too late now to correct what he had done. He would have to live with his mistake for the rest of his life, but having Emilio sure eased his guilt.

Emilio stroked the photo and stared at it for a quiet moment. "I had no idea she'd look like this. Can I keep it?"

"I want you to have it. Maybe someday you might meet her if we ever find out where she is." Rafe pulled out Emilio's new born picture and handed it to him.

"I never saw a picture of me that small."

"I took it at the hospital. You were so tiny." Rafe smiled as he remembered that moment he first saw Emilio.

"I have more pictures of you at home. I took them every time I saw you and put them all into a photo album."

"I can't wait to see it."

"So do you approve?"

Emilio nodded. "I can see some of her in me, can you?"

"Yes, I do."

Alek walked over to them. "Hey, is everything okay over here?"

"Yes. Rafe was telling me about my mother," Emilio said.

"Oh, that's great. Are you done talking?" Alek asked.

"Sure, why?" Rafe asked.

"I was just wondering what we're going to do now?" Alek asked.

"I'm going horseback riding with Kaden, so I'll see you guys later," Emilio said.

"See you later. I'm here for you anytime," Rafe said.

"Me too," Alek said.

"Thanks."

"I thought I'd take you on a boat on the lake," Rafe suggested to Alek." Would you like to do that?"

"Sure. I'd love to go," Alek said.

"I thought it would be romantic. You do know I'm trying to win your heart?"

"We'll see." Alek grinned, alerting Rafe he'd already won but keeping it to himself for the time being.

They walked down the long path to the lake and waited in line to rent a motorboat. Once the arrangements were made for the next available boat, they stopped for something to eat. When they finished, they climbed into the boat, and Rafe started the engine and steered the boat out onto the lake. Alek sat beside him.

217

"It's really pretty out here," Alek said.

"Yes, it is. Have you ever been in a motorboat before?"

"Pavel and I used to go boating, but that was a long time ago."

"It sounds like you guys were close. Do you miss him?"

"Sometimes I wish it could be the way it used to be, but I like this new adventure you're taking me on. I'm doing things I've never done before."

"My life improved since I left home, and now, with you here, it's really good. I love being with you and doing things together." Rafe bent over and kissed Alek. "You're very special to me."

Rafe's phone rang, and seeing it was Kaden, he answered it immediately. "Hey, is everything okay?"

"No." Emilio's voiced trembled. "Some crazy guys started shooting at Dante and they shot him in the leg. Kaden, Mateo, James, and Valerik returned gunfire and killed all of them. All the vans are parked at Northern Inyo Hospital. James is with Dante. I drove your van to the hospital. We're in the cafeteria right now. James said he didn't want us all in Dante's room because it would attract attention. So you guys need to take a cab to the hospital. I have your keys. We need to know where to go next."

"Are you okay, Emilio?" Rafe asked, trying to maintain his emotions.

"Yes."

"Is Dante going to be okay?" Rafe asked as he turned the boat around.

"I think his thigh was just grazed."

"Any information on the identity of the shooters??"

"James said they were all Hispanic. He thought they were from a gang. Dante said he knew three of them, so I'm guessing it's the same gang he tried to get out of."

"Are you sure you're okay?" Rafe asked.

"Yes. I'm fine. Just scared and worried about Dante."

"We're going to leave now. Tell everyone to stay put."

"I love you," Emilio said.

"I love you too," Rafe said.

"What happened?" Alek asked.

"We have to go to the local hospital. Dante was shot. It looks like it was the gang looking for him. The rest of the group is at the hospital already. When the shooting started, they returned fire and killed them all. They're no longer a threat. Emilio moved our van to the hospital parking lot. We need to call for a ride."

Rafe turned the boat around and headed for shore. Once he turned in the boat, he made a phone call to a local Uber. Within fifteen minutes, they were on their way to the hospital. As soon as they reached the emergency entrance, they headed to the cafeteria. Rafe sat down at the long table with the rest of the group. James wasn't with them.

"Okay, we're going to have to move quickly once we get Dante out of here. This time, we're flying to New Jersey. We'll stay at a resort until I find permanent housing for all of us. I'm going to look for James. I want all of you to find a movie theatre and stay there until the movie is over. I'm keeping Alek with me. Go in one van, and by then I'll figure out what we're going to do next."

Rafe and Alek headed to Dante's room. Rafe caught James's attention from the doorway, and he waved them in. Dante was wide-awake and sitting up in bed. His face was pale.

"How are you doing, Dante?" Rafe asked.

"My thigh hurts," Dante winced. "They shot me on the side of my thigh. The doctor removed the bullet. It wasn't deep but still hurts like hell."

Alek moved to the bed and smiled.

"I can't believe this has happened. They mean business. This is some serious shit," Alek said.

"I guess we need to stay with our protectors."

"Did it happen when you were sitting at the circle with everyone?" Alek asked.

"Everyone was at the circle, but I was walking to the van to get a book when they got me. Before I knew it, the men shot all of them and rushed me to the hospital."

"When can he travel?" Rafe asked James.

"He's going to be released in two hours. I got him crutches. The doctor said he can ride, but not longer than a few hours."

"I'm going to make reservations at Seaside Heights in New Jersey. We'll rent a big house to accommodate all of us. We'll be near the beach and boardwalk until we can figure something else. We're going to drop off the vans and take a shuttle to the airport when Dante gets out. I'll bring back a few things to disguise him."

"That sounds like a plan. Dante can recuperate and still have some fun. After we get there, I can push him around in a wheelchair until he can walk on his own," James said.

"I'm going to make those reservations now. Then I'll send you the online tickets to Newark. From there, I'll rent a large van to drive all of us to Seaside Heights. Right now we need to stay close to each other."

"Sounds great."

"Thanks, Rafe, I don't know what we'd do without you," Dante said.

"Maybe we should have moved sooner. Your threats are in California and the rest of ours are too. I really didn't think they'd track you down here."

"Do you think they won't leave California?" Dante asked.

"Let's hope they don't. I'll send you the information soon. We need to leave tonight."

James followed Rafe out, and turning to Alek said, "Stay with Dante while I talk to Rafe."

Alek returned to Dante's room.

Once outside of the room, Rafe closed the door and spun James around by the shoulder to face him. "Okay, James what the hell happened?"

"There were five of them. We shot at them to scare them off, but instead of running, they ran toward us, so we had no choice but to take 'em out."

"You're right. You had no other choice. You did what you had to do."

"Mateo even shot at one. He's feeling sick about it, but he stepped up when we needed him. I thought you should know that," James said.

"I'm sure he'll be traumatized, but he did the right thing. Maybe now he'll understand that we don't kill unless someone's trying to kill us. I'll go and make the plans now and send you what you need."

"Thanks," James said.

"You guys all need some downtime and fun after today. I wish I'd been there when it happened. I guess we're going to need to stay together."

"It looks that way."

CHAPTER SIXTEEN

Alek Belanov

Alek sat in the back of the van with Emilio and Liam since Rafe had Kaden beside him in the front. They were on the parkway heading toward Seaside Heights. Alek had never been there but had seen it on TV during the hurricane. He was looking forward to staying put. Dante was lying across the middle row seat. James had set him up with a pillow for his head and a blanket. Poor Dante was sound asleep. Mateo and Anouska sat in one row while Valerik and James took another. They had managed to fit the luggage in the trunk area. Alek liked the feeling with all of them in one van. There was a feeling of safety being together, almost like a family.

"I feel bad for Dante," Emilio said.

"Did you two get freaked out when the shooting started?" Alek asked.

"I did," Liam said. "Valerik told Emilio and me to go under the table. It was horrible. They were shouting at Dante in Spanish. I don't know what they were saying."

"They called him a traitor and called for his death," Emilio whispered, so Dante wouldn't hear it for a second time since he had known Spanish too.

225

"I forgot you could speak Spanish," Liam said.

"It's been an emotional day for me," Emilio said.

"It has. I was all excited to celebrate tonight with you and Rafe," Alek said.

"Yes, we all were," Liam said.

"Well, I did enjoy our meal at the airport, but Anouska had baked strawberry pies for us. She had to leave everything behind," Emilio said.

"I love strawberry pie, and the food at the airport was good. I'm glad we're getting closer to where we're going," Alek said.

"I don't know how Rafe made so many reservations so fast," Liam said.

"I'll tell you how," Alek said. "He never stopped for a second. He researched everything on his phone. I helped him with the plane tickets. He was very stressed until everything was handled."

"I can imagine. I'm so damn tired," Emilio said.

"You can lie on top of us if you want," Alek said.

"Yes, you had a big day," Liam said.

Emilio managed to get himself comfortable enough to lie on top of them.

Within a few minutes, he was sleeping.

"I'm tired too," Liam said.

"Me too. I don't want to ask if we're almost there,"
Alek said.

"We're almost there," Kaden said. "We're going to
cross a bridge into Seaside Heights, and then we'll be there
in less than fifteen minutes."

"Thanks," Alek said.

"Is Rafe good to you?" Liam whispered, making sure
Rafe couldn't hear.

"He's good when he wants me, but if I don't follow his
orders to the T, he gets really pissed at me."

"Rafe can be hot-headed sometimes," Emilio said.
"But the thing about him is he gets over it and never holds
a grudge."

Alek said, "I thought you were sleeping."

"I'm resting, but I can hear."

"So how is Valerik?" Alek asked.

"I feel safe with him," Liam said. "I can talk to him
about things that bother me. He's much older than I am, but
that makes no difference to me. I'm falling in love with
him. I can't imagine being without him."

"That's beautiful," Alek said.

When they arrived at the three-story rental building,
Rafe assigned them to their apartments. Rafe and Kaden
took the first-floor apartments, James and Valerik took the

second floor, and Mateo and Anouska took the third floor. The building had six apartments and Rafe had rented all six.

Rafe threw himself on the bed and closed his eyes.

"Can I get you something?" Alek asked.

"I want you next to me in bed. I need to relax now that we're finally settled in."

"Do you think we're all safe here?" Alek asked.

"Yes. I do. I researched Seaside Heights, and it has tons of fun things for us to do. We can go to the beach and walk the boardwalk. They even have rides there. Do you like to go on the rides?"

"Rides? Yes, I used to go to Magic Mountain and Santa Monica Pier."

"I think we're going to have some fun here. Finally after all this running around."

"I sure hope so."

***

In the morning, Alek heard Rafe in the kitchen, so he took a shower and dressed. When Alek walked into the tiny kitchen, Rafe was drinking coffee at the table.

"Hey, I made some coffee," Rafe said.

Alek poured himself a cup and sat on a chair at the small table.

"So I thought we'd go out for breakfast, just you and me. We need some time alone. Then we can join the others on the beach."

"What about beach towels?" Alek asked.

"We can buy them on the boardwalk."

Alek was so excited they were going to the beach and the boardwalk. A weight lifted from his shoulders. When he finished his coffee, they walked to a restaurant a block away. They sat in a large booth and looked over the menu.

"I can't wait to relax on the beach and swim," Alek said.

"The Atlantic Ocean is colder than the Pacific. It takes time to get used to it."

"Dante and James are here, too," Alek said.

"Of course. This is the closest restaurant. We're all going to rent cars later in the day."

"What about the van?" Alek set down his menu.

"We're keeping it for the rest of the month. We never know if something will come up and it's easier to leave all together in one vehicle."

"So, what happens after here?"

"I'll find a permanent place for all of us somewhere on the East Coast."

Kaden and Emilio stopped at their table. "Got any room for us?"

"Sure. Sit down," Rafe said.

Kaden pulled out a phone and handed it to Alek. "This is your phone. Don't call anyone other than members of our group. I plugged in all our names so you can call one of us if you're in trouble or need to talk."

"I have one, too," Emilio said. "Now we can talk anytime."

Alek examined the phone and checked out the contacts. "We sure can."

"I see Mateo and Anouska are over there. I'll give her a phone too," Kaden said.

Meanwhile the server took their orders and another person brought their coffee and juice.

"Aren't you going to invite them to sit with us?" Alek asked.

"No," Rafe said. "They need time alone. I'm going to talk to Mateo later."

"Only Valerik and Liam aren't here," Alek said.

"I saw them, and they said they would be on their way soon," Emilio said.

"I want you guys to be aware that we're going to check your phones every night. So make sure you don't call anyone other than the members of our group. As always, there will be consequences for anyone not obeying the rules," Rafe said.

"Can we go online?" Alek asked.

"Yes. Don't log on to any social media or buy anything though," Rafe said.

"So we can't look at our Facebook or Twitter?" Emilio asked.

"Absolutely not," Rafe said.

After breakfast, Rafe and Alek walked to the boardwalk and purchased beach towels for the beach. They changed into their suits and found Tower Two where they joined Mateo and Anouska sitting on the beach waiting for the others. As they sat down on their towels, the robust wind from the ocean whipped Alek's hair against his face. Salt and sand burned his eyes, so he put on his sunglasses. The sea-scented air filled his nose. He could get used to this lifestyle. It beat being in prison for two years.

"How are you doing?" Rafe asked Mateo.

"I feel sick about yesterday, but there wasn't a choice. It was either we let them gun down Dante and the rest of us, or we protect ourselves. I asked James for a gun. I hit one of them, and he never got back up. I'm sure I killed him," Mateo said.

"I'm sorry I wasn't there to help. I appreciate you helping."

"I saw a guy aim at Emilio, so I shot him before he could fire," Mateo said.

"Well, maybe now you can understand why we do what we have to, not because we want to. It's *us* versus *them*."

"I'm going to take some shooting lessons because I need to practice more. I changed my mind. I want to be a full-fledged protector. I'm needed."

"Thanks. I'm glad to hear that, and yes, we need you," Rafe said.

"Want to go in?" Alek asked.

"Sure," Rafe said.

They dove through a monster wave. Alek swam underwater for a bit, then surfaced and continued until he reached Rafe, who immediately grabbed Alek's cock, stroking it.

Without any notice, a high wave sent them both under the wave, separating them. Alek coughed up some seawater when he surfaced. Rafe swam back to him.

"Hey, are you okay?" Rafe asked.

"Yeah, just a little water, that's all." Alek treaded water beside Rafe.

"It's so damn cold, but I'm used to it now," Rafe said.

"Yes, it's the same way in Northern California, but it's warmer in Southern California."

"I swam in San Diego a lot," Rafe said.

Alek remembered reading about the roller coaster at the Casino Pier had ended up in the water. The Hydrus, a neon-green-and-blue coaster with a 72-foot-vertical drop, had replaced it. He hoped he could convince Rafe to ride it with him.

"I want to go on that new roller coaster," Alek said.

"Tonight we'll go on the rides." They continued to ride each wave.

"Hey, you look cute all wet," Rafe said. "I'd kiss you, but I'm not sure it's safe for us to do that."

"I feel the same way about you. Thank you."

"Thanks."

"I keep smelling food," Alek said.

"Are you hungry again?" Rafe asked.

"Yes. I saw lots of good food on the boardwalk."

"Okay, let's go and see what we can find."

They let the waves bring them to shore and sat on the towels to dry. Valerik and Liam showed up with a large umbrella to protect Liam's fair skin, and Valerik was rubbing layers of sunscreen on him. Alek looked at himself and noticed he was getting red.

"I need sunscreen too," Alek said.

"You sure do." Valerik threw the tube to Alek.

"Thanks."

Rafe, after rubbing sunscreen on Alek, told him to put on his T-shirt, and they'd walk to the boardwalk to find something to eat.

"What do you want?" Rafe asked.

"I want to eat at Midway Steak House. See all those lemons."

"I'm going to have the steak and cheese. What do you want?"

"Sausage and peppers and the freshly squeezed lemonade," Alek said

The amazing scent caught Alek's nose from fifty feet away. He could taste it without even having eaten it yet. They couldn't walk fast enough to get there. Rafe ordered their food and once it arrived, they sat on one of the benches overlooking the beach.

"Oh this is so good. I want to eat here every day," Alek said.

"This steak and cheese are awesome. I feel the same way as you do, but we have to try out the pizza later."

"Where are Kaden and Emilio?"

"They went grocery shopping for all of us. We'll still all eat dinner together. He bought us the basics for breakfast, so we don't have to eat out every day."

"Is that Kaden's job?"

"Yes. He likes that job. James and Valerik like to cook. Anouska likes to bake."

"Don't you like to cook?"

"Not that much. I'm usually planning things for the group, plus I'm still involved with the other groups in California."

"I wish we could live here," Alek said.

"It's not that nice in the winter. The boardwalk closes down."

"I wish it was nice all year round like in California."

"That's the problem when we move to the East Coast. We're going to have to deal with the seasons."

"Maybe we'll like it."

"Let's go to our apartment and take a break, then come out again."

"What kind of break?"

"A fuck break," Rafe said.

Alek smiled. "I hate to leave the boardwalk, but for that, I will."

As soon as they arrived back at the apartments, they bumped into James and Dante sitting on the front steps.

"Hey, you guys are back early," James said.

"We're going to take care of some paperwork and make phone calls to the other groups," Rafe said.

"How was the beach?" Dante asked.

"The water was cold, but the food was awesome. We went to the Midway Steak House. It's the one with all the lemons. I could eat there forever," Alek said.

"I'll be taking Dante out tomorrow, but he needs the wheelchair. I don't want him getting bumped on the boardwalk with all those people," James said.

"Do you want us to go and get you something?"

"No, Kaden brought us pizza for lunch, and tonight we're cooking outside on the grill," James said.

"That's great. Do you need any help?" Rafe asked.

"No. Valerik is helping."

"Did Kaden come back from shopping?"

"Yes. He put all the groceries away in our apartments, and then he took Emilio to the beach."

"Okay. Talk to you guys later."

Rafe pulled Alek inside the apartment. He locked the door and pulled him into a hug.

"Damn, we know too many people around here," Rafe said.

"It seems that way."

"Let's go to bed and play a little, or do you want to play hard to get first?"

"I'm not angry at you anymore because you saved Dante by bringing us to this place. I never want to leave here," Alek said.

"I'm happy you approve."

"How did you know about this place?"

"My mother told me about Seaside Heights. She used to spend her summers here when she was a child. So it just came to my mind when I was looking for a place for us to unwind and heal."

"I'm glad we came here."

"Take off your clothes before I rip them off," Rafe said, making Alek's cock twitch.

Alek unzipped his shorts, then shoved them down to his ankles. His cock stood up. It didn't take him long before he'd stripped. Rafe undressed a little slower since he was watching Alek. The guy was so damn sexy even when he undressed. It didn't matter what he did or didn't wear. Rafe wanted him.

Rafe pushed Alek against the wall, pressing their erections together at the same time he brushed his lips against Alek's open mouth. Rafe pushed his tongue into Alek's mouth and their tongues fought for power, rolling around each other and neither won.

"I'll never get enough of you," Rafe said as he lifted Alek and put him on top of the bed.

"I'm all yours."

"Get on your hands and knees," Rafe ordered.

Alek turned over and got into the position Rafe wanted; inhaling a deep breath. Crawling behind Alek, Rafe spread Alek's cheeks, licking him at the entrance and teasing him with his tongue. It felt so good. Alek released some loud moans and grunts without thinking. Normally he remained quiet during sexual encounters unless they asked him to be vocal or they were like the guys in prison, demanding he beg for everything, including breathing.

"Ahh… Stop making me want you like this," Alek said.

He went wild with desire for Rafe. In prison, he'd wanted a guy to fuck him and hurry about it because he didn't care for them, but he loved all the attention and teasing from Rafe. He loved being with him, feeling safe at his side. His only fear was that he wasn't good enough for

Rafe and worried he'd give him the boot if he ever found someone better. He wondered if the protectors had other sex partners beside the guy they were protecting. Rafe had said they were bonded, so Alek assumed that meant they didn't. He only hoped Rafe would honor that bonding between them.

"Fuck me. Please fuck me. I need to feel your cock in me," Alek begged, needing the connection.

"Are you trying to give me orders again?' Rafe teased as he slapped his ass.

"What?" Alek shrugged his shoulders in confusion.

"I'm in charge, not you." Rafe winked, indicating he loved every minute of dominating him.

"Sorry about that, Mr. Escobar." Alek returned a wink.

"Make noise so I know you can feel my cock inside you." Rafe reached for the lube on the comforter. He pinched the tube allowing the lube to fill his hand. He dipped his fingers in it, then stuck a lubed finger inside Alek.

"That lube is cold," Alek said, shuddering.

"That's because you're so damn hot." He stuck a second finger in and finger-banged his happy gland.

"Feels so good," he panted.

Rafe added a third finger and played more. Alek relished the power exchange between them because he felt safe with Rafe. He aimed his erection for Alek's tight pucker. He cupped his hand beneath Alek's hips tilting them, and began with a slow rhythm. Picking up his pace, he pounded hard, causing Alek's head to hit against the wall. The thunderous banging accompanied Alek's loud moans which vibrated in the room. Rafe continued to hit his happy gland with each hard thrust. Stroking Alek's brick-hard cock at the same tempo, he pumped in and out of him. Alek trembled as he tightened his ass muscles around the steel dick. The warm semen in his balls tried to flow up out of him, and he couldn't fight it as his body shuddered. He tried desperately to hold back the climax, but suddenly his cum spilled out of him onto Rafe's hand.

"Fuck. Fuck," Alek screamed.

"Oh God, oh God, oh, feels so good." Rafe's body strained with the force of his orgasm. Alek continued to milk him dry.

"I love sex with you," Rafe said, tracing Alek's lips with his finger.

"You're not so bad either, Rafe."

"You better say I'm great, the best."

"You really are the best and that's why I can't stay angry at you for too long, even though I should." Alek snuggled next to Rafe.

CHAPTER SEVENTEEN

Rafe Escobar

Rafe and Alek fell asleep and woke up to pounding on their front door.

"Who is knocking?" Alek asked, awakening from his nap.

"Don't know." Rafe got up, slipped into his jeans, and grabbed his gun from the drawer.

He answered the door, and James was standing there and said, "Time to eat."

"You woke us up to eat?" Rafe laughed.

"Come on before the food gets cold. Everyone's here."

"We'll be right there," Rafe said.

He went back to the bedroom, where Alek was already dressed. "Dinner is ready."

"I figured it was." Alek stared at Rafe while he pulled on a black T-shirt.

"What are you looking at?" Rafe asked.

"Your upper arm muscles. How did you get them like that?"

"Working out, I guess. You can work out and look like this too."

"Maybe." He hesitated, his expression pensive. "I don't think I'm as strong as you." Alek turned away, embarrassed.

"I like you the way you are. Let's go."

When they went outside, there was a banner that said, '*Congratulations to Rafe and Emilio.*'

"Join your party. We didn't get to celebrate before, but now we can," Kaden said.

James filled a plate for them and then carried it to where they were sitting. The grounds had two picnic tables that the men had pushed together, so they could all sit at the same big table. The steaks smelled so good.

"Was the grill already here?" Rafe asked.

"Sure was. No one seemed to have used it. So we christened it," James said.

When they finished, Emilio moved around to them. "You know, I keep thinking about you being my father, and I'm happy and sad. If you only could have raised me instead. I feel so confused because a part of me feels like I've been robbed of you. Though you weren't ever far away from me. I'm grateful they raised me, but to be honest, I would have rather had you."

"It's normal to feel confused and it's okay to still love your other parents. You've been loving all of us."

244

"Thanks for saying that. I do love them, too. It means a lot to be your son." Emilio wiped his tears.

"If you don't stop talking like that, I'm going to cry. I have you now, and no one is going to take you away from me. Well, Kaden can play with you. I approve of him. Yes, we missed out on a lot of things together, but not anymore." Rafe stood and hugged Emilio.

"Yes, we're together now," Emilio said.

After they devoured the strawberry pies Anouska had made them for the second time, they walked to the boardwalk leaving James and Dante behind. Dante was still in some pain and needed more rest. James was doting on Dante and he loved it.

As they walked the boardwalk, there were games, rides, pizza joints and more on every block. Two piers with amusement park rides, with twice as many games. There was so much to do and lots and lots of food. They stopped for ice cream cones. Rafe noticed there were police and security in the area, making everyone feel safe except for Liam, who clung on to Valerik. He'd made Liam wear sunglasses and a baseball cap to cover up his red hair, but they didn't hide his freckles. The protectors kept a close eye on all of them, and they stayed together the entire time.

Rafe knew Alek wanted them to go off on their own, but for the first night, he thought they should stay together.

They played at the best arcade, Lucky Leo's, and later they enjoyed the round trip sky ride from one end of the boardwalk to almost the other end. They strolled into the Casino Pier where all the rides were.

"Let's go on that roller coaster," Alek said.

"I don't know about that," Emilio said. "It's too high."

Kaden said, "You're safe with me. Come on."

They all stood in line and finally rode the roller coaster; Rafe cringed when he heard poor Emilio screaming behind him. Kaden tried calming him down, but he continued screaming. Alek enjoyed it without yelling. When they got off, Valerik said that Liam had screamed the entire ride.

"So did Emilio," Kaden said.

"Not Alek. He loved it," Rafe said with pride.

"Are we going on the rides at the other end?" Alek asked.

"No, we're going to be here for a month, so there's no need to do everything tonight," Rafe said.

"Let's go to that bar with the music blaring and have a beer," Valerik said.

"Good idea," Kaden said.

246

There was only standing room in the loud bar, so Rafe and Valerik ordered everyone cold beers and passed them around.

After their beer, they decided it was late enough and walked home. Mateo and Anouska held hands, but none of the others would dare to with the risk of being ridiculed by a homophobic person. It was always better to take the safe road, preventing any problems especially since they wanted to keep a low profile.

They sat outside on the picnic table again. James must have heard them because he came out with Dante to join them.

"I have an announcement to make," Mateo said.

"You have an announcement?" Rafe asked.

"Sure do. Anouska and I eloped."

"You're married?" Rafe couldn't believe his ears. He hardly knew her. *What had he been thinking?* Anouska held her hand out, displaying her diamond and a matching wedding band.

"Congratulations!" everyone said at once. They all got up and hugged both of them.

"What made you decide to get married now?" Rafe asked.

"Rafe, believe it or not, some people fall in love and marry. We got married in California the night we left."

"I guess they do. Congratulations." Rafe hugged his brother and then Anouska. Alek hugged Anouska and stayed to talk with her while Rafe talked to James about Dante's healing.

After a while, Rafe grabbed Alek, and they went inside.

"I have had one of the best days ever," Alek said as they entered their apartment.

"You did?"

"Yes. Everything was perfect. I love being here with you. I don't even mind living in this little apartment with you."

"I had fun too. I'm always wondering when something will go wrong. I worry about everyone and especially you and Emilio."

"I know you do, but I think you forgot some of your worries throughout the day."

"I did. You're right. Let's go to bed, and let me play with you again."

"Okay." Alek followed him to the bedroom.

"Get in that bed." Rafe's firm tone entered his voice as he stripped his clothes.

Alek moved onto the bed, and Rafe joined him with a hug.

"You feel so good. I can't imagine ever being without you." Rafe worried that Alek would eventually leave because he wouldn't require his protection anymore. He needed to find out more about Pavel. He may be the one who was the problem.

Rafe's phone rang.

"Hey, this is Eduardo. Did you hear about the deaths of the gang members in Bishop?"

"No, I haven't. What did you hear about them?" Rafe wondered why Eduardo felt the need to call him about this. *Did he know more than he was saying? How did he figure out they had been in Bishop?*

"Five guys were found riddled with bullets at the campground. All dead. The police have no idea who did this, but they found another five guys from the same gang causing trouble in Bishop. I thought I'd mention this to you since your group was in that area."

"I know nothing about it. We never went to Bishop. We left the state the morning after the party," Rafe lied.

"I heard you were in Bishop, but if you say you weren't, then you weren't there."

"That's what I just said. We weren't in Bishop," Rafe repeated.

"I didn't want you or your group set up for their deaths since your group is protecting one of their members who is running from them."

"Who told you I even had a guy who was running from a gang?" Rafe asked.

"Word gets around on the streets, I guess," Eduardo said. "I thought that Mexican with the green eyes was from a gang."

"We have no such person. We don't have any Mexicans in our group. Period. So shut down all those damn lies."

"The boy the black man had with him. He had green eyes, but he's Mexican. That's who I'm talking about."

"First of all, that boy isn't Mexican, and he was never in a gang. And the black man has a name. So use it when you refer to him."

"By any chance, have you found better accommodations for my group?"

"Are you attempting to blackmail me?" Rafe asked.

"Well, what do you think?" Eduardo's sarcastic response took Rafe by surprise.

"To answer your original question, I haven't given your accommodations for your group any thought, but I'll get back to you within the week." Rafe ended the call.

"Rafe, what's wrong?" Alek sat up.

"I don't know, but a protector from another group just attempted to blackmail me."

"About what?"

"The dead gang members."

"What are you going to do?" Alek asked as he glanced with frightened imploring eyes at Rafe.

"I'm not sure. I'm going to call Kaden. I want you to keep Emilio in here, so we can talk in the kitchen alone. This is serious business."

"Why can't I be a part of it?" Alek asked.

"It's not you. I don't want Emilio in the mix."

"Okay."

Rafe hugged Alek. "Thanks for being here with me. I know it wasn't your choice, but I'm happy you are."

Rafe sent Kaden a message to come to his apartment with Emilio. They were at the door within five minutes. Emilio went to the bedroom with Alek. Rafe shut the door, grabbed two beers, and then sat at the kitchen table with Kaden.

"What's up?" Kaden asked while he twisted the cap from his beer bottle.

"I think we have a problem with Eduardo. He called me to let me know about the five dead gang members, who were found riddled with bullets in Bishop. I told him we didn't hear about it since we weren't in the state. He also said he didn't want anyone to set us up because we were protecting a guy from that same gang in our group. He described Dante as the Mexican with the green eyes. After that, he brought up his group's housing needs."

"And you think this means what?" Kaden asked.

"I think Eduardo is turning on me. He wants to blackmail me for better housing for his group. He seems to know who shot the gang members. I told him we didn't have any Mexicans in our group or anyone from that gang."

"What do you want to do about it?" Kaden looked worried.

"My inclination is to end Eduardo. What other options do we have?"

"What if you're wrong about Eduardo? He could have just called to give you a heads-up."

"And in the same sentence he asks for better accommodations. Most groups are self-supporting. His group isn't, and that's why they were living in one big house instead of separate units."

"That's true. One of the other protectors told me that Eduardo is cutting their food and entertainment allowances by fifty percent. He's probably skimming the money."

"Maybe we should split the group and fire Eduardo?" Rafe asked.

"That won't work either. If you fire him, what stops him from reporting us for murdering the gang members?" Kaden asked.

"My head is fucking killing me." Rafe held the sides of his head.

"Where is your aspirin?" Kaden asked.

Rafe pointed to one of the kitchen cabinets.

Kaden got the bottle of aspirin and a glass of water. "Take these."

"Thanks. Some days I don't know if we'll ever stop running," Rafe said.

"Find that bastard better housing and shut him up for now. Let's see if he wants more from you. If he continues, then he's a walking dead man. We have to take care of our own right now. We don't have time for his bullshit threats."

"Okay. I'll work on something tomorrow. It's just I didn't think this would happen. I vetted Eduardo personally, and there weren't any signs of this type of behavior. I'm so pissed at his actions and threats. Why didn't I see this coming?"

"Eduardo is a snake. For fuck's sake, he may be working for your father. Who knows?"

"If he were working for my father, I'd kill him myself without any regret," Rafe said.

"You weren't there at the time of the shootings, and you can prove that."

"It's not just about me. It's our group. We're a family and if one hurts, we all hurt. This shit has to stop."

"As much as I would like to take that motherfucker down, I don't think that's the right call. We have to scare the fuck out of him and send him a message so that he doesn't ever think he can blackmail you again," Kaden said.

"I have some people back in Los Angeles. I know they can stomp on his blackmail plan and scare the hell out of him at the same time."

"Are you talking about those crazy mafia cousins of yours?" Kaden asked.

"That's exactly who I was thinking of."

"Let's wait first to see what becomes of his threats. We could be reading him wrong. Your cousins are too violent for this situation."

"We'll wait then and see what else he does."

Kaden got Emilio, and Rafe gave Emilio a goodbye hug, then returned to the bedroom.

"What are you doing?" Rafe asked Alek.

"I just finished talking to Dante. We were checking on him."

"And how is it going with him?" Rafe asked.

"James is taking him to the doctors tomorrow to check his wound. He's still in pain and needs more pain pills."

"I guess the hospital didn't give him enough. The doctor will figure all that out for him."

"He's depressed he can't go swimming or on the rides."

"I don't blame him," Rafe said.

"Let me take care of you, tonight," Alek said.

"You want to do that for me?" Rafe asked as he undressed.

"Yes. Will you let me?"

"Of course. I'd never say no to that. Not from you." Rafe watched Alek undress when he went to bed.

Alek removed his clothes and put them away. He took hold of Rafe's hard cock, licked the head, and made slurping noises. He ran his tongue over the slit and the pearlescent precum wetness on the head. Rafe moaned. Alek used his hands to fondle and gently pinch Rafe's balls. *Alek makes me feel so good.*

Swirling his tongue around the large head, Alek sucked the shaft up and down. He licked and sucked Rafe's beautiful balls leaving them wet. Bobbing his head, he deep throated Rafe's cock. Losing his breath each time Rafe's cock hit the back of his throat, he moved quicker to seek air. Rafe's cock strained and vibrated inside his mouth as he played with Alek's hair.

"You have sexy hair, and it's getting longer. I love it," Rafe said.

"I'm growing it out. I had to cut it when I was in prison." Alek quickly returned to sucking the hard cock before him.

"Good."

Rafe's erection throbbed as it plowed deeply into Alek's mouth. Rafe's entire body was soaking wet. His balls tightened as he came close to emptying them. "Stop! I want to come inside you." Rafe shoved Alek's head away.

Alek looked shocked and confused by Rafe's sudden movement. Rafe hugged him and slipped his tongue into his mouth. Alek responded by sucking and biting. Their tongues played together as Rafe's hands wandered all over Alek's body. He pulled away from Alek, staring at him with pride. *Alek is beautiful, loving, and so sexy.*

"Get on your side," Rafe whispered as he rested on his side on the bed.

Alek turned on his side facing Rafe, who reached for the lube on the nightstand. He lubed the outside area of Alek's opening. He was rock hard against Rafe's erection. He entered Alek with one finger, stretching him. Alek moaned when the second finger moved in. He arched to take more, but Rafe pulled his fingers out and replaced them with his cockhead. He moved it in deeper, more urgently, further burning him. Rafe grabbed his nipples, twisted them until Alek jerked from pain and pleasure.

"I wish you'd get your nips pierced so I can pull on them."

"I don't think so. You can play with them like this." Alek stiffened.

Rafe pounded his hole, which ignited in him a desperate need. Hitting Alek's sensitive spot made him shudder throughout. Alek was rocking in time with him, trying to pound his cock in the deepest possible way. He reached for Alek's cock, stroking it with his lubed fingers while he pounded his hole harder and harder.

"Ahh. Feels so good," Alek panted.

"Take it," Rafe moaned.

Rafe shot his cum inside him, setting Alek to spurt his.

"Fuck. Fuck. Fuck," Rafe shouted and then collapsed beside Alek.

"Ahhh. Ahhh," Alek moaned.

BURIED SECRETS

BRINA BRADY

CHAPTER EIGHTEEN

Alek Belanov

Alek woke up in an empty bed, so he took a quick shower and dressed. He walked to the kitchen with the hope of seeing Rafe, but he wasn't there. Alek poured himself a cup of the coffee Rafe must have made earlier. He carried his coffee outside to the picnic table where he spotted Rafe standing beside the grill talking to James and Valerik. When Rafe noticed him, he waved. Dante and Liam were sitting at the picnic table drinking their coffee. Liam was sunburned and wore his black baseball cap on his head. The others were probably still sleeping, so Alek took a seat beside Dante.

"How are you feeling?" Alek asked Dante.

"Still in pain. I'm going to the doctor later on," Dante said.

"Soon you'll be back to normal again," Alek said.

"Valerik said we're going to go crabbing tonight," Liam said.

"We're going to catch crabs to eat? I don't think I want to do that," Alek said.

"Why not?" Dante asked.

"I don't want to be a part of killing," Alek said.

"Do you eat crab meat?" Liam asked.

"Yes, but I don't want to catch them."

"Well, too bad because Valerik said we're all going," Liam said.

Alek drank his coffee and wondered why he didn't want to go fishing like the others in the group. These macho protectors had killed people, so catching crabs would be nothing to them. Alek was much too sensitive to be involved with either of those sadistic activities.

"I wonder what's going on between those guys," Dante said. "They've been talking for over an hour."

"Valerik said someone is trying to blackmail Rafe. Remember that party we went to?" Liam said.

"What about it?" Dante asked.

"Eduardo, the head guy of the San Bernardino group, found out about the dead gang members in Bishop," Liam said.

"Kaden and Rafe were talking about this last night," Alek said. "I don't know what they're going to do about it." He didn't think they should be discussing this with Dante. He was already feeling bad about the situation.

"I can't be involved with the police, or I'll get arrested," Liam said.

"I'm sure Valerik won't let that happen nor will any of the other protectors," Alek said.

"This is my fault." Dante's face paled. "They were after me, not you guys."

"We work as a team here," Rafe said, taking them by surprise when he butted into their conversation. "You guys shouldn't even be discussing this. We're in charge, and it's our responsibility to find a solution, not yours. Don't worry about this problem."

"We were just trying to figure what was going to happen now," Liam said

"We stand together through the good and bad times. This situation is no one's fault. I'll notify you guys if any changes are to occur. We're hoping to stay here for the month. Then we'll move to a permanent location somewhere on the East Coast," Rafe said.

James started frying bacon while Valerik was scrambling eggs in a large frying pan on the grill. The delightful bacon scent woke up Alek's stomach, making him hungry.

"I'm starving," Dante said.

"Me, too," Liam said.

Anouska carried fresh-baked rolls, butter and jam to the table, and Mateo passed everyone an orange juice carton. Kaden and Emilio finally came outside. Rafe called Kaden over to the group of protectors, so Emilio sat at the picnic table.

"Hey, did you sleep in?" Alek asked Emilio.

"No. We were doing other things that we can't do outside." Emilio smiled.

"You're so naughty," Anouska said. "I'm glad we're alone on the third floor. I wouldn't want to hear what you guys are doing in bed."

"Anouska, don't act like you're behaving upstairs with Mateo. We know you're newlyweds," Emilio said.

"So, who is going to the beach today?" Anouska straightened her shoulders and grinned.

"I think we all are, except James and Dante," Emilio said.

"I'm going to the waterpark with Valerik," Liam said.

"Rafe said we should stick together. I don't know if you'll go or if all of us will go with you," Alek said.

They ate breakfast, talking to one another. Kaden assigned Alek and Emilio to clean up. Later, they separated and went into their apartments to get ready for the beach. Alek and Rafe changed into their swim trunks and matching Seaside Heights T-shirts.

"I don't want to go crabbing tonight," Alek said.

"Why not?" Rafe asked. "It's fun. We use nets."

"I don't like killing things."

"Would you go to please me? I'd feel less stressed if we hung out together. You could just watch. It's when we go our separate ways, we encounter problems. The real reason is I want to be with you."

"I'll go if we can eat lunch at that same place on the boardwalk again."

"That's a deal. But can we swim first or do you want lunch right after our breakfast?"

"I can wait for lunch."

"I haven't seen you smoking. Did you quit?" Rafe asked.

"I smoke when I can."

They all walked to the boardwalk and the smell of pizza mingled with other delicious aromas filled the air. The game players were throwing darts at balloons, some winning prizes based on the combination of tags underneath the balloons they popped. Valerik and Liam wanted to play, so the group stopped to watch them. Valerik won a stuffed teddy bear for Liam.

"Hey, muscles, want to give it a try?" the short man behind the stand asked Rafe.

He raised his hand like a stop sign and shook his head.

A pack of aggressive young men stood around smoking cigarettes, making bets, and taking turns pounding an arcade game that measured a player's punch. Alek stood closer to Rafe, and Liam did the same with Valerik. The aromas of the food from the stands overpowered the smell of the ocean. Alek wanted to eat at the boardwalk restaurants for all three of his meals. They returned to Tower Two and walked on the hot sand nearby the water.

They had purchased passes for the beach to save money. Why were they charging anything to sit on the beach and swim? In California, they paid for parking only, not the beach or to swim. Just like those tollbooths on the Parkway, which Alek thought was crazy since he had grown up with the freeways.

They threw their colorful beach towels down, sunning in the same area. Alek sat between Emilio and Rafe. On the beach, people doused themselves with suntan lotions and oils. What irritated Alek were the lifeguards who overused their whistles, demanding the swimmers move closer to the shore. For the slightest reason, they'd close the beach, and everyone had to leave because of the rain or stormy conditions. That happened twice the day before. As soon as the rain stopped, they were allowed to return to the beach.

The California beaches were more relaxed than the ones here. He never remembered a lifeguard using a whistle or being told to leave the beach due to rain. These lifeguards were getting high from blowing their damn whistles. Another thing Alek didn't care for was the announcements coming from a loudspeaker as if they were under attack. They also had helicopters pulling messages across the sky, which Alek thought was an invasion of his space.

For no reason at all, Alek felt depressed. Everything was going okay with Rafe, and he got along with the others in the group. This stifling feeling hit him hard; he missed his home with Uncle Sacha and California. They had done many things together and now nothing. His uncle had completely banished Alek from everything he had known.

Didn't he care about me anymore?

Uncle Sacha had always told Alek that he was more of a son than a nephew, and yet the man who raised him had thrown him away. When he thought about it, Pavel must have had something to do with this. His cousin knew Alek would never take over, so why did he want him gone for good? Again, he wondered what Pavel had meant when he said he should have killed him with the rest of the traitors. His cousin had been referring to his parents and brothers as traitors, which they weren't. Pavel had implied he knew who murdered them. How would he know when he had been a child too when it happened? None of this made sense at all.

"Do you mind if I talk to Valerik?" Alek asked Rafe.

"No. Go ahead."

Alek walked over to Valerik.

"Can we talk about my uncle in private?" Alek asked.

"Yes." Valerik shot Alek a welcoming smile and then turned to Liam. "Stay here. I'm going to talk to Alek."

"Yes, Sir," Liam said.

They walked along in the water, just enough to get their feet wet.

"You said you worked for my uncle. Did you ever hear him mention my parents?" Alek asked.

"What's wrong? Why do you need to dig up things about your parents?" Valerik asked.

"I want to know who murdered them and why."

"He never discussed your parents. I'm sorry. What else can I help you with?"

"I need to know why I'm here. How can I find that out?"

"You should have asked your uncle. He has all the answers."

"Do you think he'd talk to me?"

"Why wouldn't he? He loves you. Discuss this with Rafe and see if he'll allow you to call your uncle. He'll make sure you don't breach security. That's the best I can do. I know you want more answers, but I don't have them," Valerik said.

"Thanks for talking to me. I guess I just miss him," Alek admitted.

When they returned to the others, Alek sat beside Rafe.

"Hey, are you okay?" Rafe asked.

"I think one of the Philly Cheese Steaks might help me feel better," Alek said.

"Sounds good."

After they ate and walked on the boardwalk, Rafe decided to go back to the apartment.

"You know we need to discuss my expectation for you in our relationship."

"When are we going to talk about it?"

"When we get to the apartment."

They walked the two blocks to their apartment. James and Dante had left for the doctors, and no one else was home yet. They went to the bedroom and sat on the bed.

"First, do you have any questions?" Rafe asked.

"Are you into BDSM?" Alek finally got the nerve to ask.

"That's not a simple question. I've been in a BDSM relationship as a Dom with a sub before I set up the society. Why do you ask?"

"I want to know if we are practicing BDSM," Alek said.

"No, we're not. Why would you think we were?"

"The punishment with the belt. Where did that come from? I don't know any guy who allows his sexual partner to punish him. But I guess we're not partners really, right?"

"We're bonded partners. That means our sexual relationship is between the two of us without anyone else in the mix. The punishment comes from me. Each protector deals with breaking rules in their own way. I expect you to listen to me since I'm protecting you, and I can't do that unless I can trust you. I know Kaden feels the same way. James uses punishment in his relationship with Dante because they're in a BDSM relationship. Mateo doesn't punish Anouska. Valerik uses discipline with Liam, too. The protectors will do what they have to do to maintain safety because your life is on the line here. This isn't a game with do-overs."

"Do they all use a belt like you?"

"Kaden and Valerik do, but James has an array of spanking implements. We don't use the belt to exert our power over you but to correct you. We don't abuse you guys."

"What's the difference between your discipline and BDSM?"

"Big difference. Are you interested in a BDSM relationship?"

"I don't know. I need to know what it means and how it's different from what we're doing."

"BDSM has a variety of erotic practices or role-playing involving bondage, discipline, dominance and submission, sadomasochism, and other combinations of interpersonal dynamics. There's a Dom and a sub. The Dom is in charge of the sub. In our relationship, I'm in charge, and you follow my orders, so that part is similar. The sex is different because we have vanilla sex. BDSM has other activities."

"Can we try out BDSM sex sometime?"

"Well, what are you talking about? Bondage, discipline, or what? BDSM relationships begin with a questionnaire of what you like and don't like. The Dom will give you a set of rules and jobs. The two must agree and sign a contract. If you have a contract, then you create a safeword which stops anything you don't like or can't handle during scenes."

"So you have sex during a scene?"

"Depends. You can but you don't have to. It's very subjective, and the scenes are created by the Dom which is based on your list."

"Dante has a book on BDSM. He said I could read it. What do you think?"

"Read it when you get the time. We're pretty busy here having fun."

"You didn't answer me about the BDSM sex," Alek said.

"When I was a Dom, I gave a lot of spankings to bad boys. I don't know if you could deal with that."

"What does that have to do with sex?" Alek asked.

"You better read the BDSM book."

"Don't cop out on me. Tell me," Alek demanded.

"Damn, Alek. Did Dante tell you that you weren't getting enough from vanilla sex because you weren't in a BDSM relationship?"

"No. He'd never say that. Stop changing the subject."

"For some subs, pain takes them into subspace. That's a place where you feel so good. Sex is good, but subspace is a whole new level of enjoyment if that makes sense. For others, they can go there with bondage or role-playing involving combinations of toys."

"And what do you get out of that?" Alek asked.

"It's a power exchange. It's like I take care of you in exchange for your submission."

"Would you ever want me as your sub? I mean am I good enough?"

"I want you with me. It's not about good cnough and you know you are to me. I want to give you want you need."

"So, you just don't want me that way?"

"I do want that with you, but I have to see what you really want for us."

"Would you teach me?"

"When we get settled, we'll discuss it again. To your question, of course, I'll teach you."

"Will you come up with something for us to do now?"

"I will. I sure would like to know what started this interest in BDSM."

"I guess, when Dante told me I should read the book, I wanted to know more about it."

"That's good."

BRINA BRADY

CHAPTER NINETEEN

Rafe Escobar

Rafe's phone rang while he was getting ready to go outside to talk to Alek.

"What's up, Joe?" Rafe asked.

Joe was one of his Southern Californian contacts. They had worked together for five years, and he was very reliable when it came to information about members in the other groups Rafe controlled. He also assisted Rafe with hiring new protectors and finding gay men who needed protection.

"I have some sensitive information that you might find informative," Joe said.

"What did you find out?" Rafe knew this info wouldn't be good since Joe never called unless something was wrong.

"Your man Eduardo has been talking shit about you and your group. Word has it that your group was responsible for the killing of five gang members from Los Angeles. They said you're harboring a gang member and one guy with a police warrant. I think you need to deal with Eduardo soon. He's gone rogue and can cause bigger problems than gossip."

"Is Eduardo still at Fawnskin with his group?" Rafe asked.

"He's still there."

"He's supposed to be there for a month. Anything else?"

"Where are you?" Joe asked.

"We're out of state traveling."

"I know people who can take him out for a fair price," Joe said.

"No. I don't want that. First, I'm going to talk to him about the lies he's spreading. I gave him a great opportunity when I took him in as a group leader. I set him up so he could be successful, and this is how the fucker repays me," Rafe said.

"I suggest you hire a hitman to take him out. I don't see this getting better with time."

"That won't be necessary. I'll handle this myself, but I need to find out who he's working for."

"He is supposed to be working for you, not any of your enemies," Joe said.

"That's what I thought too. Get back to me with any additional info you find. Thanks again for keeping me posted."

Rafe had too many things going on and Eduardo causing problems that could escalate only added to his full plate. He was disappointed with him since he had trusted him. Maybe the job was getting to him. There was only one thing to do and that was fire him, but he needed a replacement. He also had to make sure he didn't use his information against the group again. He knew one guy he had interviewed and placed on the waiting list. Harlan was from Kansas and had been one of his best friends at UCLA. If he were still available, then he'd hire him.

Rafe went outside to the picnic table.

"I want all the boys and Anouska to go to the third floor into the empty apartment. The protectors will stay outside for a meeting." He handed Alek the key to the apartment.

"Is everything okay?" Alek asked.

"I'll talk to you later about it. Make sure everyone stays in that apartment. Lock it."

"I will."

Anouska and the boys followed Alek inside the building. The four men gathered around Rafe at the picnic table.

"We have a problem with Eduardo. It's bigger than I had originally thought. Apparently, he's working for one of

277

my enemies. He's spreading rumors that our group murdered the five gang members in Bishop. He also knows our group has a member with a police warrant and a former gang member from the same gang of the five dead. This is serious. I know a guy who can replace Eduardo. Once he accepts the job, then I'm going to fire him," Rafe said.

"What's going to keep Eduardo quiet after you fire him?" James asked.

"That's the thing. We have to shut him down, but I really need to know who he's working for," Rafe said.

"Dante said that he thought he had seen Eduardo in Los Angeles talking to the gang leader," James said.

"So do you think he is doing this to join a gang?" Rafe asked.

"No, but he may be on the take to find Dante for them," James said.

"Why didn't you mention this?" Rafe asked.

"Dante just told me this last night. I didn't know we had problems with Eduardo until now."

"In future any new information should be brought to me immediately, and everyone should leave the thinking and deciding what is vital to their safety to me." Rafe raised his voice.

"What are we going to do with him?" Mateo asked. "I hope you don't plan on murdering him."

"No. I'm going to call Cousin Arturo and his brother to scare the shit out of him."

"Do you trust them not to kill him?" Mateo asked.

"I'll tell them not to kill him," Rafe said.

"They butcher people." Mateo rolled his eyes.

"Look, I don't want anyone calling the cops on Liam, nor do I want that damn gang to hurt Dante again. He wants to destroy me and our society by turning us in for the murders of the gang members," Rafe said.

"It makes me sick. All of this makes me sick. Do what you have to do," Mateo said.

"I think this is the best way to deal with that bastard," Valerik said. "I support you."

"And you, Kaden?" Rafe asked.

"I support firing the bastard, but I'm not so sure I trust your cousins. I feel like Mateo."

"Well, it's our boys' lives at stake here, Kaden," James said.

"That's right. Not to mention we all took part in the killings," Valerik said.

"Let's vote on it," Rafe said. "Who supports firing Eduardo?"

They all raised their hands.

"Who supports hiring my cousins to scare Eduardo into silence?" Rafe asked.

Valerik, James, and Rafe raised their hands. Mateo and Kaden didn't support it.

"Okay, since you two don't support it, what other option do we have?"

"I think we should meet him here and threaten to kill him if he opens his mouth," Mateo suggested.

"That would compromise our location. We can't do that," Rafe said.

"Two of us could go to him and rough him up with threats of killing him," Kaden said.

"I don't know about that. I need all of you here. I'm going to call my friend and see if he's still interested in the job first."

"What about two rough guys take a visit to Eduardo? I just don't think Arturo is the right man for the job. He'll cut Eduardo's tongue out. He takes shit very literally," Mateo said.

"Valerik, do you know two guys who could rough Eduardo up?"

"I do. They would do this as a favor to me if I asked," Valerik said.

"Are they Russians?" James asked.

"Yes. Do you have a problem with Russians?"

"No," James said.

"Who is in favor of hiring two Russians to shut Eduardo up?" Rafe asked.

All of them raised their hands.

"Okay, take care of it. If you need money, let me know. I'm going to call my friend."

"Is Eduardo still at the Fawnskin cabins?" Valerik asked.

"He and his group were supposed to be there for the month, but move them to the Riverside cabins after Harlan shows up to take over. Check out the other protectors and see where their loyalties are. If you think they're still loyal to Eduardo, fire them," Rafe said.

"Got it," Valerik said.

"Make sure they escort Eduardo off the grounds before you move them."

"I'll get on it now," Valerik said.

"Thanks," Rafe said. "Hey, James, can you tell the boys and Anouska to come outside."

"Sure will."

"How's Dante?"

"He's much better. I'm going to take him to the boardwalk."

"Why don't you wait until we all go later? We can never be too cautious."

"Good idea."

Rafe went inside and called his friend Harlan.

"Hey, Rafe. I thought I'd never hear from you again."

"The job is yours if you still want it."

"I told you I was available, and I still am."

"Plan to move to Fawnskin, California in the cabins and then you'll all move to the Riverside cabins. I'll send you everything you need to know in an email. We're in the process of removing the turncoat, Eduardo. Once he's gone, you can go in. If you don't want the young man he's protecting, we can send him back to the camp, and he'll go through the process again, and you can choose another one at a party. It's up to you."

"I'll give his young man a try first, and if it doesn't work out, I'll let you know. I appreciate you giving me this opportunity. This job is perfect for me."

"Thank you." Rafe ended the call.

Alek came in from outside and gave Rafe a hug. "You look like you need a hug."

"Thanks."

"What's going on?" Alek asked.

"We had to deal with Eduardo. Things have gotten worse. I hired a new man for his job."

"What's going to happen to Eduardo?"

"He's going to receive a visit this week, and I'm firing him."

"Isn't he at Fawnskin?"

"Yes. He'll be out soon. Did you want something?"

"No. I just wanted to check on you," Alek said.

"Don't mention what we discussed here to anyone else."

"I won't say anything. You have my word," Alek said.

"What did you discuss with Valerik at the beach?" Rafe asked.

"My uncle. I wanted to know if he had any additional knowledge. He told me I should call my uncle and ask him, but he said I had to make sure you approved the call first."

"I don't approve the call at all. My investigation of your family isn't complete. I don't know who the rotten one is yet. Don't call him. If he wants to talk to you, he knows how to reach me, and he hasn't called me."

"You don't get it, do you?" Alek raised his voice.

"Get what? You're pissed at your uncle, and you want to know why he sent you away. It's really simple. He wants

283

you protected from your family. What else do you want to know?"

"I want to ask him who murdered my family? I don't believe that a Mexican cartel was responsible. I want to know the truth because Pavel said the man who did this should have killed me too."

"Sometimes, it's better to let things stay as they are. Do you think your uncle would tell you the truth?"

"I need the truth. I deserve the truth. Why did he lie to me in the first place?"

"Alek, he took you in and raised you. He did more than some birth parents have done. Maybe. Just maybe, he wants to protect you from the truth. Let it be."

"Something doesn't feel right. I have this overwhelming feeling that something is very wrong."

"I don't think knowing will bring you peace. It might open a door to a room you should never walk into."

"So you're telling me I can't call my uncle?" Alek spaced out his words evenly as his anger increased.

"For now, the answer is no. Remember to obey my orders, and if you don't listen, there will be consequences like last time." Rafe's calm tone changed to his warning voice.

"I'm going to take a nap." Alek headed to the bedroom and slammed the door behind him.

After Rafe drank a beer, he went to the bedroom and sat beside Alek.

"Look, I don't want you angry at me. I know you're upset but I don't want you upset."

"I'm not really upset with you. It's just that I need to feel okay about my life."

"Let me help you with that," Rafe said.

"I'm sorry. I know you want to help me. Being with you feels right. It's just other things are upsetting me. Are we going to be okay?" Alek asked.

Rafe kissed Alek. "We're more than okay."

BRINA BRADY

CHAPTER TWENTY

Alek Belanov

Alek kissed Rafe on his cheek, but he still didn't move. He must have been exhausted since he was usually the first one up. Alek loved the way Rafe's hair splayed wildly against his forehead. The only time Rafe wasn't in control of every strand on his head was when he was sleeping. Alek inhaled his scent, which mingled with the leftover traces of their sex, reminding him of their rough night together.

Alek moved around in the bed carefully until he untangled himself from Rafe's body. He jumped out of bed, stood up stretching, and rummaged through the small dresser he had put his clothes in. A moment later, he heard Rafe turn over on his stomach. Alek looked over and the first thing he noticed was his bare ass, so he moved the covers over him. After he dressed, he made his way to the kitchen and made coffee, and carried it to the bedroom. Rafe opened his eyes, sat up with a sexy smile, and blew a kiss to Alek.

"Thank you. I need to meet with the protectors in fifteen minutes," Rafe said.

"How come?"

287

"It's a follow-up on Eduardo."

"Is he dead?"

"No, but he won't be causing us any more problems."

"That sounds horrible." Alek shuddered inwardly at the details.

Rafe got up and took a shower. They went outside and met everyone for breakfast. When they finished, Rafe told the boys and Anouska to go inside because the protectors were having another private meeting. Alek wondered what had happened with Eduardo. Dante invited them to his apartment. He passed everyone a soda.

"Does anyone know what that meeting is about?" Liam asked.

"It's about Eduardo," Alek said.

"I hope he's not dead," Anouska said.

"I heard Valerik speaking Russian on the phone last night, and he wasn't angry. So I don't think they killed him," Liam said.

"That's good, then." Alek wondered why Valerik told Liam more than Rafe had told him.

Dante handed Alek the BDSM book. "I finished it. I know you're going to want to be in a BDSM relationship after you've read about subspace."

"Have you ever reached subspace?" Alek asked.

"Last night was my first time. You guys are missing out," Dante said.

"What are you talking about?" Anouska asked.

"It's a trance-like euphoria state. It's different for each person on how you get there. I felt drunk with a high. It's like you and your Dom are the only ones existing in the moment," Dante said.

"So sex got you drunk and high?" Anouska asked.

"Not just sex. You feel like you're floating or flying. Subspace is the ultimate goal for a submissive. It doesn't always happen. When I reached subspace, I didn't want to come down, but James helped me through with aftercare."

"What did he do to you to make you go into subspace?" Alek asked.

"He paddled me really hard; the pain took me there. When I got there, I didn't feel any pain. All of you should read this book," Dante said.

"What kind of paddle?" Liam asked.

Dante left the room and returned with a large paddle.

"That's huge," Anouska said. "I don't think I want Mateo to do that to me."

"It's not just about that paddle. Don't you have to be submissive to James?" Alek asked.

"Yes. It's not just the paddle, but you're right we have a special relationship. It's just that using pain takes me to a pleasurable place."

"If Valerik could take me into subspace, then I might consider it," Liam said.

"I don't know. I would like to experience what subspace feels like, but Rafe might get too excited using that paddle on me. So, you think it's worth it?" Alek asked.

"Totally," Dante said. "Read the book because it's more than just subspace."

"Rafe used to be a Dom."

"I didn't know that." After a startled look at Alek, Emilio frowned, wrinkling his forehead.

"What about Kaden?" Alek asked.

"He hasn't discussed that with me, but did you know that Rafe and Kaden used to be together?" Emilio asked.

"Really?" Alek raised his eyebrows with disbelief.

"Don't tell Rafe. I thought Kaden was too friendly with Rafe, so I asked him where they'd met, and he told me."

"That's scandalous. He does seem closer to Kaden than the others," Alek said, wondering if he felt jealous of Kaden. Why didn't he discuss it with him?

"Are you sure, Emilio?" Dante asked.

"Yes, they were in the Marines together. That's where they had their secret relationship. He said they'd decided to be friends instead of lovers."

"I can't even picture them fucking," Alek said.

"Alek!" Anouska raised her voice in polite disapproval.

"I'm sorry, Anouska. I got carried away with myself. That image was too much for me."

Rafe sent Alek a text.

Rafe: *"You guys can come outside now."*

"The meeting's over," Alek said.

Dante walked over to Alek. "If you want to ask me any questions about BDSM, I'll try to answer them for you. You're lucky that Rafe was a Dom before. I wonder why he isn't anymore."

"I'll ask him why he stopped being a Dom. I'd like to know that too."

Alek stopped at the apartment and put the book in the bedroom for later. He reached for his phone and stared at it. What good was this phone if he couldn't call who he wanted to. He wanted to hear his uncle's voice and see if there was any truth to what he had said all these years about his parents. The man always chose to protect him versus the truth. It was time for Alek to know the truth regardless of what Rafe had said.

The front door opened and Alek walked to the front room. Rafe stood there looking quite stressed out. He looked so sexy in his tight jeans and T-shirt.

"What happened?" Alek asked.

"Eduardo is gone and won't be back in the Gay Protection Society. Harlan is now in charge of that group. I need to find a better location for them, but they must work to afford it."

"Are you sure Eduardo's not dead?" Alek asked.

"I already told you he's not dead. He's in the hospital with broken limbs and other issues, but he'll live. I don't think we have to worry about him anymore."

"Why did he try to blackmail you?"

"People are greedy. The more you give them, the more they want. Why didn't you come outside?" Rafe asked.

"I had to put away the BDSM book that Dante lent me."

"If you're really serious about learning about BDSM, I'd like to hear what you like and don't like."

"Why did you stop being a Dom?" Alek asked.

"When I became involved with the protection groups, I didn't have time to have a sub. I wasn't protecting anyone either. I was involved with building up the groups. Occasionally I'd go to a BDSM club and find a sub to play with for the night."

"Are you done with being a Dom?"

"If the situation presented itself, I'd be open to it. And before you say it, I'm not dumping you for some unknown sub. If you're interested in it, we'll explore it together."

"How did you meet Kaden?" Alek asked.

"We were in the Marines together. I thought I told you that."

"Were you just friends or something else?"

"What are you asking me?" A flash of humor crossed his face.

"Was Kaden your sub?"

"My sub?" Rafe laughed. "Oh, no. Kaden wouldn't be anyone's sub, that's for sure."

"What kind of friendship did you have with him?"

"Why are you asking so many questions about Kaden?"

"You two seem closer with each other than with the other protectors. I mean, you said they've all worked for you for five years, but you always talk to Kaden first."

"Sometimes I do ask Kaden before the others. He's the one who thinks before he acts. He sees all the sides to a problem. James and Valerik are very reactive, and sometimes they act before they think."

"But have you known Kaden longer than James and Valerik?"

"Yes, I have. What are you really asking me?" Rafe asked.

"Were you and Kaden ever together?"

"Together, as in fucking?"

"Yes, that's what I mean."

"I love Kaden like a brother, and he feels that way about me. It's not about sex for us. We're just close. We did have a relationship when we were in the Marines for a short time. It didn't work out because we both wanted to top. Taking turns wasn't what either of us wanted, so we decided it would be better to be friends only. Did someone tell you about Kaden and me?"

"No. I just noticed how close you are with him," Alek lied.

"You have nothing to be jealous about. My relationship with you is very different than mine with Kaden. I don't see you as a brother. You're my lover and partner."

"Do you think I'm sub material?" Alek's fear of rejection surfaced. He shouldn't have asked. What if he said no?

"I don't know enough about what turns you on. I don't know if you want me to control every aspect of your life in return for your submission and obedience. At this point, I don't see any signs that you would be comfortable with it. I may be wrong."

"I want to experience subspace."

"Subspace? Well, you need to submit to someone to experience that, but sometimes that's not enough. How about the next time James takes Dante to a BDSM club, we'll go with them so you can see what goes on."

"I'd love to go. When can we go?"

"I'll have to talk to James. Dante is doing much better."

"I think Liam might be interested too."

"What about Emilio?"

"I don't know. He didn't say much, but Anouska isn't interested."

"Kaden used to be a Dom too, but I don't know if he told Emilio. I have no idea if Emilio is interested in BDSM. He used to be a rent boy. That's what got him kicked out of my uncle's home with pressure from my father. I didn't know he was selling his ass, but that's why I worry about him. I don't want him to go back to that."

"He never told us about that, but it makes sense because he was so comfortable being a naked bartender. I know he's happy with Kaden."

"Yes, he makes a cute naked bartender. He gets his cuteness from me. He loves that job. The next party we have, you could work behind the bar with him if you wanted." Rafe shot him a cheeky grin.

"As a naked bartender?"

"Yes, you'll wear my red tie around your neck, so no one bothers you."

"I'll think about it."

"Want to try something new?"

"Sure."

"I'm talking about sex. What if I tie you to the bed and have sex with you?"

"What would you tie me with?"

"My belts. Just your arms, not your legs. This way you can kick me if you don't like something." Rafe smiled.

"Is that part of the bondage part of the BDSM?"

"Yes. Now, before we play, you need a safeword. Most guys choose red to stop."

"Oh, I want red too."

"That means if you want out of the scene, or in this case, it'd mean you want me to unbuckle the belts and free you."

"Okay."

"Were you ever tied down when you had sex?" Rafe asked.

"Nope."

"If you freak out, just use your safeword and everything stops." Rafe took Alek's hand and led him to the bedroom.

"I will. I wouldn't be doing this with you if I didn't trust you."

"Get naked," Rafe said as they entered the bedroom.

First, Alek removed his running shoes and socks. He carefully unzipped his jeans, in slow motion. He proceeded to unbuckle his belt while Rafe watched him. Then Rafe pushed them to his ankles with the speed of a madman. Alek stepped out of them at a faster pace. He whipped off his T-shirt.

"Facedown on the bed."

Alek landed on the bed as ordered. He waited while Rafe went through the closet, he figured to fetch the belts. Sure enough, Rafe had three belts in his hand. Fuck! Sweat rolled down his face in anticipation. He only had two hands, so why three belts? His fear ratcheted up a few notches. Could he handle this bondage play? *Shit! This is going to freak me out.*

"I'd like to blindfold you with one of the belts. Is that okay with you?" Rafe asked.

"Yes."

"When we play BDSM games, you need to say, *Yes, Sir,* to me."

"Yes, Sir." Alek almost laughed because he thought it was funny to call Rafe *Sir* in the middle of sex play.

Rafe wrapped the leather belt over his eyes, blackening his vision. With his sight impaired, he couldn't prepare for anything.

Rafe wrapped a belt around one of Alek's wrists and the headboard, then clasped the buckle. He did the same with the other side. Rafe spread Alek's legs spread-eagled across the bed with his body forming an X. His cock roused from the adrenaline rush of being in bondage. He enjoyed being bound like this for Rafe. The helpless feeling made his cock twitch just thinking about it.

"I'm going to put some warming lube on your hole. If you need me to stop at any point, use your safeword. If you want me to pause or you need to talk, say yellow. If I ask what color you are and you're good, say green."

"Yes, Sir." His voice trembled.

Rafe added lube to Alek's opening and then pushed his finger inside.

"Feels nice inside here," Rafe said.

Alek didn't respond but found he enjoyed the more intense feeling when he couldn't see.

"What color are you?" Rafe asked.

"Green, Sir."

This was the first time Alek allowed a man to tie him to a headboard. He had to admit that he had wanted a man who would take the lead and tell him what to do. It all made sense that his protector Rafe would be that man. His protection required Alek to follow his rules and if he failed to follow his rules, there were consequences. He needed Rafe to take charge of his life the way he had been doing. He felt safe and happy around him. All Alek wanted was to make sure he could please Rafe.

Rafe placed a pillow under Alek to prop up his ass. He stroked Alek's cock, sending all the blood rushing to one hot spot. He was blazing with desire. He expected Rafe to fuck him, but he didn't. He ran the edge of his shirt along Alek's back, ass, and legs, tickling him. A trail of goose bumps went down his spine. He couldn't stop Rafe from driving him crazy. Rafe dropped a featherlight kiss on Alek's cheek.

Alek arched his back in pleasure. Rafe laid his hands between Alek's thighs, running his fingers along the sweaty balls, filling his hands with them. Alek took a deep breath, not knowing what Rafe would do with them. An incredibly cool rush traveled through his body, leaving him trembling with need. He trusted Rafe with his body unlike those men in prison who demanded things. When Rafe ordered him to do something, he wanted to do it for him.

"You make me crazy when I get near you," Rafe said.

When Rafe pushed his cock in, he was surprisingly gentle, waiting for Alek's reaction, trying to make it as smooth as possible. Once Rafe was inside, he switched to pounding him hard, hitting his special spot. Without his vision, the intensity of Rafe's cock rubbing inside drove him wild. Alek's entire focus was on his cock as it thickened.

Rafe pounded Alek's butt with all the power of his muscular body. Alek clenched his ass muscles with each thrust. His moans grew in volume as the room filled with a powerful musk created between them. The wet sounds of hot sex moved them beyond lovers to lusty animals, each looking for release.

"Oh, please... don't stop," Alek moaned.

"Fuck that feels good. So damn good."

"Keep doing it to me, please," Alek begged.

Alek's muscles tightened as a swell of euphoria traveled through him at the same time Rafe's cock throbbed inside Alek's ass.

"Your ass... this ass of yours feels like velvet," Rafe said.

Alek contracted his anal muscles around the thick cock inside him. Rafe brushed his prostate repeatedly. It was rare that Alek had a lover who cared about him feeling good. Rafe took hold of Alek's erection underneath him, stroking it. He pulled out of Alek for a minute, slapping his ass hard, then rammed his cock back inside. Alek panted as Rafe thrashed his hole. Alek's cock vibrated in Rafe's hand.

"I love you inside me. So close."

"Because you belong to me." He pounded harder and continued to stroke Alek's cock.

Alek vibrated inside and out of his body. He loved every moment of it. Rafe released his cum inside Alek, and that ignited him to spurt all his cum onto the sheets. Rafe's cum felt cool on the heat inside Alek's hole. Rafe caressed Alek's sweaty back as his cock softened and slipped out.

"You were so good." Rafe unbuckled the belt from his eyes. He leaned over and kissed Alek's cheek.

He released the belts from the headboard and his wrists. Rafe rested beside Alek in their afterglow. The deep flush of Rafe's skin told Alek his lover was spent, too.

"I liked playing like this," Alek said.

"Me, too. We'll try other things, but I don't have any toys here, so we'll have to make do with what we have."

"What kind of toys?"

"Oh, so many. I think I'm going to call James and see if we can find an adult store to buy some toys for us to try. Do you like that idea?"

"Yes. Let's do it soon."

"We will."

"Will you teach me more about BDSM like this please?" Alek asked.

"I'd love to teach you."

CHAPTER TWENTY-ONE

Rafe Escobar

Rafe found James outside getting the grill ready for dinner. Since Dante wasn't with him, it would be a good time to talk to him.

"Hey, James. Where's Dante?" Rafe asked.

"He's cleaning the apartment."

"Do you know of any BDSM clubs around here? Alek is interested in checking it out. I thought we could go one night with you guys," Rafe asked.

"There's one in Toms River, called Leather Whips, not too far from here. How about tomorrow night?" James asked.

"Sounds good. I need to know where an adult store is, too," Rafe said.

James handed Rafe a business card. "We've already been to the Sex Mart adult store when you guys were at the beach. It's also in Toms River, right over the bridge. They have some good toys for BDSM. I bet Dante talked to Alek about it. I know he lent our BDSM book to him. I figured it'd be okay with you since you're a Dom," James said.

"That's fine. We're going to go after dinner for some toys. Dante has been talking to Alek about his BDSM relationship with you, but I'm not sure Alek is sub material."

"He might be if he reaps some benefits. Dante went into subspace last night for the very first time. He was probably bragging about it to the other guys. He'd make a good salesman."

"I bet he did because out of the blue, Alek told me he wanted to experience subspace."

"These newbies are always looking for drug replacements. Did Alek ever use drugs?" James asked.

"I don't know. His uncle certainly didn't mention it, and that man sent me extensive written notes on Alek."

"I think you ought to ask him. His uncle might have been sugar-coating how perfect Alek was, so you'd take him on."

"I suppose he could have. I'll keep an eye on him." Rafe hoped Alek hadn't been using drugs, but he just had gotten out of prison. He had no idea, but he didn't see any signs of it.

"I don't know Alek well enough to know if he used drugs. I didn't mean to make you distrust him."

"Alek is sweet, and I love how he expresses himself. I'll ask him more questions and check to see if his uncle has told me the truth."

"Alek might be a challenge for you if you collar him," James said.

"I don't know if we'll get that far. He really doesn't like to be told what to do."

"Did you discipline him when they ran off?" James asked.

"Yes, and he didn't really like it because he stopped talking to me for a while. He thought he was in the right when he wasn't. That's a stop sign for me. He overreacted to the punishment. I don't know if he'd be a good fit or not, but Dante is talking up a storm about it."

"I bet his rich uncle spoiled him, so he's not used to any kind of discipline."

"I've talked to his uncle several times, and he doesn't sound like a man capable of spoiling anyone. Alek did say his uncle didn't spoil him, but I see signs of the opposite. His uncle sent me this huge list of foods including name brands of what Alek does and doesn't like. I've never seen anything like it."

"Spoiled and needs discipline. I hope it works out for both of you." James was scrubbing the grill.

"Thanks. I'm taking everything slow with him. I don't want to ruin anything we already have. I love having him in my life," Rafe said.

"I can see that. Dante likes Alek too. They're becoming friends."

"Alek needs friends. We're going to visit the adult store tonight, then we'll be back to walk the boardwalk. He loves the boardwalk. Tonight, the protectors need to meet after dinner. I'll have some new information."

Valerik walked over to them. "What's going on?"

"We have a meeting after dinner, and then I'm taking Alek to the adult store for some toys."

"I need to go too," Valerik said.

"If you don't mind, we'd like to go again," James said.

Mateo came over to where the other protectors were talking. "Did I hear adult store?"

"I'm taking Alek, and the others are coming with us. Do you want to come with Anouska?" Rafe asked.

"Sure, count us in. Is it for gay people only or all kind of people?" Mateo asked.

"All kinds of people, not just gay," James said.

"Then I guess we'll all go after the meeting," Rafe said.

When Rafe saw Alek coming outside with the other guys, he waved him over.

"After dinner, the protectors are going to have a private meeting, and when it's over, we're all going to the adult store."

"Really? Everyone is going with us?" Alek asked, finding it funny that they all wanted to go with them. At the same time, there was comfort in traveling with the group he had come to love like family.

"It didn't start that way, but one by one, they asked to join us." Rafe's smile matched Alek's.

"That's great."

"I'm going to find some fun items for the bedroom," Rafe said.

After they finished with dinner, Liam and Emilio cleaned the area.

"Now that you're finished here, go into one of the apartments, and I'll send a text notifying you when it's okay to come out. After the meeting, we're taking the van to the adult shop."

When the boys and Anouska went inside, Rafe told the protectors to sit at the picnic table.

"I have an update on our new location. We have three more weeks here, but I'm looking at rent-to-own cabins somewhere in Northern New Jersey. It's deep in the woods, but you can take a bus to New York City, and it's near a few colleges. I have a few realtors looking at properties for five couples. These cabins have air and heat," Rafe said.

"What about Wi-Fi?" Mateo asked.

"Yes, of course."

"I got another update on Eduardo," Valerik said. "He's moving to a long-term rehabilitation facility. He'll remain there for a few months, and then he'll be moving back to Mexico when he's able to."

"Good. That will send a message to that gang not to fuck with our group," James said. "I want Dante to feel safe with me."

"Well, at least he's still alive," Mateo said.

"That bastard deserves to be dead. Anyone who tries to hurt Dante is a dead man walking," James said.

"I'm going to send a text for the others to come outside, and then we'll leave," Rafe said.

When everyone was settled in the van, Rafe left the driveway and drove them over the bridge to Toms River. After he parked, they broke into five couples and entered the store. From the outside, it looked like a huge house. James and Dante walked with Rafe and Alek. He had never been inside an adult store. He used to buy things online when he lived with his uncle and had them delivered to a friend's house.

"What do you think of this place?" Rafe asked Alek.

"Interesting."

A slow, naughty smile spread over Alek's handsome face. Rafe's body ached for Alek's. The store, the talk of BDSM, and Alek all reminded Rafe how much he had enjoyed being a Dom. However, he had no idea if Alek would enjoy the role of a sub.

The first area carried all the foreplay goodies, lubes with different flavors, sizes, and some edible or warming varieties. There were quite a few people around the spanking implements.

"I don't have anything to spank Alek with," Rafe said.

"We're buying a crop," James said. "Why don't you try the flogger? It's not too bad on the bare ass."

Rafe walked over to the spanking implements and picked up a flogger. "What do you think of this when we play?"

"I don't know how it feels," Alek said.

Rafe slammed the flogger across Alek's ass. His face turned red, and then he laughed.

"Well, is it okay?" Rafe asked.

"Yes. I like it."

"Good because I'm going to buy it. Maybe tonight I'll try it out."

"I think you already tried it out."

"Maybe you can get into subspace with it," Dante said.

"Dante, don't put ideas into Alek's head. He has enough of his own," Rafe teased, trying to lighten the mood.

"Let's look at the handcuffs. I don't have any here," James said.

"Do you want me to pick up some handcuffs?" Rafe asked Alek.

"I guess so." Alek shrugged, uncertain of his answer.

"Are you sure?"

"I trust you," Alek said.

"That's a good sign that you trust Rafe," James said.

"What else are you going to get?" Alek asked.

"Tell me what you want," Rafe responded.

"I want you to get rope and a spreader since there's no footboard," Alek said as his cheeks reddened.

"We need to get a spreader too," James said.

They picked up the handcuffs, rope, and a spreader.

"James, keep an eye on Alek. I want to pick up a few surprise items," Rafe said.

"I ought to put a leash on him," James said.

"I'm not going anywhere, James," Alek said.

Rafe went to the other side of the store and picked out butt plugs including vibrating ones, warming lotion, a cock cage, and nipple clamps. After paying for the items, he found Emilio with Kaden looking at paddles. He had no idea that Emilio was into BDSM. Kaden had never mentioned it.

"Are you going to paddle Emilio?" Rafe asked. Emilio wouldn't look at Rafe when he mentioned the paddle.

"He told me he wants to go into subspace," Kaden said.

"Dante must have been talking to him because Alek said the same thing. I guess our boys are interested in kinky sex play," Rafe said.

"We're going to try out a few things," Kaden said.

"Kaden, do you think Rafe needs to know about our sex life?" Emilio asked.

"Oh, I didn't think you would mind me mentioning it to him," Kaden said.

"I won't ask any more questions about spanking implements if it makes you uncomfortable," Rafe said.

"Fathers don't usually discuss things like this with their sons."

"Point taken. I'll catch you guys later."

Rafe wondered why Emilio felt he had invaded his space. He'd have to think before he discussed such matters again. He never wanted to embarrass him or hurt him in any way. When Emilio had thought they were cousins, he confided in Rafe about all his sexual experiences, but they weren't cousins. At least, Emilio was accepting the change in their relationship, even if the cost was losing his confiding in him about everything. Rafe had mixed feelings about losing this part of their relationship, but in the end, it was for the best. He was Emilio's father, and he needed to start acting like one.

"Hey, Rafe," Valerik called.

"What's up?"

"Liam wants to go into subspace so he wants me to buy a paddle."

"It looks like Dante has gotten to all the boys," Rafe said.

"Not just the boys," Mateo said, holding Anouska's hand.

"Don't tell me she said she wants to go into subspace too?" Rafe asked.

"Yes, she does. So we picked up a few things and a book," Mateo replied.

"Don't do anything to her without asking me first. You need to know what you're doing, and you're not trained as a Dom. If you don't do certain things the right way, you could hurt her."

"Of course, you'd say that, Mr. Know-it-all," Mateo said.

"I just want you both safe, that's all," Rafe said.

"I know how to read, remember?"

"Rafe, Mateo knows what he's doing in the bedroom, and he doesn't need instructions from his big brother. Trust me. He knows what he's doing," Anouska said.

"Just be careful," Rafe said.

He left them in the aisle and noticed Alek looking at the paddles hanging on the wall. He may as well pick one up since everyone else was.

"Hey, you want me to get that paddle you're looking at?" Rafe asked Alek.

"I don't know."

"Did you know Valerik and Kaden bought one for their boys?"

"They did?" Alek's eyes widened with surprise.

"Of course. They want to go into subspace like Dante."

"Okay, buy it. I don't want to be the only one without a paddle," Alek said.

313

They purchased their items and piled back in the van. After they went over the bridge into Seaside Heights, Rafe stopped at an ice cream parlor where they all crowded into the tiny shop and ordered cones.

"Are you excited about the new toys?" Rafe asked.

"Yes, but I don't know what I'm getting myself into."

"That's the fun of it. You don't know, but if you trust me, you'll find out."

"I'm a little nervous about it."

"We'll take everything slow and remember you always have a safeword to stop anything we do."

When they got back to the apartment, they all decided to turn in instead of taking a walk on the boardwalk. Rafe figured they wanted to try out their new toys.

CHAPTER TWENTY-TWO

Alek Belanov

Alek took a shower to make sure he was ready to play with Rafe tonight. He wondered what Rafe would do to him and if he'd go into subspace. In prison, he had known some men who were in BDSM relationships. He wasn't sure he'd be successful in one, but he was willing to try. If for no other reason than to please Rafe. He really didn't want Rafe to get bored with him, yet at the same time, he worried he'd be unable to do what was required.

Rafe stood in the bathroom and watched him shower, saying nothing.

"Are you going to come in with me or just watch?" Alek asked.

"I'll wait until you're done."

"I need some privacy," Alek said

"Privacy? What are you going to do in there?" Rafe grinned.

"Take care of a bottom's business."

Rafe left him alone to take care of the cleansing; then a few minutes later, he peeked into the bathroom. "Make sure you don't touch yourself. That's my job."

"I'm too busy for that right now."

When Alek finished, he headed to the bedroom. Rafe was sitting on top of the bed reading the BDSM book.

"This book will explain lots of things for you. It's excellent. I'm going to take my shower, and you can read while you're naked in the bed."

"Yes, Sir."

"Hey, I like hearing you call me Sir. It gives me a hard-on." The smile in Rafe's dark eyes contained a sensuous flame.

"Figured it would." Alek sat up in the bed and opened the book.

The first chapter covered the first talk with a Dom. It listed questions and checklists for the sub to fill out to let the Dom know what you like and don't. He wondered if Rafe had such a checklist. Alek had no interest in some of the listed items and others he didn't understand. There were many items he was curious about and wanted to try.

Rafe walked into the bedroom in jeans but with an obvious hard-on. "Do you want to play?"

"Play how?" Alek took a deep breath, trying to steady the shakiness in his voice.

"Don't you like surprises?"

"Not with something like this. I don't know what you're going to do."

"Do you trust me?" Rafe asked.

Rafe's eyes looked so bright and excited when he discussed anything to do with BDSM. *He's letting me inside a little. Maybe if I do well with his game, he'll like me more. I have to do it so he'll accept I want to please him. I must first learn what pleases him. More research.*

"Yes, I do."

"Tell me why you want to try BDSM."

"Other than the subspace, I want to please you, so you'll never look at someone else. I want to be able to give you something you want. I know you were paid to protect me, but I want to be everything you need because I know you didn't have to protect me."

"Wanting to please me is always a good start in this kind of relationship. You do have to give up everything to me. It's similar to what we're doing now as far as I'm protecting you and you obey my safety rules. With the BDSM relationship, it's more intense, and it crosses many areas in which you give up your control and give it to me. Right now, you're obeying the safety rules or trying to. It's much broader than what we have now. Part of the relationship is that we negotiate the terms of our relationship. I have friends who have a 24/7 BDSM relationship. Other friends only practice during the sex scenes. As your protector in our society, you don't get much input."

"That's not exactly true. You asked me if I wanted to be bonded to you, and you said that meant we're monogamous. I agreed to our bonding. I also had a choice to accept or reject your tie at the party, so I did have some input; more than you think."

"You're right. I hadn't looked at it quite like that. I was focused on the fact you were sent here, not by choice."

"My uncle didn't give me choices. Ever since I can remember, he told me what to do. For the most part, I trusted him and did what he said until I met Burain. I shut my ears to him when he told me to break it up." Alek lowered his head, remembering his frustrations and sadness with his uncle.

"Does it turn you on to take the back seat when we're having sex?"

"I like being told what to do. I respond sexually to your orders."

"That's a very good start. I want to try a few things. Remember, use your safeword we talked about if you don't like what's happening or you want me to stop."

"I get that part."

"Do you get the part that subspace isn't a given in every situation?" Rafe asked.

"If you say so, then I believe it." Alek frowned.

"Remember this is your idea not mine. I personally don't think you have what it takes to be a sub," Rafe said.

"You don't think I'm good enough to be your sub?" Alek felt hurt immediately from his words. In prison, he had given his body to a man who had protected him. Of course, he hadn't had to agree. If he hadn't agreed, then he might have been dead by now. One thing was for sure; he couldn't protect himself. He didn't have the stomach to fight back and defend himself. He needed a protector, and he had that much, but a Dom, he wasn't so sure. He'd have to see all aspects of the lifestyle. However, it was evident Rafe wanted to be in a BDSM relationship, and Alek wasn't sure he'd want to be a Dom to Alek. He wasn't certain he could be a sub either. He still needed to see how it'd go. He certainly wasn't going to rush into it.

"That's not what I said. I said I don't think you have submissive characteristics."

"I've always been a bottom."

"Being a bottom doesn't necessarily make you a sub. I'm not talking about sexual gymnastics. For instance, a sub can admit and accept a mistake. You're not always right especially when you're learning from your Dom. You need to feel pleasure from pleasing your Dom. That's the core of it. You need to trust your Dom."

"I do get pleasure from pleasing you. That's one of the reasons I'm here now. What about the sex part?"

"You need to be okay with taking orders in the bedroom. Can you accept another man controlling you? I don't just mean in the bedroom."

"I don't know about you controlling all aspects of my life, but I like when you dominate me in bed."

"Prove me wrong then. It's about what you want. I can have vanilla sex or not."

"When you say vanilla sex, I feel like you're settling with me and that you really want a BDSM relationship. I saw how excited you were in that store."

"Alek, I never settle for anything. I want you with me. Making you happy is important to me. I'd never force anything on you that you weren't comfortable with."

"Okay, I'll leave it up to you to figure out what to do. Keep in mind I'd love to go into subspace, but I understand that's not always possible. I wouldn't know what to tell you to do."

"Kneel on the floor." Rafe pointed to the middle of the room.

Alek paused for a moment, wondering if Rafe was serious. When Alek caught Rafe's stern expression, he knelt down on the hard tile floor before him and waited for further instruction.

"Your first lesson is to submit to me. This means you will meet my needs first and not think of your own. Can you do this?"

"Yes."

"When we are in a BDSM scene, you must say *Yes, Sir*."

"Yes, Sir."

Standing above Alek, Rafe unzipped his jeans, pushed his cock out, and pulled the foreskin a few times.

"Hands behind your head. Suck and swallow." Rafe rubbed his cock against Alek's closed lips.

Alek looked up at him while he placed his hands behind his head, but froze in position, unable to move toward Rafe's cock. His mind was traveling in circles. He'd wanted to please Rafe in every way for a long time. He wanted to be here with him.

Alek's hard-on had popped up after Rafe ordered him to suck his cock. Yet another betrayal from his stupid dick. Rafe scared him and turned him on all at once. It was different when Rafe had ordered him to suck him than when there wasn't a command. He liked the order and the sound of Rafe's voice. The line between pain and pleasure was blurred.

Alek lowered his head and wrapped his lips around Rafe's swollen cock. He couldn't determine any particular flavor other than Rafe's cock tasted clean, like his fresh scent. He slid his mouth up and down while sucking him. Alek loved the feeling of making Rafe feel good. His own erection seemed to stiffen more and his balls felt tight and ready to release. He wouldn't dare come while he sucked Rafe. That probably wasn't allowed without permission in BDSM.

"Use your hands to play with my balls," Rafe ordered.

Rafe's cock grew warmer and harder in his mouth. Alek played with his balls, lightly massaging them. Alek felt something vibrating on his tongue, and without any warning, Rafe's hot, sticky cum spurted into his mouth. Alek enjoyed swallowing it; wanted to please him. Rafe pulled his cock out of Alek's mouth and kissed him.

"You were beautiful." A satisfied light glowed from Rafe's sparkling brown eyes.

"Thank you, Sir. I wanted to please you." He couldn't believe he admitted his true feelings, something he wasn't accustomed to doing with most people.

322

"I like you, Alek. But I'm concerned that you're only playing for the high, so I want you to listen to me carefully before you answer my question." Rafe's voice, deep and sensual, sent a ripple of awareness to Alek.

"Yes, Sir." He hoped Rafe wouldn't change his mind about BDSM playtime. He needed this man and desired him in ways he couldn't understand.

Rafe collected the brown bag and set it on the bed. He pulled out a leather collar. Rafe helped him up to a standing position. He laced his fingers through Alek's long hair.

"I'll teach you what a sub is to a Dom, and then you'll make the final decision, but first you must learn what it is before you can decide. When we play, I want you to wear this collar. It signifies that our roles have changed. I'm in charge of your body. Do you accept this temporary collar so we can play tonight?" Rafe asked.

"Yes, Sir."

Rafe put the collar around his neck and fastened the clasp.

"What's your safeword?"

"Red, Sir."

Rafe slipped his hand down and closed it around his erection. Rafe traced each vein with his thumb. "You're

323

mine, Alek." He slapped his ass hard with his other hand. "And don't you forget that."

"No, Sir." Alek's twitching cock slapped his stomach.

Rafe reached for the bag and pulled out the nipple clamps. Rafe pinched both his tender nipples, not too hard, but enough to cause Alek to wince. Rafe licked and sucked hard on the left one. Alek loved the attention, the pain and pleasure blend. Rafe carefully attached a clamp to his extended nipple so that it couldn't retract again. The clamp stung and throbbed at the same time. Alek watched Rafe's every move. He tugged on it playfully.

"Hurt?" Rafe asked.

"Yes, Sir."

"Good. That's what I want it to do."

Rafe worked on the other side, coaxing it to hardness. He licked it and sucked it. He carefully attached the other one. A tiny chain connected the nipple clamps. He pulled on the chain while Alek winced. The more he played with the chain, the more Alek felt the pain making his cock twitch.

"You're going to wear this butt plug and think about who owns your ass."

Rafe squeezed lube generously over the plug. "Bend over."

Alek knew what that meant, so he made an about face and bent over. First Rafe lubed his finger, then pushed it in to stretch him and added a second one. Alek felt the burn and enjoyed the fingers moving around before Rafe slowly removed his fingers. Rafe carefully penetrated him with the rubber plug. It took him a while to notice Rafe was pushing in and out like he was fucking him with it. He had been feeding on the pain and pleasure, enjoying it. It was making him feel drunk. If he could only reach subspace tonight. He panted, trying to get as much air into his lungs as possible.

"Do you think you're worthy of becoming my sub?" Rafe left the plug inside and moved to face him.

"Yes, Sir." His words sounded strangled in his throat.

"Bed. Facedown."

Alek sprawled out, facedown on the bed as ordered. Rafe handcuffed each hand to the posts on the headboard, and then he used the spreader to lock his ankles to keep his legs far apart. He didn't fasten them too tightly.

"How could anyone not get hard, seeing your smoking hot sexy ass in all its glory?" Rafe asked, climbing over him and settling between his thighs. He tickled his thighs with the lightest touch of his fingers.

"Because no one sees my naked ass, Sir." Alek snickered from the tickling of his thighs, which was moving quickly to his ass cheeks.

"They better not see your naked ass unless you're working as a bartender for our parties."

"Only you, Sir."

"You're mine," Rafe whispered in his ear.

"I want you to use my ass and mouth for your pleasure whenever you want, Sir." The words rolled right out of his mouth without thinking, but they felt right, even though he didn't know how far those words would take him.

Rafe slapped his ass hard. "Don't demand. I'll decide what I want from you."

"Yes, Sir." Alek needed to remember he couldn't just say things without thinking about it. Rafe was very serious about respecting him.

Rafe grabbed his cock underneath him and gave it a tug, then stroked it up and down slowly.

"Beg to be my boy," Rafe said.

"Please, Sir," he whimpered. "Please fuck my ass. My dick hardens at the thought of you. Please, Sir. Please make me your boy. I want you on top of me, dominating me. I want you to. Please. Please. Please, Sir. Please let me get off on your orders. Make me do dirty things to you, Sir."

"Do you promise to obey and respect me?" Rafe asked.

"Yes, Sir. Please teach me how to be your boy. Please."

Rafe removed the butt plug and set it on the end table. He pulled out the large leather paddle and showed it to Alek.

"We can try to get you to subspace from the pain of the paddle. Use your safeword if you want me to stop because it hurts too much. Don't be disappointed if you don't reach subspace from it. Any questions?"

"I won't."

"Use Sir when you address me."

"Yes, Sir."

"Remember you said you wanted me to buy this paddle. Do you still want me to use it on you?"

Alek hesitated as he stared at the paddle. "Yes, Sir. I want it."

Rafe swiped the paddle in the air three times; the sound made Alek tremble. He clinched his ass cheeks, waiting for Rafe to strike.

"Twenty-five swats."

"Twenty-five?" Alek turned his head to face Rafe.

"Turn around," Rafe said in a Marine cadence. "You added another five for questioning me, so now you have thirty swats."

"Yes, Sir."

Rafe swiped the paddle in the air three times, the sound made Alek tremble. He clinched his ass cheeks, waiting for Rafe to strike. He banged the paddle against Alek's ass with all his strength. Alek wanted to scream, but no sound fell from his mouth. He held his breath as if he were grieving his own death.

"Breathe, Alek." Rafe reassured him by stroking Alek's back.

Alek couldn't breathe and felt sick to his stomach. He held his breath in and refused to exhale.

"Start breathing or I'll stop this session."

Alek heard Rafe, and he didn't want Rafe to stop, so he opened his mouth to exhale. He took in a deep breath and exhaled again. The nausea left Alek, but his ass throbbed with Rafe swatting him once. Twenty-nine more to go. *Fuck, I can do this.*

"Remember red is for stop, yellow is for pause or need to talk, and green is for go on. Are you ready for me to begin?" Rafe asked.

"Yes, Sir."

Rafe cracked the paddle down ten consecutive times on his right ass cheek with no hesitation between blows. Alek's right cheek numbed beyond the point of stinging.

"Yellow," Alek said.

Rafe stopped immediately. "Do you need a break or do you want something else?"

"I just needed a little break." Alek forced a smile.

Rafe trailed the side of Alek's neck with kisses while he stroked his back.

"I'm ready again."

Rafe swung another ten consecutive strikes to his left cheek. Alek floated off to a cloud. He didn't remember the final strikes. Slowly he became cognizant of Rafe removing his handcuffs and the spreader, then picking him up in his arms when he was done with all thirty. The paddle rested on the dresser.

When Alek's eyes stopped blinking, his surroundings were blurred. Rafe grabbed a bottle of water for Alek from the dresser, twisted the top off, and handed it to him.

"Drink this," Rafe said, displayed a concerned, fatherly expression.

When Alek sipped the cold water, his eyes focused more clearly. Alek didn't remember wrapping his arms around Rafe at all. Alek rubbed his teary eyes while he smiled at Rafe, staring back at him.

"Rafe, I think I went into subspace," Alek said in between the sips of his water and hitched breathing. When he finished the water, Rafe took the empty bottle and threw it into the recycling can.

Alek ran his fingers along Rafe's back. He flipped Alek on the bed; face down, for which he was grateful. Alek's ass throbbed. The numbness was wearing off and his muscles tightened with pain. His cock delighted in the midst of all this aching. The beautiful view of Rafe's upper body put him in the mood for sex. Sore and confused as Alek was, Rafe turned him on.

"I'm going to rub some lotion on your ass. It will help with the pain and healing." Rafe rubbed the lotion on his ass very gently. After he waited for a while, he heard the familiar sounds of Rafe lubing himself up drifted to his ears.

"I'm going to fuck your ass."

Rafe smeared lube on the crease in Alek's backside, then twisted his finger inside. He circled around and inserted another finger making a scissor-like motion. After a few minutes spent stretching his asshole, Rafe's hard cock speared into Alek's tight opening, pressed hard and

330

deep, then abruptly stopped when Alek whelped like a puppy.

"Hey, do you need more lube, boy?" Rafe asked.

"No. Fuck me... please. Fuck me hard," Alek pleaded.

Rafe held Alek's hips, pushing his chest against Alek's back, just so just his ass stuck up in the air. He aimed his cock into Alek's quivering hole. Rafe snapped his hips harder, making Alek pant and sweat.

"Fuck. Fuck. Fuck," Alek moaned, trying to push back.

Rafe growled, slapping his ass. "Don't move," he demanded.

Alek moaned nonstop when Rafe's hand stroked his erection. He groaned, loving the feeling of Rafe's cock in his tight ass while his hand stroked his slick erection.

"Fuck. I love your tight little ass," Rafe said.

Snapping his hips harder and faster, Rafe forced Alek to jolt forward from his thrusts. Alek screamed in pleasure when Rafe hit his happy gland.

"Rafe. Again, there," Alek sobbed deliriously, clawing at the sheets

Rafe puffed air, hitting Alek's prostate dead on. "There, Alek?"

Alek nodded, frantically panting heavily. His orgasm took him by surprise; he arched his back, blasting his cum onto the sheets with a scream. Rafe groaned loudly when Alek's butt muscles tightened and milked his stiff member.

"Fuck, Alek," he growled, flooding his cum deep inside his ass.

Alek whimpered softly when he felt Rafe come. He wrapped his arms around Alek and turned him to face him. He held him tightly in his arms and handed Alek a miniature chocolate bar.

Rafe cleaned them with a washcloth.

"So, what do you think of me now?" Alek asked.

"You surprised me in so many ways. First, you accepted the paddle and managed to go into subspace on your first day. You must approve all our BDSM play. I'm not going to do anything you don't want, but you made me very happy tonight," Rafe said.

"The subspace is just like Dante had said."

"I got worried when you didn't answer me, so I stopped everything and carried you to the kitchen for water. You didn't even say a word when I removed the clamps."

"I was too spaced out to talk. So, now what do we do?" Alek looked down and was surprised the nipple clamps were gone. He had lost some time near the end while he was into subspace.

"I don't know what you want. We can have BDSM playtimes when you ask. As far as you being my sub, you need to be ready, and at that point, we'll have a serious of conversations. I want to know if subspace would get old or if you would want to go back to where we don't do this anymore."

"I'm not ready to be your sub. I can see that. I want us to play and see how it goes."

"We have some toys, but you will learn it's not all about you when you enter a BDSM relationship. We'll explore different aspects of the lifestyle. Don't forget we're going with James and Dante to a BDSM club tomorrow night. You'll get glimpses of it at the club. Remember that it's very different when you live the lifestyle."

"My ass still hurts."

"I guess I marked you again."

"You sure did."

CHAPTER TWENTY-THREE

Rafe Escobar

Valerik called Rafe to meet him at the picnic table for an update on the Belanov family. Alek and the other boys were visiting Dante to discuss BDSM. Valerik sat at the picnic table alone, dominated by a profound sadness and fatigue engraved on his worn face, a telling sign of dreadful news. *More bad news about Alek's family.*

"What did you find out?" Rafe asked, as he sat across from Valerik.

"Alek must never learn the truth about his family's slaughter. He came to me at the beach looking for answers I didn't have. He was relentless with his questions about the true circumstances of his family's death. So I talked to several people who have worked closely with Sacha Belanov over the years," Valerik said in a somber tone.

"Valerik," Rafe barked. "Spit it out. What did you learn?"

"Sacha Belanov gunned down his younger brother and his family except Alek for a reason, not a good one. Sacha took Alek to his home before the police entered the scene."

"What reason? Why did he save Alek?"

"Alek's mother and Sacha fell in love while she was married to Alek's father. Sacha was convinced Alek was his son and demanded they give him Alek. They refused and told him that Alek was their son, not Sacha's. This battle for Alek went on for four years until Sacha finally lost his mind and murdered them all, leaving only Alek for him to raise as his son. This is why he told me that Alek was his son, not his nephew. He still believes Alek is his." Valerik lit a cigarette.

"Is Alek Sacha's son?" There was a long pause as they looked at one another with disbelief.

"No one knows because there was never a DNA test. However, in Sacha's mind, Alek is his."

"If Alek finds out the truth, it would destroy him. He couldn't deal with the truth. Why did he send him to me for protection?"

"Two of Sacha's cousins attempted to blackmail Sacha because they wanted to take over the family business. They threatened Sacha with turning him in and telling Alek the truth. Everyone in the family knew Sacha had murdered his younger brother's family and were aware of his claim that Alek was his son. Sacha wanted to keep Alek from learning the truth and spare himself prison time. After Sacha had his two cousins tortured and slaughtered, he burned their houses down and left their families penniless. No one in the family would challenge Sacha after the cousins had been murdered. They knew that if Sacha could kill his own brother, he'd do the same to anyone who threatened him or went against him."

"I don't know what to say." Rafe's stomach turned upside down.

"Pavel set Alek up with the drugs because he wanted Alek out of the picture. When he came out of prison, Sacha had to come up with a plan to keep Alek from the truth. So he called me and told me that the two families wanted Alek dead because he had a relationship with Burain. The Belanov family considered Alek a traitor. No one is after Alek. The fact is that Burain isn't dead. His family sent him away, but he's not dead. Sacha knew that too. Yet he allowed poor Alek to mourn."

"If I tell him the truth, Alek would be free to live his life without me and the protection society. I don't want him to leave. If I don't tell him the truth, he might hurt himself trying to find out who was responsible for his family's death. And from what you said, Sacha might kill him to protect himself from prison."

"Sacha loves Alek and wouldn't hurt him. My opinion is to leave the truth alone for Alek's sake. He wants to call his uncle and ask him about his family's murder. I told him to ask you, but the look in his eyes told me he's going to call him regardless of what anyone tells him," Valerik said.

"I know he wants to call his uncle. Alek doesn't need protection from me. Alek doesn't need to be living on the run, but still I don't think he can handle the truth. I don't know what the right decision is. I'm going to think about it first before I make any decisions."

"If Alek does question his uncle, it may be a death sentence in itself. We don't know what Sacha values more, his freedom, or his apparent son. I wonder how Sacha would take to Alek questioning him about the death of his parents suddenly," Valerik said.

"I have a lot to consider before I decide what to do about this."

"I know you'll do what's right for Alek. He belongs with you."

"Thank you. The truth is gruesome."

"Let's change the subject."

"Yes and let's never speak of this again until I make my decision."

"So, are you guys still going to the BDSM club tonight?" Valerik asked.

"Yes. Are you and Liam coming too?" Rafe asked.

"Liam wants to go, so we're going. I think Kaden and Emilio are going too."

"I've never asked you this, but were you ever a Dom?"

"I was a Dom for five years, but my sub left the relationship because he fell in love with his college professor. I never took on another sub."

"If Liam wanted to be your sub, would you collar him?"

"I don't think Liam is ready to be my sub at this point. He needs to learn more about the lifestyle, but what I've seen from him so far, I think he has the makings of a good sub for me."

"I think it's too soon for Alek too." Out of the corner of his eye, he saw Anouska standing to the side talking on the phone. Mateo was nowhere in sight. Rafe didn't trust her regardless that his brother had married her.

"I want to make sure Liam isn't in it for the high from subspace. Liam used to do drugs and he's attracted to the high. We shall see," Valerik said.

"Thanks for telling me the truth about Alek's family and investigating it for me. That means a lot to me, and I know it has put you at risk digging for information."

Rafe walked over to Anouska and said, "Who are you talking to?"

She covered the phone with her hand. "I'm talking to Mateo. He's upstairs."

Rafe didn't believe her. "Remember you are not allowed to call anyone unless they are in the group." He pulled the phone out of her hand and checked the incoming and outgoing calls. The last caller was from New York City. "You are risking our security here. You lied to my face and now you don't get a phone."

Rafe gripped Anouska's phone tightly, the whites of his knuckles clearly visible, as he walked away with fury in his footsteps. He went up two flights of stairs, pounded on the Mateo's door, and waited.

"What do you want?" Mateo asked when he answered the door.

Rafe walked right into the apartment. "We need to talk about Anouska."

"What about her?"

"Didn't you enforce the rule she's not to call anyone except members of our group?"

"She knows that. Why?"

"I took her phone away because she was talking to someone in New York City. Do you know who that might be?" Rafe swallowed hard, trying not to reveal his anger.

"No. I didn't know she called someone in New York." Mateo flashed him a look of disdain.

"Did you fucking check her phone every night like I told you to do?"

"I guess I haven't. I trusted she wouldn't call anyone out of the group."

"What the hell is going on? We can't have shit like this happening. Everyone is happy here, and now I have to figure out who she has been talking to since she's had the phone. If she is reporting to someone else about what we're doing, she's out of here."

"I'll talk to her," Mateo said.

"You're weak. Talking to her? She could be the reason someone might be killed. She's not allowed to use a phone or she's out of here and I mean it. She must never be left alone or leave the house unless she is with you or another protector. Stop her from undermining our security and safety of our members."

"Do you want us to leave?"

"Not you. I wish to hell that you hadn't married her. We don't know anything about her."

"Rafe, I know you think she's up to something, but she's just a lost girl. She had a horrible life. Give her the benefit of the doubt here. I'll make sure she doesn't call anyone anymore."

"See that you do. I'll get back to you about who she's been calling. I swear if she's a mole for one of our enemies, she's in big trouble with me."

"Are you threatening to harm my wife?"

"It's a warning. Call it what you fucking want," Rafe said.

Mateo shoved Rafe against the wall and pulled his arm back to swing at him. Rafe blocked him, shoved him back to the couch.

Rafe shouted, "Don't ever do that again!"

He walked out of the apartment and slammed the door behind him. What if Mateo had been working with Anouska and one of their enemies? After listening to Valerik discussing Alek's family drama, Rafe's brother might be trying to ruin him and the society. After all, Mateo and Anouska weren't gay, and this society had been created for gay men needing protection. Rafe hated this paranoid thinking but he also couldn't dismiss it as unrealistic. It was possible, and he'd have to keep a close eye on Mateo and Anouska.

When Rafe left the building, he noticed Anouska wasn't on the grounds. She either left the premises or went to visit the others. James was sitting at the picnic table with Kaden. He sat down with them.

"Is everything okay?" Kaden asked.

"Did you guys see Anouska?" Rafe asked.

"She was outside, then she disappeared," Kaden said.

"Was anyone with her?" Rafe asked.

"No. She was alone. What's going on?" Kaden asked.

"I caught her using the phone to call someone." Rafe sighed. "I need to check her phone now." Rafe pulled out her phone.

"I don't trust her." James maintained eye contact with Rafe. "I didn't want to say anything because she's your brother's wife."

"I don't know. She seems harmless," Kaden said.

Rafe went through her contacts, and they were all Russian names.

"Where's Valerik?" Rafe asked.

"He's getting some hot dogs to grill," James said.

"What did you find on her phone?" Kaden asked.

"Russian names. None of which I know."

"I don't want to sound like a conspiracy nut, but do you think she could be a mole for Alek's uncle?" Kaden asked.

"She was with Mateo before Alek got out of prison," Rafe said.

"But if Alek's uncle planned to send him here to you, he could have planted her."

"No, that can't be. She was with him before I called Mateo to join the society."

"But he knew eventually you'd be in contact with your brother," Kaden said.

"No," Rafe said. "None of that makes any sense. I don't think she's working for Sacha. I'm worried she had something to do with Eduardo. I mean how the hell did he know the details of our whereabouts? Someone told him. That someone either followed us or is part of us."

James added, "I hope you don't think any of us protectors are a part of that."

"No. I don't think our boys are either. I'm still worried Anouska is a plant. She lived in Los Angeles for a time. She could have connected with Eduardo. And she and Mateo just so happened not to attend that pool party," Rafe said.

"And got married? I wonder whose idea that was," James said.

"I don't know, but watch her and Mateo," Rafe said, planting more doubts about both of them.

"Mateo?" James asked.

"He married her. I just had a fight with him over Anouska."

"That can't be good," Kaden said.

Silence fell upon them as they lowered their eyes in deep thought.

CHAPTER TWENTY-FOUR

Alek Belanov

Alek passed out beers to all the guys in the living room. Dante opened a bag of chips and pretzels for them to munch on during their meeting.

"Did anyone play with their new toys from the Sex Mart store?" Dante asked.

"Yes. We did," Liam said.

"And?" Dante asked.

"I didn't get into subspace, but Valerik used that paddle on me. He swatted me ten times and nothing happened. But he used those handcuffs and the spreader and I couldn't move. I got really turned on spread out on the bed while he fucked me."

"Well, sometimes it takes a while to go into subspace," Dante said.

"I didn't go into subspace," Emilio said. "Kaden was so sexy last night. He ordered me to do all sorts of dirty things. He cracked the paddle on me a few times. When nothing happened, he told me I had to work up to receiving more swats. He handcuffed me too. That was fun."

"What about you, Alek?" Dante asked.

"I went into subspace. It was exactly as you described it to be. Rafe swatted me thirty times and I'm still sore, but he also used nipple clamps and a butt plug. He made me do all sorts of things. I think for me, the pain took me there."

"Thirty swats? Is he out of his mind?" Emilio asked.

"No, he's not. He knew how to take me where I wanted to go. Did it hurt? Fuck, yes, but at the end, it was all worth it."

"Alek is right. For most, it takes a great deal of pain to go into subspace. But a BDSM relationship isn't just entering subspace. Tonight, James and I will be in a private room to do a scene. You're all invited," Dante said.

"I can't wait," Alek said.

"Me, either," Emilio said.

"I'm excited too," Liam said.

Someone knocked on the door, so Dante answered it and Rafe stood there.

"Hey, I hate to break up your meeting, but I need Alek."

Alek headed toward Rafe.

Rafe turned to Emilio. "Hey, Emilio. Are you okay?"

"Why wouldn't I be?" Emilio looked confused as he smiled graciously.

"No reason. Just checking on my favorite son." A smile ruffled Rafe's mouth.

"Do you have other sons?"

"No, I'm just playing with you. See you guys tonight," Rafe said.

Alek didn't like the look in Rafe's eyes. He seemed distant and upset. Something must have happened. He followed Rafe down the stairs to their apartment. He went inside and grabbed a beer, but Alek had one from Dante's place.

"What's wrong?" Alek asked.

"Sit down and let's talk."

Alek took the chair across from Rafe. "This must be important."

"It is. A few things happened while you were hanging out with the guys."

"Like what?"

"I'm not sure we can stay here. Anouska has been using her phone to communicate with Russians. I don't know what she's doing. Valerik is researching the names of the contacts on her phone."

"What does all this mean?" Alek felt torn about Anouska.

"It means the rule of not phoning anyone unless they're in our group must be taken seriously, and this includes you. No calls to your uncle unless I give you permission. One wrong call could cause one of our members to die."

"Did you call me down here to tell me something that I already know?"

"Did you know about Anouska?"

"Well, no. I didn't know she called other people. She's probably lonely. Maybe she called a friend from the outside."

"It doesn't matter if she's lonely. She must follow the rules. And with all this shit going on, I had a fight with Mateo."

"About Anouska?"

"Yes. Mateo doesn't think he has to follow the rules here, nor does he enforce the rules with Anouska. I told him if I find out she's a mole and is working against the society, she's in big trouble with me. He saw it as a threat."

"Well, isn't it a threat? She's his wife," Alek asked.

"I'm not sure what it is. I'm just so pissed right now. Don't do anything to make me angrier than I am."

"What are you talking about? I thought we had great sex last night. Everything was good between us, and now

350

you're suggesting I would do something to fuck all that up?" Alek said.

"I'm sorry, Alek. I had a bad morning. Really bad and I have to make some decisions that are life changing. I'm not in a good place right now."

"We've moved before, and we can do it again. Don't worry about the decisions. We'll do anything you want or need to help out?"

"Don't call your uncle. I'm worried you're going to start something."

"Are you telling me never to call my uncle or to wait until the group is stabilized in a better location?"

"Part of the agreement with your uncle is that I keep you and don't allow you to contact him. If you do, he might destroy our society."

"Are you serious?" Alek didn't buy what Rafe was trying to sell him. No one could stop him from calling his uncle. He needed to know the truth. Something had triggered Rafe in this intolerance of Alek finding out what happened to his family.

"Do not call him. I don't want to discuss this any further."

"Yes, Sir," Alek said to appease Rafe's anger.

When someone pounded on the door, Rafe answered it. Valerik walked into the kitchen.

He took a seat at the table.

"Do you want me to leave?" Alek asked.

"No. You need to hear this."

"Thank you."

"So, is it bad?" Rafe asked.

"She made five calls, all to the same person. It seems this person is from Russia. He's in the US now. I don't know how she knows this man. He also left her a message that he wanted to meet her in New York City for two weeks."

"What did she say to that?" Rafe asked.

"She told him she couldn't right now but would when she could get away."

"Is this Russian man working with any of our enemies?"

"No. Not to my knowledge," Valerik said.

"Mateo is so fucking stupid. What the hell is he doing with her? When I first met her, she was sweet and helped us, but I should have known better than to trust her," Rafe said.

"Let me talk to Mateo. You're too involved and you already had one encounter with your brother. Let's try to keep this civil," Valerik said.

"That's a good idea. I don't want to talk to him right now."

"I think Anouska is lonely. That's why she wanted Sara to travel with us," Alek said.

"I'm sure she is, but why did she marry Mateo then?" Rafe asked.

"She loves him," Alek said.

"If she loves Mateo, then she can't be lonely in his company," Rafe said.

"That's all I have for you." Valerik handed the phone to Rafe. "I'll go talk to him now." He closed the door on his way out and left them with a quiet and tension filled apartment.

"So what are we going to do?" Alek asked, trying to break the uncomfortable silence and release the tension in the room.

"I'd like to find a bench on the boardwalk and maybe eat some pizza."

"That sounds good to me. Anytime on the boardwalk is good for me."

They headed to the boardwalk and ordered pizza and coke, then carried it to one of the benches overlooking the ocean.

"Which beaches do you like better? The California ones or here?" Rafe asked.

"I like the beaches in California better. They're free, and the lifeguards aren't whistle-blowing control freaks. I just miss California. But there's no boardwalk in California that's like this one."

"True. I'm going to be making a decision where we'll stay permanently very soon. You'll be able to go to school or work. Whatever you want to do. You can also do nothing as you have enough money to stay home," Rafe said.

"I want to go to school full time. That's what I should have been doing two years ago, but someone had hated me so much they had set me up. I'm still angry about it. I want to know who did this to me and why. I don't believe Burain's family did this anymore."

"Who do you think set you up?"

Alek tried to hold back his warm tears rolling down his cheeks. He fisted them away.

"Hey, I didn't mean to upset you. You don't have to answer me."

"I'm afraid of my own thoughts. Since I've been out of prison and away from my uncle, I see my past so differently."

"That's called growing up. You're seeing things like a man, not a child."

"I wonder if it's that simple. The reason I want to talk to my uncle is to find the truth. I'm so angry with him, and I still can't believe he sent me here."

"Are you unhappy with me?" Rafe asked.

"This is not about you. Of course I love being with you but I had a life before you, before prison. I was used to having choices on where I went and who I went with. Living with you under these circumstances makes me feel that all my personal choices on a daily basis have been erased."

"I'm sorry you're struggling with your past. I would like you to look forward to our future. I know you're not here by choice, and I have to limit some of your freedom to keep you safe. I want you to know that I'm happy I picked you. Maybe in time, you'll feel that way about me."

"It's not about me disliking you because you're the brightest star in my day from the moment I wake up right beside you. I never had a live-in boyfriend. I've always lived in my uncle's home," Alek said.

"Tell me, if you had met me in a bar, would you have gone home with me?"

"I sure would have. You're everything I've ever wanted. It's the loss of freedom that bothers me more than anything. I used to love to go to gay clubs to dance. I hung out at the beach."

"I'm sorry we won't be near the beach where we're going, but in the summer, we could stay here in Seaside Heights.

"What are you going to do with your home in California?"

"We'll visit when we have the once-a-month parties for new members and protectors. Right now, it's not safe in California for most of us."

After they finished their pizza, they walked to the apartment. Valerik, James, and Kaden were at the picnic table. The boys sat on the other side of the apartment grounds. Mateo and Anouska weren't outside.

"Why don't you sit with the boys," Rafe said with a gentle tone.

"Okay. See you later," Alek said.

"Remember I want to be with you."

"I love being with you." Alek blew him a kiss.

CHAPTER TWENTY-FIVE

Rafe Escobar

The sun burned strongly, forcing Rafe to slip his sunglasses over his eyes. He sat at the picnic table with all the protectors except Mateo. There was no reason for Mateo to be missing from the meeting.

"Where's Mateo?" Rafe asked.

Kaden said, "He called an Uber, and they left with their luggage."

"They what?" Rafe shouted. "No one stopped them?"

"He told me to tell you he and Anouska needed a honeymoon. He said he wanted to go before he started school," Kaden said.

"Why didn't he tell me this?" Rafe pounded the table with his fists.

"He knows you're angry with him. We all told him to wait until you came back. He said he didn't have to clear his honeymoon with you."

"He's such a spoiled brat. My father is still looking for him, and whoever called Anouska wants her. He's such a damn fool. I can't believe he pulled this shit again."

"Don't let it spoil tonight," James said. "You and Alek need to have some fun."

"I guess we do. Are you ready to hear about our next move?"

"When are we moving?" Valerik asked.

"In three weeks. We're going to a camping area where I rented five cabins. They're modern cabins with everything in them, and the college and community college are nearby. We can work there if you want to, but our cabins are away from people. It's similar to Fawnskin. We'll stay there for a year. After that, we'll see how things go and whether it's safe to return to California."

"How far is it from here?" James asked.

"About two hours."

Emilio walked over to the picnic table and waited for Rafe to stop speaking.

"Rafe, I have a note for you from Mateo." He handed Rafe the folded note.

"Thank you."

"I want you to spend an afternoon with just me, so we can, you know, talk about our new roles in our relationship," Emilio said.

"I'd like that too."

"Kaden said he'd stay with Alek."

"Okay, we'll do that." Emilio was right. They needed to spend some time alone. Somehow, he needed to enrich

358

their relationship. Maybe Emilio wanted more parental guidance from him and less friendship.

"What about dinner?" James asked.

"Want to eat out?" Rafe asked. "Let's give you guys a night off."

"Sounds good," James said.

"I'll stop somewhere on our way to the club," Rafe said. "I'm going to round up Alek and get ready for later. Meet you guys here at seven."

Rafe found Alek, and they made their way to their apartment.

"Are you okay?" Alek asked.

"I don't know. I have a note from Mateo. Give me a minute so I can read it."

Rafe opened the note and read it silently.

Rafe,

Sorry to bail on you again. I know we're not getting along and this would be the best time for Anouska and me to go on our honeymoon. I'll be back when we move again. We'll be gone for three weeks. We're going out of the country so we should be fine. Sorry about today.

Love,

Mateo

"Are they coming back?" Alek asked.

"Yes, when we move. They went on a honeymoon."

"That's good."

"Now, tonight I want you to wear your play collar so no one touches you in the club. If you walk in there without a collar, the guys might think you're available."

"I'd be honored to wear it."

"Take a shower first," Rafe said.

Alek headed to the bathroom and left Rafe alone in the kitchen. He didn't know how to feel about Mateo leaving the group again. Something seemed all wrong about them leaving. Was Anouska the reason, or did Mateo leave on his own? When Alek was dressed, he walked to the kitchen.

Rafe's phone rang, so he answered it.

Harlan, Eduardo's replacement, said, "Eduardo's boy left Fawnskin when I arrived. The other protectors said he told them he'd stay at Eduardo's side. He's living with Eduardo's brother until Eduardo gets out. I need my own boy to protect."

"I didn't expect that. It's at the boys own risk and we can't force him to remain under our protection, but I hope he's made the right decision and is, in fact, safe."

"I hope so too."

"At the beginning of next month, we'll be having another party, and you can choose one of the new ones. I'm

360

sorry to hear this, but it will give you a chance to get to know everyone and how things work."

"Excellent. I'm looking forward to your famous parties. Something odd happened here yesterday. A girl named Sara showed up on the premises. She said she worked for you and wanted to work here at Fawnskin."

"Did you tell her no?" Rafe figured that his father was determined to locate Matco and Emilio. Rafe thought his father would have fired her, but if she's the maid's daughter, he obviously gave her another chance.

"Of course I did. She was quite insistent about the job, but I told her no. I can't imagine having her work here with all the gay men."

"She's pregnant. Be careful. I think she's working for my father and looking for my brother and Emilio. She tried to work for us, but we kicked her out. I hope she's gone for good now."

"Don't worry. She's not going to get near the cabins. I drove her into town. I just wanted you to know what was going on. The group members had so many complaints about Eduardo. They see me as their savior. I'd like to stay here instead of going back to the large home."

"That's fine. Just remember that everyone in your group must work to afford their living expenses. None of

361

the boys paid for their protection, so they must work. This is an experiment for me. I wanted to see if we could protect poor gay men who were under threat," Rafe said.

"Most of them work. I think one or two don't, but they're looking."

"Keep me updated. Let me know if you get short on money for food. I don't want them to go without food."

"Will do. Thanks."

"I'll see you at the next party so you can choose someone to protect."

"Tell me how it works," Harlan said.

"We gather men who need protection or they come to us. They go to the party. We insist that they be naked and wear a tie. You can see what you're getting first. At the end of the party, you choose the one you want. You pick up the tie on a table that matches the color of the tie they are wearing. When you place your tie on who you choose, he's yours. It's a lot of fun."

"The guys here said sex goes on at the party. Is that true?"

"Blowjobs only. No one fucks. So see you there. I'll email you the info when I know we have enough new ones."

"Thanks."

CHAPTER TWENTY-SIX

Alek Belanov

After they showed their IDs at the door, Alek perked up when he walked inside the club. The rules were clear and explained at the entrance. They could watch any show as long as the drapes were open. The bouncer instructed them not to put themselves in harm's way.

No loud talking, cell phones, or anything else that would detract from the ambiance was permitted. They could only touch if the people conducting the activity invited them, and finally, no meant exactly that.

Smelling the new leather and looking around at the men in their leather made Alek's cock twitch. A few were leading other men around on leashes attached to their collars. Many were dancing to loud music while strobe lights danced over the bodies. Upon first sight, Alek spotted the Dungeon Masters wearing leather slacks with matching vests. On the back of their vests, the words *Dungeon Master* were written in bright red. Alek counted six of them spread-out through the club.

"What are the Dungeon Masters for?" Alek asked.

"They're here to keep everyone safe and comfortable. They know how to operate equipment. If you break the

363

club rules, they'll remove you, but if a Dom abuses a sub, then the perpetrator will be asked to leave" Rafe said.

They first encountered a man splayed across a spanking bench on the stage, moaning as a Clark Kent look-alike vigorously applied a paddle to his ass. At the end of the swats, the Dom massaged oil into the tender, bruised skin. The young man looked blissful and unfettered by his pain.

Alek turned his head and saw two men wearing nothing but a miniature cage padlocked to their genitals. It hurt just looking at them. Who would do such a horrible thing to a man?

"Their cocks are in jail," Alek said.

"They're wearing cock cages, which prevents them from getting an erection or coming," Rafe said.

Alek suppressed an oncoming laugh, knowing it would be inappropriate. Emilio stood beside them with Kaden.

"I don't ever want one of those," Emilio said.

"What's the point if you can't have a hard-on or come?" Alek asked.

"Many Doms practice edging with their subs," Rafe explained. "If they excite their subs to the brink of coming without allowing them to come, it makes the orgasm more intense when the Dom finally allows them to come."

"Are you boys freaked out in here?" Kaden asked.

"No, I like watching," Emilio said.

"It's very interesting in here," Alek said.

Alek scanned the room, and there was a man in leather pants, and an elderly gentleman dressed in a French maid outfit, and provocative pictures of nude men in contorted positions on the walls. Rafe found a large table to accommodate the group, and once they were seated, they ordered drinks. The boys were staring at different activities going on around them.

"So, when you're into BDSM, do you have to parade around naked with a leash?" Alek asked.

"You don't have to," Rafe said. "This club allows naked men. Most clubs don't permit complete nudity unless you're in a private room. There are rooms down the hallway in which some keep the drapes open to allow others to watch their scene. Some will display their bondage scenes, spanking scenes, torture scenes, and sex if the Dom chooses that."

James said, "Dante and I rented a room for an hour, and you're all invited into the room, or you can watch through the hallway window."

"Dante, are you nervous?" Liam asked.

"A little. I hope I don't make a fool of myself," Dante said.

"You can never do that, Dante," James said as he kissed him.

Kaden said, "We're going to check the rooms. Does anyone else want to come with us?"

They all followed Kaden to the hallway of rooms, stopping at the first open draped room. It had stocks similar to the ones in the town square years ago. After the Dom locked his sub in the stocks, he spanked his balls with a crop.

"That looks painful." Alek thought the balls were too sensitive, and the Dom should be spanking his ass.

"It gives his Dom pleasure. Remember that the sub serves the Dom, and his pleasure comes first. What he's doing to the sub's balls is called CBT, which stands for Cock and Ball Torture. Playing with a man's scrotum can be painful or pleasurable. The goal of CBT is to make it both. Some subs don't like it, so the Dom won't practice that. It's a good punishment too," Rafe said.

"My balls hurt just looking at it," Alek said.

"Mine do too," Emilio said.

"It's not that bad," Dante said.

Emilio chimed in, "Did you let James do that?"

366

"Yes, I did. My last Dom attached weights to my balls."

"And I'll be giving your balls a damn good whipping if you talk back to me," James winked at Dante as he spoke.

Dante's face turned red, and the other guys laughed.

In another room, there was a giant cage and inside was a thin naked man. The Dom was shouting at him, but they couldn't hear what he was saying. There were other people in the room, some throwing ice at him.

They moved to another room that displayed two men in a shower. The bigger man was peeing on the smaller man.

"That's a no," Alek said.

"It's a no for me too," Emilio said.

Liam added, "No, never."

Dante added, "It's not as bad as it looks."

All the other boys scrunched up their faces, looking ill. They moved down the hallway, and a man was whipping a young man on a St. Andrew's cross. His facial expression looked spaced out, not in any pain.

"We're going to be in room five, so come back in twenty minutes while I set up the scene," James said.

At the same time as they returned to their table in the main room, a man was being tied up, and then he was suspended from the ceiling, just left to hang there. The whole process mesmerized Alek. On the opposite side of the room, a man was licking another man's boots.

"Is that large shower in one of the rooms only for pissing on a guy?" Emilio asked.

"Should I tell him, or do you want to tell him, Rafe?" Kaden asked.

"Tell him Kaden."

"They are for men who are into blood play or urine or scat."

"That's disgusting," Emilio said.

"I wonder if James was ever into that," Liam said.

"Ask him. I'm sure he'll tell you," Valerik said.

"I can tell you that he's not into that," Rafe said. "We had a discussion about that and other BDSM activities when he told me he wanted to practice BDSM with Dante."

"So did you tell him he wasn't allowed to do that?" Valerik asked.

"I did, but I didn't need to. Since I own the Gay Protection Society, I wanted to make sure all the clients are safe when they play with their protector. Playing with blood and scat is dangerous. I don't dictate to any Dom unless I think it's not safe."

When it was time to watch James with Dante, they all entered the room and sat on a bench. James was fully dressed, and Dante was naked, tied to the St. Andrew's cross. His ass was visible to everyone in the room and neither seemed uncomfortable.

James said, "I'm going to lube Dante, then try the beads."

James slowly inserted the beads inside Dante's ass as he panted unable to move as they went inside. As soon as one bead popped inside Dante, the next stopped against the entrance of his butt hole ready to be pushed in. James slipped his hand under Dante, stroking his erection gently up and down. His hand slid to the base of Dante's cock, squeezing it before he moved back to the cockhead. He gradually added the next bead. Dante's ass muscles contracted as each new bead entered him; his legs shook slightly when James tugged on them a bit. Alek thought the beads looked fun and would like to try them out with Rafe.

When James pulled out a remote from his pocket, he pressed the setting on the remote, and Dante moaned. James switched the setting to a higher level, sending Dante into wiggling his ass and groaning. Then James pulled the beads out one by one.

Once the beads were pulled out, James picked up a whip and used it on Dante, beginning with his ass, and upper thighs. The whip painted thin red lines without any bleeding. James turned to the group and said, "We need privacy now. Please leave and close the drapes on your way out."

***

When they arrived home, Rafe and Alek sat up in bed.

"Tell me, what did you think of tonight?" Rafe asked.

"We were more like an audience looking in than taking part in it."

"That's true. We're not in a BDSM relationship, so of course, we wouldn't be part of what they were doing. Overall, how did you feel about what you saw going on?"

"I think I'm not ready to go public about my sexual fantasies. I like when we play BDSM with the toys, but as far as it carrying on into our daily routine, I'm not ready for it. I want to slowly learn more. I do want to please you and that makes me feel guilty because I know you'd like this with us."

"I'm a little disappointed, but I'm a very patient man."

370

"I know, but I'm just not ready yet. I hope we can still do scenes when we're having sex."

"Of course we can."

CHAPTER TWENTY-SEVEN

Alek Belanov

Alek took his phone with him into the bathroom while Rafe went outside to meet Emilio to spend the day with him while Kaden would stay with Alek. He told Rafe he'd be out after he used the bathroom. He knew he wasn't allowed to use the phone to call anyone except the members of the group. At this point, he didn't care. He needed to know more about why his uncle had banished him. Thoughts had circled in his head while he'd tried to sleep last night. He had to know the truth about his family. Before he went out to meet Kaden, he decided to call his uncle Sacha.

"Who is calling me on my private number?" Uncle Sacha asked in his thick Russian accent.

"Alek." His voiced cracked from hearing his uncle who he had loved all his life. He missed him in so many ways. Tears filled his eyes as he waited for a response.

"What's wrong?" Uncle Sacha sounded concerned about his well-being.

"I miss you," Alek said, wiping his tears with the back of his fist.

"I miss you too but I told you that I couldn't protect you anymore. It's not safe for you to be with me."

"I know that, but I need some information from you," Alek said.

"Alek, you can't come home. It's not safe for you. I'm dealing with many enemies, some in our own family."

"I don't want to come home. That's not why I'm calling you." Alek felt justified when he finally said something that might hurt his uncle. He was still angry over his banishment, but still missed him.

"You sound upset and angry. What do you want, then?"

"I want the truth about my family's death. You know the truth, but you lied to me. Pavel told me *he* should have killed me too since I was a traitor just like my family was. Who is the *he*?" Alek's voice rose as his stomach twisted. This was the first time he had ever confronted his uncle. It was easier on the phone because he didn't know if he could have done this in person.

"Why do you want to go over history?"

"Are you listening to me? I just told you why. When Pavel dropped me off at the party, he told me the killer should have murdered me too. He said I was a traitor like my family."

"Pavel was playing games with you. He means no harm to you."

"No, he wasn't playing. He's always wanted to take my place, and now you've allowed him to replace me. Why did you even bother taking me in only to cast me out of the family? What are you hiding from me?"

"No one can ever take your place. I've only loved you. My decision to send you away wasn't an easy one. I had to protect you from my enemies. You should not have to pay for things I've done. My enemies threatened to take you out to punish me. I won't allow anyone to touch you, even if it means we must be apart until I can fix this. Please believe me. I never did anything to hurt you. I'm suffering without you here. I was praying you'd find a happy life with Rafe. He's just your type, and that's why I wanted him to protect you. You're safe with him. Tell me you do like Rafe."

"I can't lie. I do like him very much. He's good to me, and you made a good choice with him, but that doesn't answer my questions about my family. Why didn't they kill me?" Alek knew his uncle was trying to sidetrack him and avoid the subject at hand.

"You were hiding in the toy box. Remember I was the one who told you to do this if you heard gunshots?"

"My father told me to do that if I heard guns going off."

"He may have told you that too."

"It doesn't matter about all that. I want to know who took my family away from me."

"I told you who. They didn't know you existed."

"Are you still trying to tell me that my parents were working with a Mexican cartel?"

"Yes. I know you don't want to hear this, but your parents made a bad deal, and the Mexicans took them down."

"I don't believe you." Alek shouted. "You're lying to me. Please tell me the truth."

Alek heard someone knocking on the front door and figured it was Kaden. He had to answer the door before he broke into the apartment. But he also needed answers from his uncle.

"I'm working on fixing the problem so you can return home to me. I want you to finish school. This isn't fair to you, but I hope you enjoy your time away until then."

"Why did you allow Pavel to see where I was going?"

"He's my driver and your cousin. Why not?"

"I think he set me up with the drugs because he was the only one who would gain something with me in prison. He wants me out of the picture permanently."

"Pavel would never do that. I don't know why you think Pavel wants to hurt you. He doesn't. He loves you."

"No, he doesn't. Thanks for raising me, but I'm never coming home." Alek ended the call and raced to the living room.

Kaden had already unlocked the door and stood inside the apartment. "What's going on in here?"

"I was in the bathroom, not feeling very well," Alek said.

"Do you want to go back to bed?" Kaden asked.

"No, I'm going to have something to eat."

"How about we eat on the boardwalk?"

Alek heard Kaden's words but was unable to answer.

"What's wrong, Alek?" Kaden asked as he inched closer to him.

Alek's thoughts weren't clear enough at this point to understand, but he knew something was terribly wrong. Knowing his uncle wouldn't ever tell him the truth troubled Alek even more. The old wounds of losing his family haunted him again. His uncle defending Pavel deepened the pain after the phone conversation. His uncle had discounted Alek's questions.

The pain in his chest was agonizing, hurting like a deep gash. Even breathing and swallowing pained him, and at the same time, Alek's stomach tightened as he became overwhelmed with thoughts. Within moments, his knees weakened. His vision blurred and he couldn't see properly. He barely registered the fact that it felt like all the blood was rushing from his head to his feet. Little black dots swarmed his vision, the corners slowly fading into black. His knees gave out and he collapsed into blackness. Beside him, a voice chattered nonsense, the words unclear. Darkness pulled him into a cloud. He tried to fight the blackness, but it was too strong. He finally gave in, it overtook him. Everything faded out and nothing mattered.

Alek had collapsed into Kaden's arms. He had no idea where he was or where he needed to go to be safe. Kaden held on to him, preventing him from hitting the floor.

Kaden helped him to the bed and sat alongside him. Alek's phone rang; Kaden removed it from his pocket and answered it. That's when Alek opened his eyes.

"Give me my phone," Alek said.

"Relax, Alek. Don't worry about the phone. I'm going to get you some water. You need to rest. You fainted."

"Who called me?"

"Wrong number." Kaden left the bedroom and returned with a bottle of water.

"Thanks," Alek said.

"You need bed rest."

"Why did I faint?" Alek's head throbbed.

"Not eating could be a reason, but you said you didn't feel well."

Alek's tears rolled down his cheeks, and he wiped them away with the back of his hand. He hated that Kaden was witnessing him crying. Sadness overwhelmed him and nothing would lighten his mood.

"Hey, tell me what's wrong," Kaden said.

"I can't talk about it."

"Why did you call your uncle when Rafe and I told you not to use your phone?"

"How do you know I called him?" Alek's head throbbed again.

"He called back. That's one way I knew, but there are other ways."

"What did he want?"

"He wanted to talk to you. He said you hung up on him."

"I did. He continues to lie to me. I don't believe anything he has to say."

"Do you want to call him back?"

"No."

"I'll be right back. Don't move."

"I'm too miserable to move."

Alek closed his eyes, wondering if his uncle had changed his mind about telling him the truth. Kaden returned with hot soup and a sandwich on a tray.

"Eat, you'll feel better."

"Are you going to tell Rafe about the phone call?"

"I don't know. I should tell him, but I understand your need to know the truth. I guess I won't this time."

"Thanks." After Alek finished his soup, he nibbled on his sandwich and drank the water.

"You know I'm glad you're here with Rafe. He hasn't had anyone in so long. I know he wants you here with him."

"I want that too. At first, I didn't. I wanted to go home and live my life. I see now, I never really had a real home. My uncle took me in, but he also threw me out. He refuses to tell me what happened to my family."

"I'm sorry you lost your family when you were a boy. Rafe told me about it."

"I was also set up with drugs and sent to prison for two years. It would have been longer if I didn't have good behavior. Going to prison was a nightmare. I'm not used to those sorts of men. My uncle could have done something, but he told me I was safer in there. What the hell does he know about being in prison? I wasn't safe at all."

"No, you weren't safe in prison. You're too pretty for those ugly guys. You'll never go back because when Rafe has your back, you're safe from any danger. Trust me, I know him, and he has never turned his back on someone he commits to protect."

"Do you still like Rafe?"

"I see you've been talking to Emilio. Figures. I love Rafe like a brother. As I told Emilio, we had a short relationship in the Marines, and that part didn't work out for us. But we remained very close to each other."

"Rafe told me, not Emilio," Alek said.

"I'm surprised he mentioned it. It doesn't matter really because we each have someone we love and care for now. I hope you don't dislike me because of my history with Rafe."

"I don't dislike you, but I don't really know you other than what Emilio has to say, and he speaks highly of you."

"How are you feeling?" Kaden felt Alek's forehead.

"Depressed. I don't know. I just feel like I'll never find out the truth. It makes me feel hopeless."

"Don't feel hopeless. Rafe is investigating your family situation. Until then, try to enjoy your time with him. I want you two to work out."

"Thanks."

CHAPTER TWENTY-EIGHT

Rafe Escobar

After Rafe instructed Emilio how to steer the boat, he took over. Rafe wanted to teach Emilio all the things he hadn't had the opportunity to when Emilio was a boy.

"Great job, Emilio," Rafe said.

"I don't know why I feel so strange around you. A part of me feels like I lost my favorite cousin. It feels like Rafe died. And now that you're my father, I don't know you. What happened to our relationship?"

"Nothing we shared is dead. What we had as cousins still exists. What we felt toward each other remains. We can deepen our relationship because now we both know I'm your father. I want that with you. What do you want?"

"I want to be able to talk to you about everything like I used to. Those special conversations we had, I'd never discuss with my father who raised me."

"Here's the thing. Not all fathers raise their children the same way. If I had raised you, I would have allowed you more freedom and choice. Many times when Uncle Reuben made some decisions that I didn't agree with, I had to bite my tongue. He didn't allow you enough freedom.

But all that's in the past. I want us to grow even closer than we were."

"I want that too. You were always my hero and still are," Emilio said.

Rafe hugged Emilio and kissed him.

"So, how is it going with Kaden?" Rafe asked.

"He's perfect for me. I hope he's not with me as a favor to you."

"Kaden wouldn't ever do me a favor when it concerns who he sleeps with. You caught his eye. He told me he's so happy with you and cares for you."

"Do you think it's weird that he used to be with you and now me?"

"Not at all. Kaden believed you were my cousin. So no. Did he tell you about our relationship?" Rafe asked.

"I asked him because I thought he was too close to you."

"Yes, we're best friends. I'm sure he told you we didn't work out as lovers. He prefers you, and I prefer Alek."

"He said the same thing, so that makes sense."

"Did you tell Kaden about your past?" Rafe asked.

"No. I was afraid he'd ask you to send me to the Ranch."

"Kaden is very understanding. He wasn't perfect when I met him. You might be surprised to learn about who he really is."

"Did you tell him about my past?"

"No. I told him you were my cousin and that my father wanted you murdered because you were gay. That's all he knows. It's up to you two to tell each other about your pasts, not me."

"I wish your father loved me. I know he hates gays, but you're gay."

"My father doesn't really believe I'm gay because I had you. I refused to take over his business, which angered him, but he thought he had Mateo. He didn't want to take over either, and my father blames me for brainwashing Mateo. One of the reasons he hates you is to hurt me. When he found out you were selling your body to men, that's when he wanted you gone."

"I don't know how he found out."

"He finds out about everything. I learned that at an early age. It doesn't matter what you do to cover; he'll find out. He was a mean father, and I wouldn't wish him on anyone. In a way, you were lucky you didn't have to grow up in his home."

After Rafe took Emilio to lunch, they returned to Rafe's apartment. Kaden was sitting on the couch watching TV.

"Where's Alek?" Rafe asked.

"We need to talk alone. He's sleeping right now. Emilio, hang out here while I talk to Rafe."

"Okay." Emilio sat down and changed the channel.

Rafe followed Kaden across the hallway to his apartment.

"What's going on?" Rafe asked.

"Before I tell you, I need you to promise not to act upon what I say. I promised Alek I wouldn't tell you, but it's too important not to."

"Why would you do that?"

"Alek fainted in my arms today. He's not feeling well. He needed me to lean on when he was so upset," Kaden said.

"I won't act on it, but don't do shit like that again. I'm in charge of him, and he's my lover."

"I know who he is to you, but he needed attention at that moment, not when you returned."

"What happened?"

"He called his uncle, and it didn't go well. He wanted to know about his family. His uncle continued to tell him the same lie. Alek was so upset that he hung up on him."

"He wasn't supposed to use the phone outside of our group," Rafe said. "Is this what you didn't want me to act on?"

"Yes. He wants to know the truth, and he'll find out himself. He's very upset. His uncle called back, and he told me to have Alek return his call. Alek didn't want to talk to him. I think you need to tell him the truth."

"He can't handle it. He'd be devastated if he knew. I don't want him hurt anymore."

"The problem is you can't stop him from learning the truth. He'll find out without you. He'll also figure out you knew, and then he'll leave you for keeping the truth from him. I would if you knew something that was that important to me," Kaden said.

"I don't see anything positive coming out of telling him."

"He's an adult. Shouldn't he know who murdered his family in cold blood? Shouldn't he know Pavel set him up?"

"I don't know that there's a good outcome either way. I need to think about it."

"You're going to regret not telling him," Kaden said.

"I'll decide after I think on it more. Thanks for being there for him. I guess you weren't expecting to be his confidant today," Rafe said.

"I don't mind at all. I know you'd do the same for me."

"I would, especially since you're with my son."

"How did your day go with him?"

"It was okay. He shared how uncomfortable he was with the change of our roles. I think it will work out when we spend more time together."

"You do need more time with Emilio. I'm sorry you have to go through all this with Alek. I wished things with him would be easier on you."

"Thanks. I'm going to check on Alek, and I'll send Emilio back here."

"Good luck, Rafe."

"Thanks."

Rafe left the apartment and entered his. Emilio turned off the TV and left.

Rafe's head pounded, and he took two aspirins. When he walked into the bedroom, Alek was sitting up in bed staring out the window. His face was so pale that it troubled Rafe. *How could I ever tell him the truth?*

"Hey, I missed you." Rafe sat on the side of the bed.

388

"I missed you too." Alek's voice was soft, almost as if the wind had been knocked out of him.

"How are you feeling?"

"Not that good. I don't want to get up."

"You don't have to. You can stay in bed until you feel better." Rafe stroked Alek's hair.

"Did Kaden say anything about me?"

"No. He said you didn't feel well."

"I had the worse day ever."

"Do you want to tell me about it?"

"It's about my uncle." Alek fiddled with the blanket.

"What about him? You can tell me anything. I'll listen to you."

"All my life I've been trying to find out who murdered my family. My uncle told me a story, but it was just that: a story."

"There are things in my life that I never understood. Finding the truth may be impossible. Are you unhappy living with me on the run?" Rafe asked.

"This has nothing to do with us. I want to be with you, but I need to know what happened. I'm still very angry about going to prison for something I didn't do. I wasted two fucking years. I should have been in school."

Rafe pulled Alek into his arms. "I know you're angry, and you have every reason to be. I don't want you to be so upset that you can't enjoy being here."

"I love it here, but something inside me demands that I find out the complete truth. I couldn't sleep last night thinking about it."

"What set this off?"

"I think in circles and can't sleep."

"Do you want to call your uncle?"

"No. I don't ever want to talk to him again."

"Okay. Do you feel like going to the boardwalk?" Rafe asked.

"No. I don't feel like doing anything. I just want to be left alone." Alek pulled the covers closer to his chin.

"I'll watch TV in the living room. Call me if you want something." Rafe hated leaving Alek alone but that's what he wanted at this time. He really must be depressed when he declined going to the boardwalk, one of his favorite places. Feeling frustrated that he couldn't solve Alek's sadness, he had to do something.

"Thanks."

Rafe left the apartment and stood in the hallway to call Alek's uncle.

"Rafe, what's going on with Alek?" Uncle Sacha asked.

"He's not feeling well. I understand he called you," Rafe said in a firm tone.

"Yes, he did, and he hung up on me. He's never done that before."

"What happened?" Rafe asked.

"Alek refuses to accept the circumstances of the death of his family. It was hard for him to understand what had happened in the past. I've tried to make him a good home, but now that he's older, he thinks there's more information."

"He wants more details to make it real to him. He's also very angry he went to prison for something he didn't do."

"I know all this. Can you keep him safe?"

"Yes. He doesn't want to talk to you. I guess in time, he'll find the peace he needs."

"I'm pleased with your services and talking to Alek, he told me I made a good decision in choosing you. He has not felt anything for anyone since he lost Burain. I'm sure he has mentioned him."

"Is your family after Alek?"

"Some are. They want my position and money, but everything I have goes to Alek. I want him safe from them. He never needs to work, but he wants to work with animals. I trust you to see that he gets his wish."

"Yes, he'll return to school soon. I need to know his active enemies to protect him."

"I told you some in my family and those in Burain's family." Sacha's accent thickened.

"What about Pavel?"

"What about him? He's Alek's cousin, and he's not his enemy. They were like brothers."

"Are you certain of that? Alek believes Pavel set him up with the drugs. Pavel also seems to know who murdered Alek's family. Do you know about this?" Rafe asked.

"I'm Alek's family. I know Alek believes Pavel is his enemy. Trust me, he isn't."

"Who set Alek up?" Rafe noticed when Sacha lied, his accent grew stronger. Why wouldn't he tell the truth to the man who was protecting Alek? Sacha was hiding pertinent information from Rafe.

"Burain's family set Alek up since they believe we murdered Burain. We didn't hurt him, especially since Alek loved him."

"You really don't know the truth about Alek's enemies. It's imperative that I know their names," Rafe repeated.

"We know that Burain's father was angry that his son was with Alek. He refused to accept his son was gay. This is the truth I know."

"Who killed Burain then if you didn't?" Rafe asked.

"I don't believe he's dead. I never mentioned this to Alek because he'd look for him to the end of the earth. It's best for both families they aren't together."

"If that's true, then why would they be after Alek?" The more Sacha spoke about the situation, the less Rafe understood. The man spoke in circles as if he had lost his mind. Either Burain was dead or not. There couldn't be two outcomes, yet in their conversation, he spewed out one lie after another. No wonder Alek felt the way he did.

"I believe they are. I could be wrong."

"I don't see any signs of them looking for him. But still, who in your family wants Alek gone?" Rafe was determined to find the truth, but the conversation only reaped confusion without understanding or facts.

"What are you asking me?" Sacha sounded angry and upset with Rafe.

"I need to know what family members want Alek dead."

"I can't say because I have no proof, only what my men told me."

"Well, if Alek is gone, which he is, why would they still be after him?" Rafe tried to make sense out of Sacha's comments.

"That's just it. They aren't after him since he isn't here to go after. Sending Alek to you for protection was a preventative measure only. I'll fix this problem within my family so he can return to me, but he told me he doesn't want to come home."

"He's angry at you because he believes you lied to him. Unless you're ready to tell him the truth, he wants nothing to do with you. Don't worry about Alek. He's well taken care of here. I'll get him through his anger and depression."

"I believe you will. I miss Alek. Without him, my home is empty, but I'll fix the problem between us. Keep me posted on Alek and tell him I love him." Sacha ended the call.

CHAPTER TWENTY-NINE

Alek Belanov

Alek was standing by the door listening to Rafe talking to his uncle. He could tell by Rafe's responses. Why would Rafe be speaking to Uncle Sacha? Did he know about the phone call? Rafe didn't say anything about it if he knew unless his uncle called Rafe.

When Rafe entered the apartment, Alek was standing near the door.

"Were you listening to my phone call?" Rafe asked, inching closer to him with concern written on his face.

"Yes, you were talking to my uncle. Why would you talk to him?" Alek asked.

"I called him to see if I could get any more truth out of him."

"What did you learn?"

"Sit down, and we'll talk."

Alek and Rafe both sat on the couch.

"I asked him about your enemies, and he wouldn't give me names."

"What did he say about Burain?"

"He said he doesn't know for a fact that Burain is dead," Rafe said.

"He what?" Alek jumped up and paced the living room floor. *How could his uncle lie about Burain's death too? How many damn lies has he told Alek?*

"Alek, when I pressured him on who had killed Burain, he said the Belanov family didn't kill him. I asked him who did, and he said he doesn't think he's dead."

"Another lie that bastard has been telling me all these years. How could he tell me Burain was dead when he didn't know that to be true? He said they blamed our family for his murder, and that's who set me up. That explains why I wasn't allowed to go to his funeral. I'm sick of all these lies. Why do I need protection then?" Alek asked.

"He claims someone in the family wants you dead so they can take over. Then he told me that he's left everything to you and what they want doesn't matter."

"So again who is after me now that I'm not around?" Alek asked. He had known his uncle would leave everything to him so it was no surprise about his future inheritance.

"He said sending you away was a preventative measure, and that he was going to fix the situation so you can return."

"Never. I will never return to a man who lied to me time after time."

396

"I agree. You should stay with me. I want you here."

"What else do you know about Pavel?"

"I think he set you up. Your uncle thinks Burain's family did at the same time he said Burain wasn't dead."

"You found out something without telling me?" Alek's voice was full of anger.

"What are you talking about?"

"You already knew Pavel set me up and if I hadn't listened in on your call to my uncle, I bet you weren't going to tell me."

"That's not true. I would've told you. I've always been honest with you," Rafe said with a poker face.

"No, you haven't. I bet you know who murdered my family and why. Tell me what you know." Alek's voice trembled.

Rafe raised his hand and put it on his forehead as if he had a headache.

"I know who killed your parents and why. I also know Pavel set you up."

"Tell me!"

There was a knock on the door, interrupting their strained conversation.

"Tell me. Fuck the door," Alek shouted, losing his patience.

"Let me get rid of who it is first."

Alek glared at Rafe.

Kaden stood at the door with a concerned look on his face. "Is everything okay in here?"

"No, Rafe has been lying to me this entire time. He took money from my uncle to protect me when I didn't even need protection. He knows who slaughtered my family and who set me up to go to prison. Yet he chose not to tell me." Alek's voice grew louder.

"Did you tell him?" Kaden asked.

Alek glared at Kaden for a moment as he quietly absorbed the shock and hurt, and then he faced Rafe. How could he discuss who murdered his family with Kaden first? His pain turned into anger.

"What? You told Kaden too. Not me. So who the fuck murdered my family?" Alek shouted to Rafe.

"Please sit down, Alek." Rafe looked at him with a kind and sympathetic expression as he spoke with a quiet voice.

"No."

"Just tell him," Kaden said. "He deserves the truth."

"I know he does," Rafe said.

"Tell him," Kaden repeated.

Rafe looked down at the floor as he let his breath out fast in sheer distress. "Your uncle murdered your family and saved you because he believes you're his son."

For a moment, he was shocked by his words and stared at Rafe. "How could he do that?" Tears trickled down his cheeks. "Why would he believe I'm his son?"

"Your mother and your uncle had an affair. So he wanted to raise you, but your parents claimed you were their child. This went on until your uncle went crazy. It's why you weren't killed with them. This is also why he was the one to bring you to his home right after the shootings. He was there. He did it. Two cousins wanted you and your uncle dead so they could take over. He killed them when they threatened to tell you."

"Were you ever going to tell me?" Alek glared at Rafe with hate clear in his eyes.

Alek could only lash out at Rafe for not informing him. To accept the truth was beyond him at the moment. The question about his uncle being the shooter had always been in the back of his mind. As he got older, he hadn't been able to understand how his uncle scooped him up from the toy chest within minutes of the shootings. His uncle had said he was in the neighborhood and heard the gunshots. Instead of calling the police or ambulance, he had chosen to take Alek home. He remembered seeing blood on his uncle's hands and clothes, and Alek had asked about it. Uncle Sacha had explained it away. He told Alek he had checked to see if anyone was alive. It all made sense now. *It was Uncle Sacha. He was the one who slaughtered his family. No. No. How could he?*

"I was going to tell you, but I was trying to find a way to do it without upsetting you." Rafe broke the uncomfortable silence between them.

"I don't believe you," Alek shouted.

It dawned on Alek that he had been the cause of his family's deaths. If he had never been born, his parents and brothers wouldn't be dead. How could his uncle shoot Alek's brothers? They were children. Uncle Sacha murdered his brother and his family, and he lied about who had done it. No wonder everyone in the family feared him. Was he really his uncle's son? He didn't think so. His uncle's sick mind had taken over all the good inside him. Uncle Sacha was pure evil. Alek had lived with him for a long time and became part of him without choice.

Alek headed for the door because he couldn't face anyone right now. He had to leave so he could breathe. He didn't need protection. He didn't care if something happened to him. Nothing mattered.

"Where are you going?" Rafe shouted.

"Away from you and your lies," Alek said. "Don't follow me."

"Let him go. He needs to think," Kaden said. "Alek, call me if you need anything."

Alek left the apartment in tears and bumped into Emilio in the hallway.

"Alek, what's wrong?" Emilio asked.

"I'm leaving. I can't stay anymore," Alek said.

"Please stay with us. It's not safe for you out there. Don't leave the society. I need you here," Emilio begged.

"I'm sorry, but I have to leave."

Alek stormed out of the apartment, ran down the street toward the boardwalk, and entered a bar. He ordered a whiskey and beer chaser. His entire body shook.

"Alek, what's wrong?" Emilio asked as he took the seat beside him at the bar.

"What are you doing here alone?" Alek worried that Emilio would get into trouble with Kaden. He didn't want to be responsible for causing any problems for them.

"I followed you because I was worried about you."

"Everything is wrong. You should go back before Kaden gets pissed off."

"Tell me. Don't worry about Kaden. He's talking to Rafe."

"Did you know too?" Alek asked.

"Know what? I don't know what's going on," Emilio said.

"My uncle was the one who murdered my family, and Pavel set me up. My uncle sent me away so I wouldn't find out what he had done."

"What are you going to do about it?"

"I'm going to do my own checking and see if I need protection. I don't think I do. I'm also going to look for Burain."

"You said Burain is dead." Emilio widened his eyes in alarm.

"They all lied to me."

"Can I go with you?"

"No. Go back, Emilio. I'm going to get a room on the boardwalk and do my own investigation. Please leave. I don't want you to get into trouble."

"You have my number if you need help," Emilio said.

"Thanks."

"Stay safe." Emilio hugged Alek, then left the bar.

After he finished his drink, Alek stumbled onto the crowded boardwalk and found another bar. He stood beside the door, looking through the glass window. The bartender caught his eye and proceeded to watch him with great interest. He sat down, pulled a twenty-dollar bill from his wallet, and slapped it on the bar. He was glad that Rafe had given him emergency money, but he had his debit card if he needed more. The place smelled of smoke, alcohol, and greasy, fried foods. Alek didn't care because his goal was to forget his pain.

After his third drink, the bartender said, "I'm cutting you off. You look stoned."

Alek left the bar, the half door swinging behind him, as he staggered down the boardwalk. He stopped at a liquor store and purchased a bottle of vodka and cigarettes. He found a sleazy hotel on the boardwalk and rented a room. He needed a place away from everyone to think and investigate. He sprawled on top of the bedspread and found this place was too noisy to sleep at this hour. He heard the screams coming from the rides. Of course, he could hear the lifeguards blowing their whistles too. He hoped that later on, the boardwalk would quiet down enough so he could sleep.

His phone rang, but he ignored it. He got out of bed to remove his clothes except his jeans, threw himself on the bed again, and picked up the bottle of vodka on the end table. After he drank almost half the bottle, the room whirled around like a merry-go-round. He sat up and tried to ride out the dizziness before he staggered in front of the mirror. His eyes were bloodshot from the combination of tears and vodka. If he didn't watch the amount he was drinking, he'd end up dead from an overdose. He wouldn't become an alcoholic like his uncle.

Did everyone in the Belanov family know that his uncle had murdered his entire family? Not one of them had seen fit to tell him the truth. Had any of his relatives been involved? He doubted it, but he couldn't be certain of anything anymore. Pavel had known about it and didn't give a fuck either. He only mentioned that he should have murdered Alek because he was a traitor. His parents and brothers weren't traitors, and yet Pavel had continued with that narrative.

He had to think about what he was going to say to his uncle. He took his phone and called Burain's home instead.

"Pavlenko's residence," Mrs. Pavlenko said.

"This is Alek Belanov. I'm looking for Burain."

"Burain has moved to New York."

"May I have his phone number please?"

"How are you? I heard you were in prison because your cousin set you up."

"My uncle told me that your family set me up."

"No," she paused. "I'm sorry, but your uncle lied to you."

"How do you know who set me up?" Alek asked.

"Oh, sweet Alek. I thought you knew by now. Your cousin shouldn't have done that to you. You didn't deserve to be treated the way you were. All the lies."

"Did you always know?" Alek asked.

"Yes, word travels fast."

"Can I please have Burain's number," Alek repeated.

"His private number is 212-504-3345. I'm not sure he wants to talk to you."

"Can I speak with Mr. Pavlenko?"

"Yes, you can."

"Hello, Alek," Mr. Pavlenko said.

"Did you put a hit on me?" Alek asked.

"A hit on you? No. That's bullshit. Who told you that?" Mr. Pavlenko voice rose.

"Why did you lie to me about Burain being dead?"

"Your uncle and I thought that was the best way to keep the peace between our families."

"My uncle told me you put a hit on me," Alek said.

"I'd never do that. You were young and innocent. All you ever did was love Burain. I had no reason for you to disappear."

"Thank you, I appreciate your honesty."

"Burain has moved on now. He's married to a woman and has two children."

"How can that be?" Alek felt a knife cut his heart in half.

"Alek, he isn't available to you, so it would be best to stay away from him. I don't want to hear that you broke up his marriage. I wish you the best, but stay away from Burain." Mr. Pavlenko ended the call.

Alek wasted no time; he immediately called Burain.

"Who is calling me on this number?" Burain asked.

"Alek."

"Alek? How did you find me?"

"How could you let me think you were dead all this time? I grieved for you for so long. You couldn't get one word to me? How could you let this horrific lie go on and on?"

"Who gave you my number?" Burain asked.

"Your mother."

"Don't call me again."

"Why would I call you again? You hurt me for a lifetime."

"You were the love of my life once, but I could see it would never work out. Our families wouldn't allow it. My father moved me away, so I'd be safe from your crazy uncle. Your uncle lied to you again. You were so innocent that you didn't know you were living with the man who murdered your family. I wish you well, but please don't call me again."

Alek ended the call because Burain's words brought him more pain than he could endure. He'd grieved the loss of his lover for years, and after all that, he told Alek never to call him again. Alek didn't understand anything. Burain had known the truth about his uncle and had never told him, just like Rafe. *How could I be so stupid and not figure it out? I'm not innocent now, Burain. Not after prison.*

Alek cried, thinking about all the hate and misery in his life. Was it even worth living at this point? He picked up the bottle of cheap vodka and swigged it down. He was getting dizzy and soon he would pass out. He had no idea what to do or where to go. The noise of the people enjoying life while he suffered from the lies of his past was too much for him.

He woke up at four in the afternoon; he left the room and got a Coke with some crackers from the hallway machines. With trembling fingers, he turned off the sound on his phone. He was in no frame of mind to talk to anyone, not even Rafe. He'd be angry if he knew how weak Alek was, not to mention how drunk he was. What was he doing to himself? Nothing fucking mattered anymore.

Alek should have been crying, but he was too numb. There was a giant hole in his heart, and he knew nothing would ever be the same. When he looked into the mirror again, his reflection scared him. He looked like death, and he didn't care. His eyes were puffy from crying, and he felt dehydrated too. Alek pointed to his face in the mirror. "Uncle Sacha, how could you do this to my family?"

He threw himself on top of the bedspread and grabbed his phone to call his uncle. The alcohol made him forget how he felt about Uncle Sacha. Alek didn't really want to speak to him, but he had to confront him.

"Alek. Talk to me," Uncle Sacha said.

"I know what you did." Alek's voice shook.

"I did nothing wrong. Do not accuse me of wrongdoing. I raised you because I knew you belong with me."

"I belong with my parents. How could you do it? My brothers were children. Why them? What did they do to you?"

"Alek, you sound like your mind has left you. What are you talking about? Where did you hear such lies?"

"I talked to Burain. Do you remember you told me he was dead? You watched me cry for months. I was inconsolable, and you watched me suffer from being heartbroken."

"I'm sorry about that, but Burain's father and I both decided it would be best. Our families were going to go to war over you two. We had to prevent the bloodshed between us. It had to be done."

"I hate you for what you did to my family. I hate you. I never want to see you again. You and Pavel can celebrate that you put me in prison. This isn't love, Uncle Sacha. You hate me."

"I never did those things you said. My life was always about you. I don't know who told you such lies about me. It's not true."

"You killed my family because you thought I was your son. How could you do that? I don't even know you anymore."

"Out of respect to my brother and your mother, I never told you. It's true you're my son, but I didn't slaughter your family to take you from them. If this is how you want to end our relationship with lies, I will do nothing to harm you. I'm displeased that you'd believe the lies of our enemies instead of me. Maybe someday, you'll understand the truth. I did nothing wrong. I only loved you." Uncle Sacha ended the call.

The more Alek drank, the more he cried. Everything good was gone, and everything bad was here.

CHAPTER THIRTY

Rafe Escobar

Rafe didn't know what to do about Alek leaving him. Most likely Alek wasn't in imminent danger unless he confronted his uncle or cousin. Once Alek had heard about his family and that Burain might be alive, he'd left. Of course, he blamed it on Rafe lying to him, which he did. He should have told him sooner.

"He'll come back," Kaden said.

"I don't think he will. Should we go look for him?" Rafe asked, feeling defeated and devastated.

"Let's call a meeting and talk about what happened so everyone can look for him."

"Send everyone a text to meet here. Keep the boys in Valerik's apartment."

Kaden sent the texts. "I'm going to talk to Emilio and tell him to go upstairs."

"Thanks."

Kaden returned and said, "Emilio is gone."

"Maybe he left with Alek," Rafe said.

James and Valerik stepped into the apartment without knocking.

"What's going on?" James asked.

411

"Alek left, and Emilio is missing," Kaden said.

"Why?" Valerik asked.

"I told Alek the truth, and now he's angry at me for not telling him sooner. Emilio was supposed to be in his apartment, but he's not there. I think he went after Alek," Rafe said.

"Boardwalk," James said. "I bet he's on the boardwalk."

"I don't know where he went, but we all need to look for him and bring him back," Kaden said.

"Kaden and I will go to the right side of the boardwalk, and you two go to the left side. Take the boys with you. I don't want Dante and Liam left alone," Rafe said.

Rafe and Kaden headed for the boardwalk. With the volume of people milling around on the boardwalk, they couldn't walk as fast as Rafe would have liked.

"I can't believe this is happening," Rafe said.

"Let's check the bars," Kaden said.

They walked into one of the loudest ones, full of drunk young people or well on their way at least. There was no sign of Alek. They continued to walk the boardwalk and noticed Emilio on a bench eating a chocolate ice cream cone.

"Would you look at that?" Kaden said to Rafe.

"What the hell?" Rafe said.

They walked over to him and blocked him on the bench.

"What are you doing here?" Kaden asked.

"I followed Alek. I'm sitting here because he's in that hotel." Emilio pointed to it.

"Why didn't you call to let us know?" Rafe asked.

"I didn't have my phone on me. Alek started running toward the boardwalk, so I followed him. I talked to him."

"And what did you find out?" Rafe asked.

"He wants to find the truth about his past. He thinks he doesn't need protection."

"I know he thinks that," Rafe said. "You two can go back. Tell the others we located him. I'm going to check inside the hotel."

"I already sent a text to the others," Kaden said.

Emilio got up, and Rafe hugged him. "Thanks for following him."

They left Rafe sitting on the bench. He called Alek, but of course, there was no answer. He walked inside the hotel and asked if he could have the room number of Alek Belanov.

"We don't generally give the room number out."

"He's my cousin, and I got in later than he did," Rafe said.

"He's in room 304."

"Thanks."

Rafe took the elevator to the third floor and found room 304. He leaned his ear against the door only to be met by dead silence. He pounded on the door, but no answer. He didn't hear anything moving. What if he had hurt himself? After taking the elevator down to the main floor, Rafe went straight to the check-in desk.

"Excuse me. I need help now on the third floor."

"What's wrong?" the clerk asked.

"I think my cousin is sick or has hurt himself. I need you to open the door. He received devastating news today."

The man behind the desk told another employee to take over, and he followed Rafe to the third floor.

"I'm so worried about him," Rafe said.

"Which room?"

"Room 304." Rafe pointed to the door.

The clerk knocked on the door, but no one answered. Rafe held his breath until the clerk unlocked the door. A blast of alcohol hit Rafe's nose upon entering. Alek was lying flat on his back on the floor, and his face was white with his eyes closed as if he were sleeping. Rafe stooped and shook him. "Wake up, Alek."

At first, Alek was unresponsive. Chewing on his bottom lip, Rafe was lost in thoughts of dire consequences for allowing Alek to leave him. His stomach contracted into a tight ball, and he took a deep breath. He continued shaking him. *What if he doesn't wake up?*

Alek had *take care of me* written all over his face. Many of Alek's actions and choices hadn't caused his current problems. Rafe couldn't help but he felt sorry for Alek. The circumstances he was forced to endure during his life were unfair. Rafe's need to take care of him ran strong, even now. What part did Alek play in his current situation? None. He simply wasn't responsible for the disturbing circumstances that surrounded him.

Within minutes, Alek opened his eyes and looked at Rafe. "I don't feel very good."

"I can handle it from here. Thank you," Rafe said to the clerk.

Rafe lifted Alek from the floor and carried him to the shower. He ran the water and helped Alek inside. He was a mess, reeking of alcohol.

"Everything hurts," Alek said.

"I know. You had too much to drink, and you're going to need to rest."

"I haven't eaten. I'm so hungry."

"What do you want to eat?"

"A steak and cheese hoagie, but I don't think I can walk to get it."

Rafe helped him out of the shower and dried him. He led him to the bed.

"Get under the covers. I'm going to call Kaden, and he'll bring clean clothes for you. He can get us a steak and cheese hoagie with cokes."

"I'm sorry I left." The pain in his chest twisted with regret.

"You don't have to be sorry for anything. You've been through a lot and need time and rest to heal. I want you to come back to our apartment when you feel up to it. Right now, I'm going to stay here with you." Rafe's lips met Alek's.

"Thanks." Alek closed his eyes.

Rafe called Kaden and told him to go to his apartment and get Alek clean clothes. He asked him to pick up two steak and cheese hoagies with two cokes. He also told him to bring Emilio.

Rafe rested beside Alek and wrapped his arms around him.

"Are you feeling a little better?" Rafe stroked his back.

"My life is in shambles. I called up Burain's parents, and they verified Burain wasn't dead. His mother gave me his number, and I talked to him." Tears rolled down his cheeks.

"How did it go with Burain?" Rafe was more confused by the minute with the conflicting details that had come out of Sacha's mouth earlier. So the family enemy gave Alek Burain's number. The man's words never matched the truth when he had spoken to Alek. No wonder Alek was overwhelmed with all the lies.

"Not good. Burain wasn't even sorry for the pain I'd gone through. His father told me he and my uncle told me Burain was dead on purpose to save the families from fighting."

"That is so wrong on so many levels. So, do you feel upset with Burain?"

"It hurts, and then he told me I was so innocent that I didn't know my uncle slaughtered my family. It was like he was laughing at me. All that we had meant nothing to him. His father said I was too innocent and young for Burain, and he didn't put a hit on me."

417

"I'm sorry you're hurting all over again."

"I'm devastated."

"What are you going to do about this information?" Rafe asked.

"I called Uncle Sacha. He lied and lied to me. He did say it was true I was his son. He claims he didn't slaughter my parents. He also said he had nothing to do with Pavel setting me up. He still said Burain's family did that. He told me he was upset I believed our enemies over him." Alek turned away and cried.

"I hate to see you suffering like this. You need to process all the pain. I'm here with you and will help you through it."

Two knocks on the door prompted Rafe to answer it. Kaden and Emilio stood there with clothes and their food.

Emilio rushed over to Alek and sat on the bed. "Hey, I'm worried about you."

"Thanks." Alek wiped his tears away.

Rafe took the clothes and set them on the dresser. Kaden passed out the hoagies and cokes.

Alek sat up in bed and ate his sandwich.

"We want you to come back," Emilio said.

"I don't need protection anymore," Alek said.

"But what about Rafe?" Emilio asked.

"We need to talk about that," Rafe said.

When everyone finished, Kaden and Emilio left.

"I want you to stay with me. I don't care if you need protection or not," Rafe said.

"How would that work?" Alek asked.

"The same way as before. You do need protection from Pavel and others since your uncle is leaving all his money to you."

"I don't have the same threat I thought I had. It was fake. How could he do this to me? I'll never forgive him for killing my family and sticking me in prison. I want nothing to do with him."

"Take the money. I said the same thing about my father's money, but I'm using it for a good cause."

"I guess so. I feel so upset about all of this."

"You have me to lean on. I'm your solid rock that will always have your back."

"Thank you."

CHAPTER THIRTY-ONE

Alek Escobar

The next day when they returned to the apartment, everyone was sitting at the picnic table eating breakfast. Rafe and Alek made a plate and took it inside because Alek didn't want to socialize. They sat in their small kitchen.

"Let's talk about us," Alek said.

"I want you with me whether you need protection or not. Your uncle paid me to take care of you. He put money in your account to live on and gave me money to meet your basic expenses. Right now, the future of our relationship is up to you. If you stay with me, you'd be on the run like all of us. You wouldn't be allowed to break our security by ignoring the rules. Things between us would remain the same, and we could add a BDSM component if that's what you'd like to do. I want you to think about this," Rafe said.

"When I was alone in the hotel room, I felt like I had no one who cared about me. No one. Living with you and joining this protection society gave me a lover and a new family. I don't like all your rules, but I love being with you. I understand breaking the rules could cost one of the guys their life. Like Dante. If those gang members had been around when we went to the store, we would have been targets."

"That's right. I don't make rules for the power, though I do love having the control and power in a relationship," Rafe said.

"I want to stay here with you, and I understand things would stay as they are for the benefit of the safety for the others."

"I would be messed up if you left me. I want you with me, and soon we'll be moving. You can go to school and things should be more relaxed," Rafe said.

"Sounds good. I'm looking forward to returning to school."

Someone knocking on the door sent Rafe to answer it. When Valerik walked into the apartment, Alek went to the living room.

"I have some news to share with Alek," Valerik said.

"Good news, I hope," Rafe said. "He's been through enough."

"Pavel is dead. Your uncle was hospitalized from multiple gunshot wounds, and he's asking for you. He's ready to tell you the truth. I spoke to him."

"What happened? Who killed Pavel?" Alek's voice trembled.

"I don't know, but I guess his enemies caught up to him," Valerik said.

"What about Pavel's brother?"

"He's fine. I need to see your uncle one last time. If you want to see him, I'll take you there," Valerik said.

"I don't know." Alek lit a cigarette, walked outside, and sat on the steps of the building.

All the happy times with his uncle passed through his mind. Alek recalled wishing his uncle was his father because he had loved him so much. Now that he knew he was his father, he felt hate and disgust. Did he owe his uncle anything? He had no idea what was the right thing to do. This was the same man who ordered Pavel to set him up with drugs, or so he'd thought. He had no idea what was true or not. Alek was sure his uncle had taken out his family. Everything was mixed up in his mind, but his uncle was on his deathbed and asking for him.

Alek returned to the apartment and said, "I want to go to California to hear the truth."

"Do you think that's a good idea?" Rafe asked.

"I don't know, but I need some kind of closure. He was like a father to me for years before I found out how evil he is."

"I don't know if it's safe for you. It could be a trap," Rafe said.

"I don't care. I need to see him. Would you and Valerik come with me?" Alek asked.

"I can leave Liam with James. We've already discussed it. I'm ready to go when you are. He doesn't have much time," Valerik said.

"I'll make the plane reservations. Pack us some clothes," Rafe told Alek.

***

Within three hours, they boarded the plane to California. Once they arrived, Valerik rented a car and drove them to the hospital. Alek was nervous to see his uncle now that he knew what he had done. Valerik decided it would be best if he went in first. Rafe and Alek waited in the waiting room for him. After ten minutes, Valerik returned and told Alek that his uncle wanted to see him.

Valerik pointed to his uncle's room down the hallway. Two guards stood by the door, protecting the area. When he slowly walked toward the room, the guards nodded for him to go inside. His pale and sickly looking uncle was staring at the ceiling.

424

"Alek, come here," Uncle Sacha said.

Alek inched closer and stood beside him.

"Thank you for coming. I'm ready to tell you everything. Please sit." Uncle Sacha patted the bed. His voice was so low and deep.

Alek sat down. "I can't believe you did what you did. I loved you, and now, I hate you." Tears trickled down his cheeks.

"Let me explain. When I'm done, you'll hate me, and I understand that. But you deserve the truth as you requested on the phone. A long time ago, your mother and I had an affair. It was very messy because your father was my brother. She got pregnant and had you. I was convinced you were mine. I asked her and your father to let me raise you. They refused and told me you weren't mine, but I had DNA tests proving you are my son. I battled with your parents for four years. I wanted to tell you that you were my son. They refused me that too. One day, I just had enough, and I let my anger take me to a very dark place. I went to your home and murdered them. I took you home with me and raised you. I don't expect you to forgive me for this."

"I won't ever forgive you. How could you hurt my brothers? They were children." Alek wiped his tears away.

"And your brother and my mother who you say you loved. How could you?"

"I have no answer to your questions. I allowed my insanity to do some evil things in my lifetime. I never wanted you to find out, but as I thought about it, I knew you deserved the truth from me."

"Why did you lie about Burain?"

"I told you that his father and I spoke and believed this would be the best thing for both families. I'm sorry for doing that because you should have not been lied to about a person you loved."

"And what about you and Pavel setting me up with drugs so I'd go to prison?"

"I had nothing to do with that. Pavel did that on his own. I didn't know this until recently when I spoke to a few people to investigate what you claimed. I put a hit on Pavel, and he's dead. He had to pay for setting you up for something you didn't do."

"I thought you told him to set me up."

"No. I have done horrible things, but I wouldn't have put you in prison."

Uncle Sacha picked up a pill on his tray and swallowed it without water.

"I left everything to you. It's in your account. I'm sorry for everything I've done that has hurt you, but I'm not sorry for raising you. I love you, Alek." Uncle Sacha closed his eyes and began trembling and moaning in pain.

"What's wrong?" Alek asked.

"I...love...you," Uncle Sacha whispered as he held Alek's hand.

Alek pressed the emergency button for the nurse, ran out of the room, and shouted for help. Three nurses ran into the room with Alek right behind them. She checked his pulse two times.

"He's gone," one nurse said.

"Just like that?" Alek asked. "He took a pill that was on his tray, and then he was shaking all over in pain."

Alek ran out of the room, down the halls to the waiting room, where Rafe and Valerik were.

"What's wrong?" Rafe asked.

"He's dead. He took a pill and killed himself right in front of me," Alek said.

The doctor walked over to Alek. "We're going to be doing an autopsy on him, but he wasn't going to make it anyway. I don't know where he got that pill. I didn't prescribe him any."

"I just got here," Alek said. "I don't know how he got the pill. He asked for me, and now he's gone." Alek wiped his tears away.

"We have instructions on what to do. He requested to be cremated. He doesn't want a showing or anything," the doctor said.

"Do you want to stay or leave?" Rafe asked.

"I want to leave. Now, I don't want to be here anymore."

***

Within three hours, they were flying back to Newark, New Jersey. Valerik drove a car to Seaside Heights while Alek cried on and off during the ride. When they returned, they went straight to their apartment. Alek went to bed without saying anything. Rafe stayed in the living room making phone calls for their move. Kaden and Emilio entered the apartment, and Emilio made his way to the bedroom.

"Hey, Alek, do you want some company?" Emilio asked.

"Yes, stay here with me."

"What happened?"

"He took a pill, and then he died holding my hand. It was sad, so sad. I get upset when I can't separate the man who loved me and the man who brutally murdered my family. It was the hardest thing I've ever had to do."

"I can't imagine seeing him die right in front of you."

"I'm staying with Rafe. We belong together. He is able to make me see what I'm feeling is okay and that I'm going through a process. I hated myself for... caring for my uncle after what he had done. Now, he's gone. Whatever we had all those years is gone."

CHAPTER THIRTY-TWO

Alek Belanov

Six months later

New Jersey Cabins

When Alek walked into the cabin, Rafe stood in the living room waiting for him. He wasn't smiling the way he normally did when he came in from school.

"We need to talk now," Rafe said.

"What's wrong?" Alek asked.

"Follow me. We're going to take a walk to the lake. I don't want to talk in our cabin."

Alek trailed behind Rafe, quickly hiking on a path through the woods without understanding why they were leaving the cabin to talk. He checked where he stepped along the path. The slight nip in the air caused the fine blond hairs on his arms and legs to stand amid goose bumps. As he walked behind Rafe, Alek rubbed his arms and legs to ease the chill.

"Keep up with me." Rafe paused his trudging, turned around, and studied him. "What's the problem?"

"I'd like to know what we're going to talk about. You seem pissed off at me. I can't see any reason for you to act like this."

Alek bowed his head, checking out the path for any signs of snakes. It appeared safe enough; no rocks or stones, just leaves and dirt. Rafe must have been really upset because he refused to answer his question.

Rafe stopped at the large oak tree near the lake and waited for Alek to catch up to him.

"Last night, I checked your phone. And do you know what I saw?" Rafe asked.

"There's no reason for you to check my phone anymore," Alek said.

"So, now do you know why I'm pissed off?" Rafe inched closer to Alek in a threatening way.

"No. Please tell me."

"You've been talking to Burain. I saw the calls he made to you."

"Oh, that."

"Talk to me about Burain," Rafe demanded.

"I got a phone call from him. He apologized to me for telling me not to call him. He said his wife was in the room when I called the first time."

"When was the first time *he* called you?" Rafe asked.

"Two weeks ago."

"Did you see him?" Rafe asked.

"I needed closure and wanted to make sure I didn't have any leftover feelings for him."

"Did you fucking see him?" Rafe asked again.

"I did see him. We talked for three hours, and then it was over for me."

"I can't believe you kept that from me. So, this is why you were always unavailable for sex and too tired?"

"My feelings were all fucked up. So many things have happened to me. I felt like I had no control over my life. I don't expect you to understand how confused and upset I was with Burain. I thought he was dead, and then he wasn't. It just messed me up."

"Did Burain fuck you?"

"No! I would never cheat on you like that."

"What did Burain want from you then?" Rafe inched closer to him.

"He wanted me to leave you for him."

"What about his wife and children?"

"He said he left her, but I don't know if that was the truth. He wanted to begin all over again. I told him I couldn't forgive him for not telling me he wasn't dead. He also knew that my uncle murdered my family but never felt the need to tell me."

"Why did you keep talking to him for two weeks?"

"I guess this is the saddest reason. I really believed he owed me an apology for not telling me where he was. He never attempted to let me know he wasn't dead. And each time I talked to him, I waited for his apology, but he only blamed my uncle. He wasn't sorry because he moved on with his life, and he didn't give a shit about me."

"Do you still love him?"

"I needed to see if there was anything there. Whatever we had wasn't there anymore. Every time we spoke, I hurt. I didn't feel any love for him or from him, just pain from his lying. I don't love him anymore. I hate him." Tears rolled down Alek's cheeks, wishing he wasn't so sensitive and emotional.

"He hurt you like your uncle did. He just brought up all the pain from your past."

"I know I should have told you that I was talking to him. I didn't know how to explain my feelings when I didn't know what they were or what I was doing by talking to him."

"What about us?" Rafe asked.

"I love you, Rafe. I'm willing to live on the run with you. I don't think I ever had a person who really cared for me the way you have. I feel safe and for the first time, I've experienced real love."

"I love you, Alek. But…I'm not about to share you with Burain."

"Last night, I told him not to call me anymore. I want to be with you, only you."

"From here on in, let me know what you're doing. I was very upset that you didn't want sex with me. I knew something was wrong. That's what I'm here for. Let me take care of you."

"You have. Thank you for taking care of me." Alek put his arms around Rafe and kissed his lips. Alek had wanted to do this for a long time, but now Rafe was giving him an opportunity.

"Let me take care of you at home."

Alek followed the path with Rafe, who placed his arm around his shoulders. They walked in silence to the cabin. Rafe unlocked the door. All the walls had been painted forest green with white trim. It matched the outside of all the cabins.

They removed their boots and set them in the wooden shoe tray. Rafe pinched Alek's backside when he bent over. Alek quickly turned around and shook his head with a boyish grin. Rafe could be so much fun when he played, but not so much when he was upset with him.

"I think you need a bubble bath." He took Alek's hand and led him to the bedroom.

Alek nodded, unable to speak because all his emotions were surfacing. This was what he'd always wanted, a lover who loved and cherished him. He didn't want to have to worry about anyone taking it away from him. He promised himself he would try harder to open up to Rafe. Later, if he could, he would discuss his fears about their future. He needed to lay it all down to Rafe the way he expected.

Alek watched Rafe light the scented candles in the bathroom. He ran the bath water, added the bubble crystals, and returned to the bedroom. He undressed and gestured for Alek to remove his clothes. Alek stripped off his jeans and shirt. Taking a bubble bath with Rafe was one of his favorite things to do. For some reason, sitting in bubbles with Rafe made him feel secure and safe.

Rafe took Alek's hand, lacing their fingers together, and led him into the hot, steamy bathroom. First Rafe stepped into the bath and sat. He motioned for Alek to sit between his legs. When Alek stepped into the steamy bubbles, he lowered himself between those muscular legs. Rafe wrapped his strong arms around Alek's thin waist and kissed the top of his head. Alek leaned back into Rafe's hardness. All was good when Rafe was beside him.

"I don't like seeing you unhappy and confused." Rafe caressed Alek's stomach, making small circles.

"Being close to you always makes me feel better." Alek's cock had hardened. He knew Rafe wanted his honesty and submission, but he hadn't felt he was ready to be a sub.

"I want you to give me all your worries." Rafe lubed his fingers.

"I'm sorry I failed you again." Alek twisted around and brushed his lips over Rafe's.

Rafe backed away from the kiss. "That doesn't mean I've forgotten what you did behind my back."

"I know I said this before, but I mean it this time. I won't keep my feelings a secret from you anymore."

"Time will tell if you mean what you say." Rafe's dark eyes sparkled with kindness and love.

Rafe tilted him to the right against the tile and slid his slippery finger into his hole. The stretch burned Alek in a good way, and the burning further aroused him. Rafe slipped in another digit and fingered him with fast deep trusts. He continued fingering him until Alek needed more. Rafe pulled his fingers out and aimed his cock at his entrance. He squeezed Alek's hips with his thick hands while he pushed his cock against his tight opening. Alek pushed into the hardness and flexed his hole to force the thick cock deeper into him.

"Your ass…feels so good," Rafe said.

"I love your hard dick inside me. We're so close, almost one."

"Because you belong to me and no one else." He pounded Alek and took his erection in hand, stroking him roughly. Precum oozed out from the head of his cock.

"Fuck me harder," Alek begged.

"Bend over the side of the tub on your knees."

After Alek got into place for Rafe, he knelt between Alek's legs. Rafe's hard cock carefully moved into him, while at the same time he caressed Alek's erection, pumping at a slow, balanced pace. He switched to faster movements with a deeper penetration. As Alek's prostate vibrated again and the sensations seized his body, he was moaning and groaning.

"Come for me," Rafe commanded.

Alek wasn't far from coming and tried to hold back. He relaxed enough, feeling the warm semen filling his balls, needing an exit soon. The blood surged from his fingertips to his toes. He tried to throttle down the dizzying current racing through him. His insides trembled with excitement from the closeness of Rafe's heated body.

"I need you to pump harder. Please fuck me harder so I can come."

Rafe picked up the pace. He grabbed Alek's long hair, pulling his head toward him almost painfully as he pounded his full length in and out of his ass. Rafe's motions got even more powerful. His hands grabbed Alek's hips, strangling them as he pounded harder. The last grueling thrust ignited Rafe to explode inside him. Shot after shot of his sperm painted Alek's insides as Rafe bit down on his shoulder, his dick ramming in and out as he kept shooting, marking him as his own. Alek's entire body shook from the power of his orgasm. He thought he might pass out from being so light-headed. His surroundings grayed out as all sensation focused on his cock shooting against his stomach.

Rafe caught him in his arms. They held on to each other until they stopped shaking. After they rested for a couple of minutes in each other's arms, Rafe pulled Alek to standing position. He drained the tub and turned on the shower to rinse them off.

Rafe washed Alek's hair, then sponged his body with shower gel. The scent was a familiar one. The soapy sponge brushed his balls, cock, and asshole. Alek laughed as he often did when Rafe washed him. When it was his turn, he took great care when it came to Rafe's cock.

Maybe he spent more time there than anywhere else. He belonged to Rafe, and no one was going to take him away.

"Alek, is my cock that dirty?"

"What do you mean?"

"You've been washing it for a long time, and now I'm hard again."

Alek laughed, then rinsed the suds from his lover's cock. Rafe pulled Alek closer to him. When Alek turned his face up to him, Rafe's lips met his, the tip of his tongue slipping into Alek's mouth. He felt the heady sensation Rafe's taste caused. After they rinsed off, they fell on the bed and relaxed into each other's arms.

"You and I belong together. I want to keep you as mine," Rafe said.

"I want to belong to you. I knew you were the right person when I first saw you at that party. And when you put that red tie on me, I knew my life would change for the better and it did."

"I love you, Alek. I adore you."

"I love you, too."

***

The next day when Alek woke up, Rafe was gone. As Alek walked into the kitchen, he saw Rafe standing near the back door as if he was waiting for him. He had a gigantic smile on his face.

"What's going on?" Alek asked.

"I have a present for you."

"Why? I didn't do anything to deserve a present."

"Yes, you did. I'm sorry, but I opened your mail by mistake this morning. It was your grades. Straight A's."

"Really? Where's my present?" Alek scanned the room.

"Your present is on the back porch."

Alek rushed through the back door and found a beagle puppy sleeping in a basket.

"A puppy!" He picked up the puppy, waking him up.

"I picked him up this morning when you were sleeping."

"He's adorable. I love him already."

"He's waiting for you to name him," Rafe said.

"How about Sparky?"

"That's a great name. Let him sleep. He ran around all morning while you were sleeping."

"Thank you so much. I've always wanted a puppy."

"Don't worry, if we need to go anywhere. We have our group to keep Sparky overnight."

"You really make me happy. I'm sorry if I hurt you when I was talking to Burain."

"I understand. I want you to have closure on your past so we can make new memories."

"I can't thank you enough."

"Just choosing to be with me when you don't have to is enough of a thank you."

"Now, we're a family."

"Yes, we are."

The End

ABOUT THE AUTHOR

I am from Huntington Beach, Ca. I taught various subjects at a Continuation High School in Los Angeles, California for 27 years. I obtained a Bachelor's of Arts Degree in history, Secondary Social Science Credential and a Master's Degree in Secondary Reading and Secondary Education from California State University, Long Beach. I also enrolled in some creative writing classes at UCLA.

Connect With Brina Brady

I would love to hear from my readers, so please drop me a line.

My email address:

mailto:brinabrady@gmail.com

Please visit my WordPress Blog here:

http://brinabrady.wordpress.com

Friend me on Facebook here:

https://www.facebook.com/brina.brady.3

Follow me on Twitter here:

https://twitter.com/BrinaBrady

Follow me on Pinterest here:

http://www.pinterest.com/brinabrady/

Follow me on Google+ here:

https://plus.google.com/+BrinaBrady/posts

Join my Reader's Group here:

https://www.facebook.com/groups/146904702344189/

.

BRINA BRADY

OTHER BOOKS

RENT ME SERIES 1-5

"Rent Me" by Brina Brady

Rent Me Series Book 1

http://www.amazon.com/Rent-Me-Book-ebook/dp/B00KLNSLBQ/

"Own Me" by Brina Brady

Rent Me Series Book 2

http://www.amazon.com/dp/B00VDQLDZ6/

"Make Me" by Brina Brady

Rent Me Series Book 3

http://www.amazon.com/dp/B016B6MZZY/

"For Mc" by Brina Brady

Rent Me Series Book 4

http://www.amazon.com/Me-Christmas-Story-Rent-ebook/dp/B018PWUVFI/

"Find Me" by Brina Brady

Rent Me Series Book 5

https://www.amazon.com/Find-Me-Rent-Book-ebook/dp/B01MT9S6PD/

BEND OVER SERIES 1-4

"Bend Over" by Brina Brady

Bend Over Series Book 1

http://www.amazon.com/Bend-Over-Book-ebook/dp/B00P2XO5YM/

"Don't Throw Me Away" by Brina Brady

Bend Over Series Book 2

http://www.amazon.com/gp/product/B0117VIQW4/

"Spanked in the Woodshed" by Brina Brady

Bend Over Series Book 3

https://www.amazon.com/Spanked-Woodshed-Bend-Over-Book-ebook/dp/B01BOEWBB6

"Breaking Roadblocks" by Brina Brady

Bend Over Series Book 4

https://www.amazon.com/gp/product/B07649W6RF

IRISH RUNAWAY SERIES 1-3

"The Runaway Gypsy Boy" by Brina Brady

Irish Runaway Series Book 1

https://www.amazon.com/Runaway-Gypsy-Boy-Irish-Book-ebook/dp/B01FIFE3Q8/

"Master Cleary's Boys" by Brina Brady

Irish Runaway Series Book 2

https://www.amazon.com/Master-Clearys-Boys-Irish-Runaway-ebook/dp/B01M0AF8DR/

"Master Braden's Houseboy" by Brina Brady

Irish Runaway Series Book 3

https://www.amazon.com/dp/B07HX2HR3G

STANDALONES

"Cabin Commotion" by Brina Brady

https://www.amazon.com/dp/B079Y29G5V/

"Sir Ethan's Contract" by Brina Brady

https://www.amazon.com/dp/B07DZ18WZ7

Made in the USA
Middletown, DE
27 December 2019